DAMNATION
BOOK FIVE OF THE EMPTY BODIES SERIES

Zach Bohannon

DAMNATION
Zach Bohannon
www.zachbohannon.com

Edited and Proofread by:
Jennifer Collins

Cover design by Johnny Digges
www.diggescreative.com

CHAPTER ONE

The boy's screams echoed off the surrounding trees. They'd muted the crack of the machete's blade as it severed flesh, tissue, and bone on its way into the tree stump. The others cried out as well—most of all, Mary Beth. Through this, Will remained calm, controlling the situation. If he didn't, Dylan's intense pain would be for nothing, and the boy would die.

"Keep holding him down," Will told Charlie and Holly. He put the t-shirt back into Dylan's mouth and the boy sunk his teeth into it, trying to reduce the pain.

Dylan stared to the sky, eyes wide. His cheeks began to pale.

"He's going into shock," Charlie said.

Will would worry about that in a minute. For now, he just wanted to stop the bleeding. He had severed the arm just inches below the elbow. He'd wanted to take only the boy's hand, amputating at the wrist, but he had been worried that the demon wouldn't be vanquished unless he amputated farther up the arm. It still remained to be seen whether the amputation had fended off the possession or not.

Will wrapped the t-shirt around the boy's arm, just above the elbow. He pulled the knot tight, applying intense pressure. Convulsing, Dylan kicked his legs and flayed his remaining arm.

"Hold him still," Will commanded, speaking to both Charlie and Holly.

They pinned down Dylan's shoulders, and Will finished tying off the knot. He now just had to hope that it would hold.

"Charlie, I need your shirt," Will said.

Charlie removed his jacket, then his t-shirt. He gave it to Will, who turned to Holly.

"I need you to hold this against the wound and apply pressure. Charlie and I are gonna have to pick him up and carry him back to the cabins. You've gotta stay next to us and keep this pressed against his arm the entire time, okay?"

Eyes red from crying, Holly nodded.

Will turned to Mary Beth. The girl cowered a few feet away from the scene, sitting down on the ground with her head tucked to her knees. Will kneeled down next to her. The girl's eyes were bloodshot from her having cried so much. Her body quaked, and she sniffled continuously.

"Sweetie," Will said. "I'm gonna need you to stand up now. Dylan's going to be fine, but we have to get him back to camp right away. Can you stand up and walk fast with us to get him back?"

Mary Beth didn't move. She stared past Will, past the others, looking off to the gunmetal sky. Staring off into nothingness. When Will reached down and grabbed her arm, she screeched and moved back. Her eyes met his.

"We have to do this, Mary Beth. We have to go, now."

Behind Will, Dylan cried out. He no longer clenched the t-shirt with his teeth, and the sound filled the air around them as he screamed. Mary Beth looked at Dylan, and she began to cry even more.

Growing impatient, Will said, "If we don't go now, he's going to be screaming a lot more. The only way that we can help him, that *you* can help him, is by getting onto your feet and going with us back to the cabins."

She stared past him again, and Will grabbed her by the shoulders.

"Mary Beth." He said it firmly, but not aggressively. "Please."

They held each other's gaze for a few moments before Mary Beth nodded. Will stood up, offering his hand to her. She accepted and he pulled her onto her feet.

"Stay with us," Will told the girl. "Pay attention, and don't get behind us, or ahead of us. Understand?"

"Yeah," Mary Beth mumbled.

Will turned to Charlie. "We're going to have to carry him. You get his legs, and I'll grab under his arms."

Dylan's mouth was open, and slobber dripped down from the edges of it. His eyes were wide. He had stopped kicking his arm and legs, making it easier to pick him up. Charlie grabbed onto his ankles, and Will took the boy under the arms.

"Keep a lot of pressure on it," Will told Holly, speaking of the wide open wound at the end of Dylan's arm. Will then looked down to Dylan. "You're going to be all right, buddy. I'll be sure of it. This might just hurt a little."

He placed his hands under Dylan's arm pits, and the boy screamed. As Will choked back tears, he looked to Holly.

"Keep it together," he told her. She nodded, and Will looked back to Charlie. "On three."

They lifted the boy on the count and, again, Dylan cried out. Will closed his eyes tight, still fighting back tears.

"Come on," Charlie said. "Let's move."

As they moved through the trees, the rain came all at once. It didn't drip for a few minutes, easing into a steady fall. Instead, it came crashing down.

Will picked up his gait, not wanting to have to carry Dylan through the mud.

With no Empties along the path in front of them, their biggest enemy now was time.

By the time they arrived back at the cabins, Will found himself thanking God for the rain. Smoke from the fires filled the air surrounding the area, even visible through the storm. But the rain had extinguished much of the fire, allowing them to safely walk onto the campgrounds.

The muscles in Will's arms pulsated from his forearms all the way up to his shoulders. They hadn't set Dylan down since picking him up. And even though all Will wanted to do was lay the eleven-year-old boy down and rub his arms, he continued to pace toward the cabins.

"Let's set him down by the SUV," Will said.

They hurried past the playground and arrived at the vehicle.

"Holly, grab the door," Will said.

Holly directed Mary Beth to sit in a spot fifteen feet away from the SUV, and told her not to move. She opened the vehicle's rear passenger side door.

"Easy," Charlie said as they eased Dylan onto the back seat.

"Holly, grab a bottle of water."

On the floor of the back seat lay a towel, and Will grabbed it.

"Keep pressure on his arm with this," Will said.

Tipping the water into Dylan's mouth, Holly shook her head. "It's too dirty. We can't risk him getting an infection."

"We also can't risk him bleeding out on us," Charlie said.

"Charlie's shirt wasn't clean either. It's going to have to work until we can find something else," Will said. "We'll have to take each scenario one at a time."

Holly said, "But, Will, we can't—"

"Just do it, Holly!"

Holly stopped arguing. She pressed the unwashed towel against the wound.

Inside the SUV, Will grabbed the first aid kit out of one of the duffel bags. He opened it and found bandages, scissors, Band-Aids, and cream to aid burns. But no clotting powder.

Will turned around to assess the cabins. The fire had taken out all but two of the units. A flame still rose from the bannister on the front porch of one of the cabins, but the rain made sure it wouldn't spread.

"Stay here with them," Will said to Charlie. "Holly's got Dylan; just be here if she needs any help, and try to keep Mary Beth calm. And make sure Dylan drinks plenty of water. I'll be right back."

Will ran to the nearest cabin of the two that remained standing. Charlie had been staying there. He ran up the patio, and tapped the doorknob with his palm. When it wasn't hot, he entered.

Though flames tickled the air outside, the inside of the cabin appeared to be untouched. Will hurried back to the bedroom. Charlie's suitcase lay on the bed and Will flipped through it. He pulled out several shirts, as well as a belt.

He went to the kitchen and opened the pantry. On the second rack sat an array of spices. Will checked each one, tossing aside the spices he didn't need.

"Bingo," he said.

In his hand, he held a small bottle of cayenne pepper. Will had once read about how the spice could help to clot blood. He stuffed the canister into his pocket, then reached to the back of the shelf and grabbed a half-full container of iodized salt. The cayenne pepper supposedly stung far less than the salt upon hitting an open wound. The salt would be option B to stop the bleeding.

Will turned around and went to a cabinet above the sink. Inside, he found a bottle of aspirin, and stuffed it into his pocket. He checked the other bottles, but this was the only pain reliever, so he shut the cabinet and hurried to the door.

Will ran across the muddy courtyard. Charlie was inside the shaking SUV, helping Holly hold down a bucking Dylan.

"He's coming in and out of shock," Charlie said. "It's becoming harder to hold him."

"How's the bleeding?" Will asked.

"It's getting worse," Holly said.

"All right, well, we're gonna stop it."

"How?" Holly asked.

Will set the first aid kit on the seat, then pulled the cayenne pepper out of his pocket.

"You've got to be kidding me," Holly said.

"It's the only way," Will said. "If we don't stop the bleeding soon..." Will didn't finish the sentence. He opened the first aid kit and pulled out the bottle of aspirin. "We'll give him this. Not sure if it's going to do shit to help with the pain, but it's all we've got." Will opened the bottle, removing three of the capsules. "Open his mouth."

Charlie held Dylan down while Holly reached to the boy's face and peeled his lips apart.

"You have to take these," Will said. He dropped the pills into Dylan's mouth. "Make sure he doesn't spit them out."

Holly fed Dylan water, and he swallowed the pills without protest.

After the boy had swallowed the pills, Will wrapped the belt around the top of Dylan's arm. He pulled it tight, hoping it would help stop blood flow to the open wound.

"We're gonna have to do this quickly," Will said. "As soon as you remove the towel, I'm gonna pour cayenne onto the wound." He handed Holly one of the clean t-shirts. "Once we're done, put this one on his arm."

"Then what do we do?" Holly asked.

"We wait until the bleeding stops," Charlie said.

"And hope that we don't have to use the salt," Will added.

"Is he going to be okay?" Mary Beth asked, having approached the vehicle.

"Don't look," Holly snapped. Mary Beth jumped back. "I'm sorry, but we need you to go sit back down, okay? He's going to be fine."

Mary Beth bowed her head and turned away, going back to the spot Holly had asked her to stay put at.

Holly wiped her eyes, trying to calm herself.

"You ready?" Will asked her.

Taking a deep breath, Holly nodded.

Will unscrewed the top off of the cayenne pepper. The container was three-quarters of the way full. He hoped that it would be enough to stop the bleeding, as he had no desire to have to try using the salt.

"He's going to squirm like hell once this hits the wound," Will said. "You're going to have to hold him down with everything you've got, Charlie."

Charlie nodded.

Will looked back to Holly. "You stay behind me. As soon as I get this on the wound, I need you to be ready with that clean shirt. I think we can stop the bleeding if we can get some pressure back on it right away."

Will closed his eyes and drew in long, deep breaths. *Please, God, let this work,* he thought. He looked up and told Charlie to hold Dylan down. Charlie pushed down on Dylan's shoulders.

Will pulled away the dirty towel, and dumped the spice onto the wound.

It was the loudest scream that Will had ever heard.

CHAPTER TWO

Jessica was the first among the group to wake. All four of them had slept in the middle of the main room of the Welcome Center. The temperature had dropped significantly overnight. Fortunately, they'd slept close to each other, absorbing one another's body heat.

The smell of cleaning supplies surrounded her, but it still beat the smell of rotting flesh from the bodies they'd pulled out of the inside of the building.

After lying on her back for a few minutes, she decided to get out and go for a short walk before the others woke. She knew that Gabriel would be ready to head out as soon as he was up. In fact, if he'd had the ability to set an alarm, they'd probably already have been on the road by now. But he'd hardly slept lately, and that had caught up with him as he lay with his eyes closed, breathing heavy as he rested.

Careful not to wake Gabriel, Thomas, or Claire, she walked over to one of the bags containing their firearms, removing a pistol from the inside. She stuck it in the back pocket of her jeans, put on a coat, and tip-toed across the room to the door.

A gentle Autumn morning's breeze brushed against her face. She ran her hands together to warm them, then stuck them into her pockets. It was a typical North Carolina Fall day, like so many she'd lived through. The mornings and evenings would be chilly, while the middle of the day would almost feel like Summer. Soon, every hour of each day would be cold, and she wondered where they'd be when those days came.

In front of the Welcome Center, a group of abandoned cars sat on the highway. She tried her best not to look at them, wanting to forget about the world she lived in. Instead, she looked off in the opposite direction at all the trees which covered much of the property.

As she stared off to the distance, one question loomed heavy on her mind: had she made a mistake?

The decision to come with Gabriel had been an impulsive one. On one hand, she'd simply become bored at the campground, which was strange for her. An introvert by nature, Jessica rarely found herself looking for adventure. As long as she had a pen and paper and somewhere quiet where she could be on her own, she was content. At the cabin, she'd had those things, but it hadn't seemed to quite fulfill her. Somehow, she'd gained a new sort of love for adventure and a craving for the adrenaline rush that came with it. Sitting inside of a cabin wasn't going to feed that hunger.

Jessica also wondered if she'd let the jealousy take hold of her.

Because she was in love with Will.

She couldn't put a finger on why she'd fallen for him so quickly—she just knew it to be true. Perhaps it had been the bond she'd built with his parents before the two of them had even met. She'd already seen so much of their fighting spirit inside their only son. Maybe part of it was the fact that she'd been there when Will had 'died'. She felt a connection to him through that that would be impossible for Holly to understand. When she'd seen him lying in the middle of the road, the feeling hadn't been so different from walking in on her dead parents.

But had her jealousy of Holly gotten the best of her?

Jessica reached the far side of the parking lot and stared out onto the desolate highway. Part of her wanted to keep walking and return to the camp. Another part of her wanted to jump into a vehicle and just drive away. To get away from Gabriel, who would only remind her of Will every time she looked at him. Additionally, she worried that Gabriel's recklessness and desire to reach his family would end up getting her killed. She could head south to Florida, and leave the threat of an impending Winter behind her. Others would surely be there, and she could hook up with another group and lean on them for survival.

All these ideas swam around inside her head, but they didn't matter. The thought of going at it alone was appealing, but stupid. As careless as Gabriel had become, he was smart and, like Jessica, he was a survivor. The same could be said for Claire, and especially for Thomas, who wasn't going to put up with a lot of bullshit. He would help keep Gabriel on track and focused.

Jessica set aside the asinine idea of leaving and retraced her steps back to the building. As she approached the Welcome Center, the door opened and Gabriel came walking outside. Immediately, he covered his nose, remembering the bodies they'd left to rot near the building. He met Jessica near the bathrooms, out of range of the stench.

Gabriel asked, "How'd you sleep?"

Jessica shrugged.

"Yeah, same here. What are you doing out here?"

"Just wanted to get some fresh air and take a walk before we left. I knew you were going to want to leave pretty much right after you woke up."

"Already packed up my bed and got my stuff together," Gabriel replied. "I purposely made noise in hopes that I'd wake those other two up, but they sleep like rocks. Neither of them moved."

Jessica smiled.

Gabriel looked off toward the road. He put his hands in his pockets and drew in a deep breath. "Can I ask you something?"

Jessica nodded.

"Do you think I'll find them?"

The question threw Jessica. She of course knew that Gabriel was speaking of his wife and daughter. Was she supposed to tell the truth? That, no, he wouldn't find them. That the chances that they'd survived all this were astronomical. From how he'd described her, Gabriel's wife didn't seem built for a survivalist world.

But, in this new world, hope was all they had. It was, perhaps, the only thing keeping air in their lungs.

"I do," Jessica said. "I do think we're going to find them."

Gabriel frowned, looking down at the sidewalk.

She asked, "What's the matter?"

"What if I'm not sure that I *want* to find them?"

"What?" Jessica asked. She'd heard what he'd asked, but couldn't believe it.

Gabriel looked up. "I haven't been the best father, and I damn sure haven't been a great husband. And look around us. Look at what the world has become. Look at what *we've* become. We're goddamn animals out here trying to survive. This isn't a way to live. I just wonder if it would be better for them to be dead. How am I supposed to have a family in a world like this?"

Jessica found herself at a loss. She really wasn't sure what to say.

"Gabriel, that isn't true. Look at what you've done with Dylan. You had no responsibility to take care of that child, yet you protected him like he was your own."

Gabriel looked away, unable to make eye contact with Jessica any longer. She grabbed him by the hand, and he turned to face her.

"We're going to get to Alexandria, and we're going to find your wife and your little girl, all right?"

It took a few moments of staring vacantly into Jessica's eyes, but he finally nodded. She wrapped her arm around him, just like she would have if he were her brother. She smiled.

"Come on," Jessica said. "Let's go wake those rocks up."

***

With Thomas and Claire now awake, and everything loaded into the SUV, Gabriel went to the two picnic tables at the far end of the Welcome Center. Jessica sat at one, writing in her journal. As Gabriel approached, she closed it, almost as if she didn't want him to see what she was writing. He wondered what she wrote about, but also knew that it was none of his business. She stood up.

"We ready to go?"

Gabriel nodded. "Yeah."

"Thanks for letting me have a little bit of time to myself," Jessica said.

"No problem." Gabriel cleared his throat. "Thanks for your encouragement earlier. You have to understand that, in a way, the closer to home I get, the more scared I become. I *have* to find my family."

Jessica hugged Gabriel.

"We'll find them."

Gabriel broke their embrace, then looked Jessica in the eyes and smiled. They turned around and headed back over to the SUV. Thomas and Claire stood near the back of it, watching as the two approached.

"You guys ready?" Thomas asked.

Gabriel nodded.

Thomas smiled. "Then let's blow this joint, shall we?"

***

Gabriel sat in the back seat, chewing on a tough piece of jerky. He'd never been a fan of the stuff, but now the dried meat may as well have been a tender slab of filet mignon. Thomas had several packs, and eating it in-between the cans of processed soup had become a luxury. Gabriel reminded himself of how fortunate they were to have any food at all. That they weren't to the point yet where they were hunting rabbits and squirrels.

Thomas sat in front of Gabriel, taking the first shift at driving. Gabriel had offered to drive, but Thomas had adamantly said he was driving. Whatever. Gabriel had no issue riding along, just as long as he made it home. That's all that mattered.

"Any idea how far we are from Alexandria?" Thomas asked.

"God willing, we should be there by day's end," Claire said.

Gabriel snorted to himself at the word 'God'. He then said, "Yeah, if we're lucky and don't come up against a ton of resistance." Other than the occasional straggler, they'd so far only run across one small herd of Empties. Thomas had been able to easily maneuver around it.

They'd passed a few gas stations since leaving the Welcome Center, but hadn't stopped at any of them. They'd each looked like they'd been empty since before The Fall, with windows busted out, random auto parts and trash outside, and gas prices that Gabriel hadn't seen in a decade. The weather was nice, but clouds in the eastern sky said that they could hit rain within the hour. So they'd driven on, trying to get as far as they could before the sky fell open.

Jessica sat in the back seat with Gabriel. She had her head buried in her journal.

"What're you writing about?" Gabriel finally asked.

Jessica looked up from her journal and glanced over to him. She shut the book, leaving her pen inside. "Nothing," she said.

"I'm sorry," Gabriel said. "I didn't mean to pry. It's none of my business. Go on, keep writing."

Jessica turned away from Gabriel, and stared out her window. "It's okay. I was finished anyway."

Gabriel looked out his own window. Nothing but vast open fields covered the landscape. He had spent so much time traveling and living in the city that he often forgot that his home state of Virginia had such beautiful scenery.

"Hey, look," Thomas said.

A large gas station sat in-between the eastbound and westbound lanes of the highway. It had at least one fast food restaurant joined to it.

"We've gotta check this place out," Thomas said. "We're in the middle of nowhere, and there's hardly any cars in the parking lot. Maybe this place hasn't been raided."

Gabriel doubted that. But Thomas was right that the gas station didn't appear to be a threat—at least not from the outside. And it had a restaurant attached that might have food.

"All right," Gabriel said. "Let's stop and have a look."

CHAPTER THREE

After a period of screaming, Dylan finally passed out.

"Check his pulse," Will said.

Charlie placed his index and middle fingers on Dylan's neck. "He's alive. Must've passed out from the pain."

Outside of the SUV, Mary Beth sat on the ground and cried.

"Go take care of her," Will told Holly. "I'll keep pressure."

Holly wiped her own eyes and stepped out of the vehicle.

"Come on, sweetie, let's get out of the rain." Holly led Mary Beth to Charlie's cabin.

Ten minutes later, the bleeding had almost completely stopped.

"I think it worked," Will said.

"Where did you learn that about cayenne pepper?" Charlie asked.

"My old boss, I think. He was one of those survivalist types. Loved being outdoors and shit, and always read a lot of books about Navy SEALs and the military. I thought I remembered him saying one day in the break room that you could clot blood with cayenne pepper."

"He's still going to need medical attention," Charlie said. "If that thing is infected, he'll—"

"I know," Will said. "The bleeding's stopped, so let's just be thankful for that. We'll tackle one problem at a time. For now, hand me that first aid kit so I can dress this wound."

Charlie opened the box and passed a large bandage to Will, who dressed the wound. The white of the bandage showed spots of blood, but not nearly as much as the t-shirt and the towel had. He tied the extra shirt around Dylan's arm, just above the wound, using it as a tourniquet. When he'd finished, the two men backed away, allowing the boy to rest.

Outside, the rain had stopped, and Holly and Mary Beth sat on Charlie's porch. The young girl appeared to have calmed down some, and Holly's eyes were dry, as well. She looked over to Will and he gave her a thumbs up as a signal that the bleeding had stopped.

"Thank God," Holly mouthed.

Charlie had moved ten yards away from the front of the SUV, standing near the playground. His hands gripped his hips, and he looked down to the ground.

Approaching Charlie, Will asked, "Do you know of any doctors around here?"

Charlie shook his head and looked up. "There's not even a hospital around here that I know of. And even if there was, I doubt we'd have any luck finding a doctor."

"Then we're gonna have to load up in the car and leave. We can't afford to stay here."

"Agreed," Charlie said. "But where are we gonna go?"

"I suppose we'll head North for Roanoke."

"You still want to go and try to find that preacher?" Charlie asked, puzzled.

"I want to get him help," Will said, gesturing toward the SUV. "That is my *only* priority right now. But if we're able to find him help, then yes, I want to go and try to find Father Bartman."

Charlie nodded. "I just hope that we can find a doctor, and soon."

Me, too, Will thought.

Holly and Mary Beth approached from behind them.

"How is he?"

"I wrapped the wound in bandages. He's still passed out, but he's breathing steady."

"What're we gonna do?" Holly asked.

"Charlie and I both agreed that it's best for us to leave. We still have good shelter here, but we really have no choice but to try and find a doctor. Salt, aspirin, and bandages are only going to take us so far. We need to get him checked out for an infection, and see if we can find someone who can properly close that wound."

"We need to raid the two cabins and grab anything that we can use," Charlie said. "Clothes, more medicine, food—anything that we can take with us."

"You and I can do that," Will replied. He looked at Holly. "Stay out here and keep an eye on the kids." She nodded and took Mary Beth by the hand.

Charlie went to his cabin while Will checked on the only other one still standing, which had been vacant when The Fall had happened. He wasn't sure that he would find much inside. At most, he hoped that he would find some more medicine, or more canned food.

The door was already unlocked when Will turned the handle. The fire hadn't made its way over to this building at all, and the place was clean like it hadn't been touched in weeks. There were no empty bottles or cans left on any of the tables in the living room. In the kitchen, the counters were spotless. The trash next to the refrigerator was empty, and the sink was clear of any dirty dishes.

Will opened the refrigerator, and shut it almost as fast. A rotten smell permeated out of the appliance. It smelled of a mix of spoiled milk, aged meat, and rotten vegetables.

He checked the pantry next. Inside, he found a few cans of beans, canned vegetables, and some spices. He looked for cayenne pepper and didn't see any, but he made sure to pick up the container of salt. This one was almost full.

Next, he walked to the cabinet above the sink. It was also mostly empty, but he found a bottle of aspirin, some cough syrup, and a first aid kit that was even smaller than what they had. He set the first aid kit down on the counter and popped it open. Inside, he found a large bandage, gauze, some tape, and Band-Aids. He closed it and put it under his arm, stuffing the bottle of aspirin into his pocket and carrying the cough syrup.

Two bedrooms were located in the back of the cabin. He'd hoped that he would find some clothes, as he'd lost most of his in the fire. He checked the closets, the bathroom, and the laundry room, but found nothing useful. Even still, one of the beds had clean sheets, a comforter, and four pillows. All the linens on the bed in the second bedroom had been stripped, likely by the survivors at the campground. Will removed the blankets and the pillows from the bed, and set them down near the front door.

He made one last sweep through the building, looking to see if he could find anything that would be of use to them. When he didn't, he headed back out the door.

Outside, Holly was playing with Mary Beth in the middle of the campground. For the first time in hours, the child finally appeared calm. It put a smile on Will's face to see her happy.

"You guys want to come over and help me carry some of this stuff to the car?" Will asked.

"Sure," Holly yelled back.

Will threw the bedding onto the porch and asked Mary Beth

if she could carry the pillows to the vehicle. Her arms weren't quite long enough to grab all four of them, but she managed to grab three.

"What else did you find?" Holly asked.

Will sighed. "Not a lot. I found a little food, more aspirin and bandages, and those blankets and pillows. That's about it."

After handing Holly the bag of food and the first aid kit, Will picked up the blankets and the remaining pillow. As he stepped off the front porch, he heard Charlie come out of his cabin. Will stopped in the courtyard to wait on him.

"Did you find anything?" Will asked.

Charlie carried a duffel bag and two reusable grocery bags.

"Pretty much just my clothes and some food. I cleared out the rest of the medicine cabinet. Never know when we'll need that stuff. I've got one more load just inside the door."

"I'll grab it," Holly said.

Charlie nodded, and he and Will made their way to the SUV.

The back door of the SUV was open, and the two men set their things in the rear cargo area. Will peeked over the top of the seat and saw Dylan still fast asleep, his stomach rising and falling. The bandage on his arm showed red spots, but it wasn't soaked.

"Still hard to believe that cayenne pepper actually worked," Charlie said.

"Thank God it did," Will said. "I don't know what I would've done if he would have..." Will stopped the sentence short. "Gabriel left him with me, and he trusted that I would take care of him."

Charlie put his hand on Will's shoulder. "You can't beat yourself up over what happened, man. We didn't know those things were out there, or that they would come here and start a fire. We just didn't know. We'd been here all this time and hadn't seen any. It's not your fault."

Will sighed. "I know."

A few moments later, Holly returned, carrying the remaining bags.

"This was all I saw."

"That's everything," Charlie said.

"So, does that mean we're ready to go?" Holly asked.

"I think so," Will said.

"Where are we going?" Mary Beth asked.

"We're going to go and try to find a doctor for Dylan."

"Is he going to be okay?"

"Yes, sweetie, he's going to be fine. He just needs a doctor to check some things." Holly grabbed Mary Beth by the hand and led her to the rear of the truck. "You're gonna have to squeeze in back here. We need to let Dylan lay down on the back seat."

"Okay," Mary Beth said.

With Holly's help, she loaded into the cargo area of the truck in a small area they'd left clear for her.

"Comfortable?" Holly asked.

Mary Beth shrugged.

"Would you rather sit in my lap?" Holly asked.

"I'll be fine here."

"All right, sweetie. It's just until Dylan gets better."

"When will that be?"

Shaking her head, Holly said, "I'm not sure. Now, watch your hands." She shut the back door.

Five yards from the SUV, Charlie stood with his back to the vehicle, his hands on his hips. Will stepped up behind him.

"You ready to go, man?" Will asked.

Charlie didn't respond. He raised his hand to his face and

wiped his eyes. Will walked around to face him and saw that he was choking back tears.

"I really thought we'd have this place forever," Charlie said. "I can't believe it's gone. I can't believe *they're* gone." He looked at the cabins that had burned, clearly thinking of the friends they'd lost within the campground.

"Nothing is forever," Will said. "Especially not now. But we're going to be all right." Will put his hand on Charlie's shoulder. "Come on, man. Let's get out of here."

Charlie turned around and walked with Will back to the SUV. The passenger side rear door was open, and Holly sat inside.

"I'll sit back here with Dylan," she said. "You can ride up front with Will."

Will got into the driver's seat, adjusting it so that it was comfortable for him. He looked over to Charlie, who stared outside at the destroyed cabins, his hand on his chin.

"It's gonna be all right, brother," Will said.

There was a moment of silence, and then Charlie said, "For us, it's possible." He shook his head. "But not for them."

Will drew in a deep breath, put the truck into drive, and headed for the campground's exit for the last time.

CHAPTER FOUR

They headed East on I-40—the same way they'd gone when they'd driven to Durham.

"We should hit I-77 in about an hour," Charlie said. "Between here and there, we aren't going to pass through any cities. Just a lot of rural areas and smaller towns."

"I know we didn't see many people on our way toward Durham last time, but let's just keep our eyes peeled," Will said. He glanced into the rearview mirror at Holly. "How's he doing back there?"

"Still passed out and breathing fine," Holly said, speaking low.

"I can't believe he's still out," Charlie said.

"Just enjoy it while you can," Will said. "It's gonna be hell when he wakes. How are you doing back there, Mary Beth?"

Whispering, Holly answered, "She's asleep."

"Oh, sorry," Will said.

"Poor girl went through a lot today," Charlie commented.

"Yeah," Will said. "More than any girl her age should have to."

As they cruised down the interstate, they looked around for any signs of life. They saw no moving cars, no live people walking. Nothing but abandoned cars and the occasional Empty. The farther away from the camp they moved, the dryer the roads became as the rain had apparently avoided this area.

They reached I-77 in just over an hour and headed North.

Less then ten miles down 77, Dylan sighed, and his eyes

cracked open.

"He's waking up," Holly said.

Dylan's breathing got heavier. "Where are we? What's going on?"

"You're in the car, and we're all here. We're heading to Virginia, and we're trying to find you help."

"We're all here," Mary Beth said, poking her head over the seat.

The boy picked his head up and looked down to his arm, now half the length of the other. He panted heavily.

"It's okay," Holly said. "Calm down."

"My arm, it's really gone? I thought I was dreaming."

"We need to pull over," Charlie said.

"Oh, God, it hurts." The time between Dylan's breaths shortened, his chest rising and falling.

"Sweetie, you're going to be fine. We're going to get you help," Holly said, continuing to stroke Dylan's hair.

"No, my arm!" Dylan thrusted his hips. In the back of the SUV, Mary Beth cried.

"Stop the car, Will," Holly said. "He needs fresh air."

Approaching an exit, Will veered off, and headed toward a gas station when he reached the end of the ramp. He turned into the parking lot and pulled the SUV in front of one of the pumps. The parking lot was clear of Empties.

Will stepped out and opened the rear driver's side door, where Holly sat next to Dylan's head. Charlie opened the other door to Dylan's kicking legs.

"Let him sit up," Will told Holly.

Holly got out of the back seat and stood beside Will. Panting, Dylan sat up, his back against the seat. Mary Beth continued to cry, but Will ignored it. He looked down at the dressing on the boy's arm, which had turned a little redder since Will had checked it last. Dylan looked up at Will and Holly, his eyes full of tears.

"Is this real?"

Holding back his emotions, Will nodded.

Dylan just stared at Will for a few moments before looking back down to his arm. He then grabbed the bandage and ripped away at it.

Holly said, "No, Dylan, don't—"

Will cut her off. "No, it's fine. Let him."

"But, he—"

"He needs to see it."

Holly walked around to the back side of the SUV and opened the rear compartment.

"Come on," she said to Mary Beth.

"But I want to—"

"Now," Holly demanded.

She grabbed Mary Beth by the hand and pulled the girl out of the vehicle. They stepped away toward the convenience store.

Dylan continued tearing off the bandage until nothing was there. Nothing but a bloody open wound, half of his arm gone forever. Dylan went to remove the belt, but Will reached out and grabbed his arm.

"You can't take that off, buddy. You'll start bleeding again."

Will let go and Dylan lowered his arm. He still didn't speak. He just stared down at his missing limb. Will couldn't even imagine what was going on inside the boy's head. Ever since the accident, Will had been wishing that he could have traded places with Dylan. The child didn't deserve this.

"We need to clean it up and get another bandage on there," Will said. "I promise you that we'll find a doctor who can fix this up right." He looked over to Charlie. "Can you hand me the first aid kit?"

Will got inside the SUV, sitting next to Dylan. The boy didn't look up at him. He just continued to stare down at his arm.

"Here you go," Charlie said, handing Will the first aid kit.

Will opened the box and pulled out a large bandage, a small stack of cotton pads, Neosporin, and the aspirin.

"Can you also grab a bottle of water out of the back?" Will asked Charlie.

Will opened the bottle of aspirin, dropping two pills into his hand. Charlie handed the bottle of water to Dylan, the top already twisted off. Dylan tipped the bottle to his lips and took a large swig.

"Take these. They should help ease some of the pain," Will said, handing him the two pills.

Dylan shoved them into his mouth.

Will stretched out the bandage, preparing to rewrap the boy's arm, and then he opened the tube of Neosporin and dropped some of the cream onto one of the cotton pads.

"This isn't going to feel good," Will said. "But we have to do it to keep this clean and try to keep any bacteria out. Turn my way and let me see your arm."

Will drew in a deep breath and then pressed the cotton pad against the boy's wound. Dylan jerked away what was left of his arm, his rear rising off the seat as he cried out.

"I know it hurts, buddy," Will said. "But we've got to do it. It'll only take a second." Will reached into the back and grabbed a t-shirt out of one of the bags. "Here, bite down on this."

Dylan put the shirt in his mouth and gritted his teeth. He grimaced as Will applied the Neosporin, but it only took a few moments before he was done.

"Boom, there we go," Will said, smiling. "Now we can wrap it back up."

"It hurts so bad," Dylan said.

"I know, buddy. We're going to find you some help soon." Will had no idea if he was telling the truth in saying this, but continued to stay positive. "Just hang out here. I'll be back."

Will looked to Charlie and signaled him to meet him at the front of the vehicle. The two men met at the edge of the parking lot where an air pump sat.

"That wound is only going to get worse if we don't find help soon," Charlie said.

"I know," Will said, looking down and massaging his temples.

"We've gotta start thinking about searching some of these exits for help. I know it makes sense to keep moving until we hit a more populated area, but I'm not sure we can afford that anymore."

"All right," Will said. "Let's see if we can—"

"Don't move."

The male voice came from behind them, and Will and Charlie both turned.

Holly and Mary Beth stood outside the convenience store, their hands raised in the air. Behind them were two people: a man and a woman. Will took three steps toward the SUV before the man spoke again.

"We've got guns buried into each of their backs."

The man stood behind Holly, and the woman behind Mary Beth.

"It's true," Holly said. "They're both armed."

Will could see the woman almost in tears, clearly uncomfortable that she held a gun on a child. The man looked similarly shaken. Raising his arms into the air, Will looked over to Charlie and signaled him to do the same.

"What do you want?" Will asked.

"We just want to get out of here without any trouble," the man said. Now that he spoke, Will could hear the slight tremble in his voice. "What do you have in the truck?"

Will bit his lip, nearly drawing blood. He closed his eyes and breathed. "I can't give you any of our supplies."

"I don't think you're really in the position to make that decision," the man said.

"We can spare some extra ammunition, but that's all."

The man shoved the gun into Holly's back, and she cried out as she arched forward. Will felt the sweat drip down his forehead, still not sure if the man was bluffing or not.

"We have another child in the car," Will said. "He's in the back seat. He's badly injured, and we're trying to find him help. We can't afford to give you any of our food or medicine. They're all that's keeping him alive. Now, like I said, we can spare some ammunition, but that's all. Please, just let us be on our way."

The man and woman looked at each other. The woman's face reddened; she now had tears in her eyes.

"I can see that you aren't bad people," Will said. "We've seen our share of evil. You just want to survive, like us."

The man frowned again. "If any of you move, you're dead, understand me?" He moved from behind Holly and started toward the SUV, walking slowly. He shifted his head back and forth, checking on Holly behind him. Will and Charlie remained still and with their hands in the air. Walking up beside the SUV, the man peeked inside. His facial expression changed. Where he had once held a sour demeanor of anger, he now looked concerned. Several moments of silence passed.

"Put your gun down," the man told the woman, a sense of calm in his voice.

The woman, her face flushed, continued to hold the gun against Mary Beth's back. She'd frozen. The man looked over to her.

"It's okay, Laurie," he said. "Really, put it down."

After a few more moments, Laurie lowered her hands and stepped away from Mary Beth. Holly wiped her eyes and leaned down to hug the young girl, assuring her that everything was all right.

Will and Charlie still had their arms up when the man approached them. He came to within a couple of feet of Will and holstered his weapon, and he offered his hand to Will.

"I'm Karl."

Will looked over to Charlie and nodded. Both men lowered their arms, and Will grasped onto the man's hand, shaking it.

"I'm Will."

"Nice to meet you, Will. Now, let's see if we can get this boy some help."

CHAPTER FIVE

The gas station looked like it had been abandoned long before the apocalypse. Most of the windows were busted out, and it appeared as if the inside of the store was empty. Even so, Thomas still felt the need to stop.

"There's no way we're finding anything here," Gabriel said. "Look at this place."

As Jessica looked around, she found herself agreeing with Gabriel. Only one vehicle remained in the parking lot of the gas station. It was an old, beaten pickup truck, its body rusted and rotted out. The place had the vibe of a scene from a horror movie, and something felt off about being there.

"Let's just check and make sure they don't have any gasoline here," Thomas said. He stepped out of the SUV.

Gabriel looked over to Jessica and rolled his eyes. "We aren't gonna find shit here." He opened the door, then slammed it behind him.

Claire looked back to Jessica, her eyes narrowed and showing her frustration.

"He's just ready to get home," Jessica said, speaking of Gabriel.

"He needs to chill out," Claire said.

No one said y'all had to come.

Jessica opened the door and stepped out of the SUV. Gabriel stood at the edge of the parking lot, looking out at the vast, open landscape. Thomas cupped his hands and looked through the front of the building. Jessica glanced at the gas tanks and got the first clue they wouldn't be finding anything. The gas pumps displayed a price of $1.18. The last time she'd put gas in her own vehicle, she'd paid almost $2. She walked over to Gabriel.

The entire landscape in front of them was nothing but flat lands. Fall had almost taken root, as much of the grass had started to brown. A cool breeze chilled her face. Jessica tucked her hands into her coat pockets as she stood next to him.

"You're right," Jessica said. "No way we are getting gas out of those tanks. I haven't seen prices that low in years."

"It's fine," Gabriel said. "I understand why he wants to stop and look. You never know if we'll find something."

Glass shattered behind them, and Jessica turned. Thomas had taken the butt-end of his rifle and slammed it through the front door. It had been one of the only windows still in tact. Thomas and Claire ducked through the new opening in the door and headed inside.

"I'm gonna go check the pumps for gas," Jessica said.

She walked back over to the SUV and opened the driver's side door. She bent over and popped the gas tank, then inserted the nozzle into it. Nothing happened. She withdrew her knife and sawed through the rubber hose. When she'd sliced a hole in it, she looked inside.

Bone dry.

Jessica replaced the fuel pump, closed the gas tank, and then walked to the backside of the SUV. She checked the clouds again in the eastern sky, which had grown darker and moved closer. They were possibly only a short drive away from hitting the storm head-on. Hopefully, the roads would be mostly clear of debris and of Empties.

A gleam of light stung her eye and drew her attention.

She looked off the way they'd come from, and saw a speck growing larger. The glare of light had come off of the headlights or hood of a fast-approaching vehicle. And there wasn't only one. It was a small pack of vehicles. The one leading was a pickup, and she could've sworn, even from far away, that someone was standing in the bed of it. Behind the truck was a camper, and two sedans flanked it.

"Gabriel," Jessica said. She heard feet punishing the gravel beneath, and within a few moments, Gabriel was at her side.

"Get in the truck," Gabriel said. "Now!"

Jessica didn't hesitate. She turned and loaded into her spot in the back seat of the SUV.

"Thomas!" Gabriel shouted. "Claire!"

Claire looked out through the window, confusion covering her face.

"Get out here, now!" Gabriel said.

Claire disappeared from the window, and soon emerged outside with her brother.

"What is it?" Thomas asked. "We think we may have found some food in the back that we can take with us."

"We've gotta go, now," Gabriel said.

"Gabriel, wh—"

Gabriel pointed down the highway. Thomas and Claire followed the direction of his finger toward the oncoming vehicles, which were now less than a mile away.

"Shit," Thomas said, and grabbed his sister's hand and ran to the car.

Jessica's heart raced as she loaded back inside.

***

Gabriel jumped into the driver's seat and cranked the SUV.

Thomas joined Gabriel up front, and Claire hopped into the back next to Jessica. Before they could even shut the doors, Gabriel punched the gas. The tires squealed as he raced out of the parking lot.

Now only about a quarter of a mile behind them, the men held their weapons in the air like warriors. Gabriel floored the SUV, its V-8 engine creating distance between them and their followers.

Jessica looked out the back window and watched the two vehicles flanking the camper pull away from it.

"They're gaining on us," Jessica said.

Thomas checked his gun to make sure it was loaded. It was.

The first gunshot went off, and Claire screamed. It hadn't come from Thomas' gun, but from one of the vehicles behind them. A second bullet hit the back window, creating a spiderweb-type crack.

"Get down!" Thomas demanded of his sister and of Jessica.

Gabriel had to shout over Claire's hysterics, as the woman continued to cry. "Jessica! When Thomas starts shooting, be ready to reload his weapon!"

"Got it," Jessica said. She said it with a calmness that put Gabriel at ease. One panicking passenger inside the vehicle was enough.

The oncoming group fired their weapons again, this time shattering the back window completely. Claire cried out again as glass spilled down upon her. Gabriel swerved, the shot having startled him.

Gabriel glanced into the rearview mirror again. The two oncoming vehicles had gained on them.

"I'm gonna go back there," Thomas said. "I can fire out the back window. We can't just keep driving and do nothing else."

"All right," Gabriel said. "Be careful."

"You just keep your damn foot on the gas," Thomas said. He unbuckled his seatbelt and squeezed between the two front seats.

The convoy fired another round of shots, and Thomas dived into the back seat. His sister screamed again, and so did Jessica.

"You okay?" Gabriel asked. "Did you get hit?"

"I'm good," Thomas said.

Thomas had just poked his head up when another shot rang through the air. The bullet zipped through the vehicle, just missing Thomas, as it shattered the front windshield.

Gabriel ducked out of the way, swerving again. He was now unable to see out the front window.

Thinking quickly, Jessica leaned between the front seats and hit the windshield with a shotgun, knocking it out.

"Thanks," Gabriel said.

He glanced down at the speedometer, which read 100 miles per hour. He looked in the mirror and watched Thomas jump all the way into the cargo area.

Gunshots went off again, and Gabriel ducked his head.

The next round of gunfire came from within the SUV. The caravan behind them had stopped shooting, and Thomas was finally able to fire off a few shots. Gabriel looked into his side mirror and saw one of the vehicles swerve, nearly going off the road completely.

Thomas stopped firing and ducked down. "Give me another round!"

Jessica handed him ammunition and he reloaded.

Gabriel had now accelerated the SUV to 120 miles per hour. The highway ahead was free and clear of Empties. Most vehicles that had been left abandoned were off the side of the road., giving them a clear path.

The pursuing caravan didn't return fire until Thomas poked his head up to shoot the rifle again.

Thomas screamed.

"No!" Claire yelled. She started to get up from the floorboard, but Jessica held her down.

"Thomas, are you all right?" Jessica asked.

"What happened?" Gabriel asked.

"My arm," Thomas mumbled. "Son of a bitch."

"He's hit, Gabriel," Jessica said.

"Just stay down!" Gabriel yelled back to Thomas.

Jessica poked her head between the seats.

"Is there any way you can get back there and help him?" Gabriel asked.

"I don't think so," Jessica said. "There isn't enough room back there for me to duck out of harm's way. I'd be an open target."

Gabriel bit his lip as he looked into his side mirror again. Somehow, the vehicles had closed the gap even more. They were now only a hundred yards back or so. How the guy in the truck had hit Thomas from that distance was somewhat of a miracle. It had either been a lucky shot, or they were packing the proper artillery and skill for such a shot.

Another minute or so passed before the men fired again. After a few shots, each spaced wide apart, there was a loud pop. Gabriel's control on the SUV dissipated, as one of the rear tires blew out.

"Shit!" Gabriel yelled. "They hit a tire!"

He looked down to the speedometer, and it had dropped from 120 all the way down to 95, and continued falling. He looked in the rearview mirror and saw that the truck was now between the two sedans. The man standing in the back pumped his fist, his rifle now pointed to the air.

But Gabriel wasn't going to give up easily. These men would kill them, he was sure. He kept his foot down on the gas, all the way to the floor. In the rear, Thomas still groaned, and Gabriel's control of the SUV continued to weaken.

"You two have to get up in your seats," Gabriel said to Claire and Jessica. He was worried about a bad accident now. If that happened, the girls would be thrown around the SUV like clothes inside a dryer. When neither girl moved, he yelled, "Now!"

Jessica moved first, before she realized that Claire was remaining still in the floor. She went down and said something into the girl's ear, and then Claire finally got up into the seat. No more gunshots came, and they were each able to make it into their seats and get buckled in.

"Duck your heads," Gabriel said.

"What about Thomas?" Jessica asked.

Gabriel didn't answer. He could only hope they didn't get into an accident, tossing Thomas around the inside of the SUV.

Another round of gunfire came from the pursuing caravan. There were three shots before the other tire in the back of the SUV blew.

This shot was the fatal one.

Cruising at 90 miles per hour and losing another tire, Gabriel lost all control of the SUV. The back end got away from him, and by instinct, he slammed on the brakes.

The vehicle fishtailed, and then it flipped.

When the SUV finally stopped rolling, Gabriel groaned. Everything hurt. He clutched at his ribs as he tried to cough. Though the seat belt had saved his life, it had constricted his midsection. Gabriel now found it hard to take in even a single breath.

Outside, tires squealed and the smell of burning rubber permeated the air.

"Jessica?" Gabriel asked. "Claire?"

No one responded.

Car doors slammed and men laughed.

Gabriel reached around, trying to find a weapon. He looked for the shotgun Jessica had handed him, but he couldn't even gauge in what way the SUV had landed.

One of the doors opened, and as he stretched to try and look, his side screamed at him and he cried out.

"We got one movin' in here," a man said.

Another said, "Get his ass out."

A set of hands reached down, and Gabriel's vision was too blurry for him to even see them clearly. He was on the verge of blacking out. As his seatbelt unbuckled, he slapped at the arms in front of him, but it was of no use.

"Get your ass up," a man said, and began to lift.

Gabriel cried out as the man tried to pick him up, and his entire body fell limp. He now realized that the SUV had come to a stop on its side. He looked up, and the sun shined into the cab of the truck, blocking out the face of a man.

The man said something, which sounded muffled.

The last thing Gabriel saw before he was out cold was the man's fist coming down into his face.

CHAPTER SIX

"Are we sure we can trust them?" Holly asked.

Will shook his head. "Let's just wait it out and see what they have to say."

Karl and Laurie had stepped away from the group to talk amongst themselves. A couple of minutes passed, and they finally returned to Will and the others.

"All right," Karl began. "It's clear that if that boy doesn't get some attention soon, he's going to be in serious trouble. We have a doctor back at our camp. It's only a couple of miles down the road from here."

"You can help him?" Holly asked.

Karl shook his head. "I didn't say that. I'm not the doctor, and I'm not sure we even have the proper tools to do what needs to be done to help him. But we're going to take you there to try."

Will rubbed his forehead and then shook Karl's hand. "Thank you. Thank you, so much."

"Our group isn't going to like us bringing someone else in," Laurie said. "There's no guarantee that they're going to agree to let you stay, or that they're going to help him."

"How could they not help a child?" Charlie asked.

"Do you want us to try, or not?" Karl asked.

Will and Charlie looked at each other, and Will said, "Yes, of course."

"Then get in your vehicle and follow us."

***

Karl and Laurie led them through a rural area, passing nothing but trees on a country road. The group hardly spoke any words to each other. Holly sat in the back, cuddling up to Dylan and running her hands through his hair. Over and over again, she told him, "We're getting you help."

After several miles, Karl turned into a suburban neighborhood. The concrete sign outside the subdivision read: Lake Forest Estates. The entrance was blocked with a rod iron gate. Large slabs of wood covered the openings between each rod.

"Damn," Charlie mumbled.

Karl stepped out of the vehicle and looked back to the SUV. Staring at Will, he held up his index finger, signaling that he needed a moment, and then he walked to the fence.

"I wonder how many people are here," Charlie said.

"They sure could house a lot of people, I'll tell you that much," Will said. Houses lined either side of the street beyond the gate.

"You think they're going to help us?" Charlie asked.

Will glanced into the rearview mirror at Holly. She wasn't paying attention to the conversation in the front seat. She continued to run her fingers through Dylan's hair, keeping the boy calm. In the cargo area, Mary Beth remained silent, but she stared at Will in the mirror.

"I hope so," Will said.

Ahead, Karl stood at the gate talking to someone on the other side through a square opening. He made different hand gestures, and several moments passed with no movement.

"What's taking so long?" Charlie asked. He was hardly able to get the words out before Karl stepped back from the fence and gave Will a thumbs up.

"Thank God," Holly said.

The gate opened, and Karl pulled forward.

Will sighed. "Here we go."

Two men guarded the rod iron fence, each armed with assault rifles. As the SUV passed through the gate, each man kept their eyes glued on Will and the others.

"They didn't look too happy," Charlie said.

"Your group wasn't too happy when they first saw us, either," Will reminded him.

Houses lined either side of the street. Some of them looked as if they'd been unaffected by mankind's fall, while others appeared to barely be standing. Blood stained the doors on some of the homes, the grass on others. It didn't look like any people were currently living in any of these houses. Karl continued down the street until he came to a stop sign and turned onto Chapman Drive. He drove down Chapman for three blocks before turning onto Mallory Court.

That's when other humans appeared.

Ten houses lined the road on either side, funneling into a cul-de-sac at the end of the road. In front of one house, a man and woman stood in front of a barbecue grill. Two houses down, a man kneeled in front of a generator, looking up as the SUV passed by. On the other side of the street, three kids played in the front yard of a two-story house. A woman sat on the front patio, watching the children.

Charlie said, "It looks..."

"Normal," Holly said, finishing his sentence.

Karl stopped in the middle of the road, at the end of the cul-de-sac. He didn't bother to pull up next to a curb or into one of the driveways. Will came to a stop at half of a car length behind Karl's sedan. Laurie stepped out of the passenger seat and Karl exited the driver's seat.

"Stay here with the children, Holly," Will said. He looked over to Charlie. "Come on."

Will opened the door and stepped out of the SUV. He looked around, seeing now that more people had come outside from the houses.

There were people of varying age, ethnicity, and gender. Will counted at least a dozen people. At the end of the cul-de-sac, a man and a woman, each looking to be in their mid-50s, walked outside. Karl approached, meeting them halfway through the front yard. He spoke to them, pointing back to the SUV. Looking over Karl's shoulder, the woman stared at Will. She didn't smile, instead holding an expression that asked a thousand questions.

When she looked back to Karl, she slapped him across the face.

"Oh, shit," Will said. Karl raised his hand to his face, massaging it. The man stood in Karl's face, his finger pointed at him. When he was finished, both he and the woman walked past Karl and approached the SUV.

"Just stay calm," Will said.

"This was a mistake," Charlie said. "We've got to get out of here, now."

"Everything's going to be fine," Will said. "We have a child with us. They've got to help us."

As the man and woman approached the SUV, Will took another glance around the cul-de-sac. More people had emerged from their houses. He was sure that it was least two dozen now. People had also gathered in the street behind the SUV, forming a sort of wall. Even if Will wanted to jump back into the vehicle and try to race out of there, it would prove nearly impossible. They were trapped.

Will looked through the windshield of the SUV to Holly in the back seat. She held Dylan in her arms, her eyes wide as she stared out at him. Mary Beth had joined her and Dylan on the back seat. Will mouthed the words, "Stay in the car."

The man and the woman stopped just a few feet away from Will. The man looked Will up and down, and then he smiled and extended his hand.

"Hello," he said. "My name's Timothy."

Will hesitated before he reached out and shook Timothy's hand. He still didn't understand why the woman had slapped Karl.

"This is my wife, Samantha."

Samantha didn't offer a handshake. Instead, she simply smiled at Will and Charlie.

Timothy was silent for a moment before he shrugged his shoulders. "Well, do you have names?"

Charlie started to respond before Will butted in.

"Why'd she slap Karl?" Will asked.

Timothy looked over to his wife, and then chuckled, turning his attention back to Will.

"Ya know, it's awful rude for you to not tell us your names. You are, after all, asking for *our* help."

Will furrowed his brow. "I'm just not sure I can trust you yet."

Timothy looked past Will, into the SUV, shaking his head.

"From the looks of it, you don't seem to have much of a choice."

Will glanced back over his shoulder. Holly was kissing Dylan's forehead while holding Mary Beth tight to her chest. Their eyes met again and her look told Will everything he needed to know. He turned around to face Timothy again.

"My name's Will. This is Charlie."

"Hello, Will. Charlie."

"Do you have a doctor here who can help us?" Charlie asked.

Timothy walked to the side of the SUV. Will wanted to reach out and stop him, but Charlie grabbed his arm before he could.

Opening the driver's side rear door, Timothy looked into the back seat. Holly continued holding Dylan and Mary Beth tight. Timothy ducked inside, observing the boy. Will clenched his fist, ready to go after Timothy if he made any sudden moves.

When Timothy pulled his head out of the truck, he looked to his wife.

"Samantha, go get Doug. Tell him it's urgent."

Samantha nodded, and ran toward one of the houses.

"Is Doug the doctor?" Will asked.

"No," Timothy said. "I am."

CHAPTER SEVEN

Will and Charlie loaded Dylan onto a folding table. The legs had been completely removed, leaving only a solid table top. Will remembered the way Dylan had cried when they'd had to carry him through the woods, and how he'd had to pick the boy up under his arms. He was thankful for the make-do stretcher.

They hurried through the yard of one of the nearby houses, Timothy and Doug walking in front of them. As he approached the house, Timothy shouted directions at two people standing in the yard. Then he and Doug turned around.

"Let's each grab a corner to get him into the house," Timothy said.

Five stairs led up to the porch. Wind chimes sang in the breeze. Two empty wooden chairs sat near the door.

The front door was already open when they reached it. A woman with blonde hair, held up in a bun, stood just inside the house against a wall, making sure the door remained wide. She looked to be in her late 30s or early 40s, and wore a flowered apron over the top of a worn, long sleeve shirt. There were dried blood stains mixed in with the images of roses, dandelions, and magnolias on her apron.

"Everything's ready in the living room," the woman said.

"Thank you, Maureen," Timothy said. He signaled his head toward an open doorway. "Come on, let's take him over here and set him down."

A waist-high table sat in the center of the living room. It appeared much sturdier than the throw-away one they'd loaded

Dylan onto.

Timothy said, "Just set the whole thing down on top of that table."

The four men lifted Dylan's stretcher and set it down on top of the other table. A smaller table stood just over Dylan's head. On top lay a collection of surgical tools, including a scalpel, scissors, and a small bone saw. Will was thankful that they were in a place where Dylan couldn't see them. The tools made Will cringe. He thought back to when he'd had to amputate the boy's arm, remembering how it had felt when the blade of the machete passed through flesh and bone. He shuddered, and then was drawn back into the moment when someone grabbed his arm. It was Doug.

"You guys should probably step outside."

Will shook his head. "I don't want to leave him."

Doug pulled Will a few feet away from the table and stood closer to him. "It will be better if you leave. Timothy needs to be able to concentrate, and you're not going to want to be in here."

Will bit his lip.

"Maureen will show you and your group somewhere you can rest for a while. Please, trust us."

Will still wasn't sure that he could trust them. But now that he'd seen they appeared to have the proper tools and skills to help Dylan, he had little choice. He would have to have confidence that Timothy knew how to help. He sighed, then said, "Okay."

Another hand grabbed him, and he turned around to see Maureen, smiling, if only a little.

"Come on," she said. "I'll show you where you can relax."

Will walked over to the table and looked down into Dylan's eyes.

"You aren't going to leave me, are you?" the boy asked.

Will grabbed onto Dylan's remaining hand. "We won't be far. These gentlemen here are going to help you. They're going to take the pain away. I promise you that we will be back over here as soon as it's over."

Dylan cried, and his body trembled. Will leaned down and kissed him on the forehead.

When Will turned around, Timothy stood there, wearing a pair of latex gloves.

"Don't worry, we have a little bit of anesthetic left. We're going to administer it to him before we start," Timothy said. "He won't feel a thing."

"Please, just take care of him."

"We will."

Will took one more look back to Dylan. The boy's eyes were red, full of tears. Will smiled and mouthed the words, "Stay strong."

He walked out the door, where Maureen and Charlie were already waiting on the porch.

***

After Will and Charlie went to the SUV to fetch Holly, Mary Beth, and their things, Maureen led them to another house. The front door opened into a large, open living room with all the furniture still in place. With the power out, the large windows lining the front of the house illuminated the living room. On the wall near the staircase were pictures of a family featuring a man, a woman, and four kids ranging in age from 7 to 17. Will didn't recognize any of the faces as people he'd seen in the street.

Maureen smiled and leaned down to Mary Beth, her hands on her knees.

"Are you hungry?"

Mary Beth nodded. The trails of tears from her eyes were visible through the dirt on her cheeks.

Standing up, Maureen asked, "Do you guys want anything?"

"I'm starving," Holly said.

"Yeah," Charlie said. "We could use something to eat, thank you."

"All right," Maureen said. "I have to run a couple of houses over, but I'll be back. You folks just make yourselves at home."

"Thank you," Charlie said.

Maureen smiled again, focusing it on Will, who still held a blank expression of apprehension on his face. She walked past him and exited through the front door.

Will went to the fireplace and picked up a picture off the mantle. The photograph showed the same man from the other photos, but now dressed in a swimsuit, pointing a hose at one of his daughters and one of his sons. The children laughed, holding their arms up to try and block the blast of the water. It looked like the kind of cookie-cutter, all-American family you would find in an apparel catalog.

"Do those people live here?" Mary Beth asked.

Will set the picture back on the mantle. "I don't think so."

"Then why are their pictures in here?"

Forcing a smile, Will ran his hand through Mary Beth's hair. "Why don't you hang out on the sofa until that nice lady comes back?"

"But I wanna go look around the house."

"You need to stay in here with us," Holly said. "Maureen will be back soon with something to eat."

Plopping down onto the couch, Mary Beth asked, "When can I see Dylan?"

"Soon," Holly said.

"Is he gonna be all right?"

"Yes," Will said. "Now just rest, okay?"

Mary Beth laid down on her back, staring up to the ceiling with her arms crossed over her chest.

A few minutes later, Maureen arrived back in the house. She carried a large bowl and a bucket, as well as a plastic bag looped through her arm.

"There's some spaghetti in this bowl. We've got a couple of generators and a microwave, so I was able to warm it up for you. Unfortunately, we ran out of pasta sauce a while back, so you'll have to eat it dry." She set the bucket down on the table. "I've also got some clean water here that the girl can use to wipe her face off with. If the rest of you want to wash up, I can always go grab another bucket."

"Thank you," Will said. "We might take you up on that after we eat."

"Is there a bathroom nearby were we could take this bucket and get Mary Beth cleaned off?" Holly asked.

"It's just down the hallway over here," Maureen said. "Come on, I'll show you."

While the girls went into the other room to get Mary Beth cleaned up, Will and Charlie each found a seat at the dining room table. Will found some plates that appeared to be clean in one of the cabinets and set them down on the table. Assuming that there was no running water at the house, he checked the tap on the sink anyway. As expected, nothing came out.

When the girls arrived back, Will and Charlie had prepared each person a plate of pasta. They'd set a fork and open bottle of water next to each dish. Mary Beth walked into the room with a big smile on her newly cleaned face. Will smiled back at her.

"You look beautiful," Will said.

"Well," Maureen started, "I'm going to let you all have some time to eat and rest up. Whenever we have some news on the boy, we'll come let you know."

"Thank you," Charlie said. "And thank you for the meal."

"It's no problem." Maureen turned and exited through the front door.

Mary Beth sat down at the table in front of one of the plates. Hungry, she started to dig into the pasta, but then hesitated.

"Go ahead," Holly said. "We know you've got to be hungry."

Mary Beth blushed. "Shouldn't we... say something? Like a prayer, or something?"

"Absolutely," Will said. He hadn't been one to believe in a God, but with everything he'd been through over the past few weeks, he'd come to believe that *something* was out there.

"Do you want to say something, Mary Beth?" Holly asked.

The girl nodded. "Bow your heads." Everyone did, and she started. "Lord, thank you for this food and for this shelter. Thank you for keeping us together and keeping us safe. Lord, we pray that you watch over Dylan, and make him okay again. I don't know what life is going to be like for him now, but please be with him."

There was a moment of silence until Charlie said, "Amen." The others followed.

No one spoke as they ate.

After they finished eating, the group gathered in the living room to relax on the sofa while they awaited news on Dylan.

They didn't have to wait long.

As the day was making its transition into night, the door opened. Sitting in a chair, and leaned over with his hands clasped together, Will looked up to see Doug.

"Please, come with me," Doug said.

CHAPTER EIGHT

Fluorescent lights and silence.

That was all Gabriel would remember about waking up.

Aside from the pain.

When his eyes opened, he squinted. The lights above him were so bright. He threw his hand to his face and let out a groan when his ribs screamed at him. It felt like someone driving their knuckles into his side—twisting, turning, and digging into his ribs.

"He's awake," someone said. It was a male voice. An unfamiliar male voice.

Gabriel tried tilting his head to the side to look at the person, but his neck wouldn't allow the range of motion.

As he regained his conscious mind, he came to the realization that he wasn't dreaming. This was real. The pain was real. The male voice had been real. The bright lights above his head were real. But where was he?

Furthermore, where were the others? If Jessica, Thomas, or Claire had been inside of this room, surely one of them would have said something by now.

He started to speak, but his throat felt as dry as asphalt on an August day in Tuscon. He'd been to Arizona on many sales trips. How long ago were they now?

"Are you all right?" the male voice asked.

"Yes," Gabriel muttered. It came out raspy.

"We're going to get you help," the man said.

We?

Who else was in this room? And, for the love of God, if someone only could have turned out the lights. At least the ones beaming down upon Gabriel from just above him. Even closing his eyes did little to shield him from their power.

"When they come in," the man said, "don't ask questions. None. Just let them tend to you."

"Who?" Gabriel asked, but the man didn't answer.

Heavy footsteps replaced his voice, pounding on tile flooring. With each step they became louder, moving closer to wherever Gabriel was.

I am home, Gabriel thought. *Not home, but near home. Maybe I'm in a hospital and those steps belong to a doctor, coming to bring me to my family. Yes, to Katie and Sarah. Oh, my Sarah. Will she be in that dress her mother and I bought her for her birthday? The robin egg blue one that makes her look like a princess? Yes, that's the one.*

Just then, everything started to come back to Gabriel. What had happened, where he'd been.

The accident.

"They've drugged you," the man said.

"Drugged me where?" Gabriel said, laughing on the inside.

"Not *dragged* you, but injected you with something."

Gabriel wondered, if they had drugged him, how could he feel the pain?

"Not drugs for the pain, but for your mind," the man said.

How did he answer my question? Is this man inside my head?

"Who else is in here?" Gabriel asked.

The footsteps stopped right outside the door.

No response from the man inside the room.

He coughed, and then asked, "Where are my friends?"

The door opened.

"Dammit, tell me," Gabriel said.

Those heavy footsteps now slapped the floor inside the room. Whoever it was did not speak, but they moved closer to Gabriel, in no rush to make their way through the room. Gabriel tried to move his head again, but it was of no use. It was as if someone had put a padlock on his neck.

"Who's there?" Gabriel asked.

"Thank you for letting us know that he's awake, Joe," a new male voice said. It had a slight Southern twang to it, but the man sounded more articulate than most. Each word carried its own certain bit of elegance with it as he spoke.

The heels of the man's boots clicked against the floor as he worked his way nearer to Gabriel. Out of the corner of his eye, Gabriel saw the man briefly before he moved down near Gabriel's feet. Anyone else who was in the room held their tongues.

"What is your name?" the man asked.

Gabriel, still trying to work past the sharp pain in his neck, ignored the question. Standing still, the man awaited an answer he would not get.

"All right then," the man said. "Want to play that game? Fine. In lieu of your apparent secrecy, I'll just call you Bob."

Gabriel couldn't help but smile, and he wondered if the man had noticed the gesture.

"Though, I must warn you, Bob, that I will find out your name eventually. I always do, don't I, Joe?"

"Y-yes, sir," Joe said.

"But," the man continued, "if you want to do this the hard way, well then, I suppose that's fine."

The man whistled, and a collection of new footsteps sounded

through the room.

The man said, "Get him up," and then left the room.

Gabriel cried out when his back came off of the surface he was lying on. Hands, at least four of them, picked him up under his arms. They sat him straight up, and it felt like all his insides shifted. His internal injuries stormed alive, and burned like someone had flicked a Zippo lighter inside him, the flame licking his organs. Gabriel tried to open his eyes again, but they still didn't want to stay open.

The hands returned to under his arms and lifted him up. Again, he cried out. His captors stayed at either side of him, holding him up. That was good, because his legs felt like they would've folded if he hadn't had the support.

The men on either side of him began to walk, much faster than he'd anticipated. They apparently didn't care that he'd been in a car accident, and then had been lying on his back for however long. Gabriel pulled from the little strength he had to keep himself from falling down. He knew he'd much rather try to move on rubbery legs than have to go through the agony of being peeled off the ground if he fell.

As they moved, his vision finally started to come back, and he was able to keep his eyes open at a squint. For the first time, he was able to look around the room he'd been held in. Just before they exited through the door, Gabriel glanced around to see nothing but men scattered around the room. Their faces appeared old and tired, though many of the men looked around Gabriel's age or younger. Most of them sat on the ground, and a few sat in small desks like the ones they had in high school classrooms.

They moved out of the doorway, and then the desks made sense. They entered a long hallway, lined on either side by two rows of lockers, one on top of the other. Gabriel had indeed been brought to a school. The sun bleeding in through the windows provided the hallway's only light. It was dim, telling Gabriel it was either later in the day or overcast outside.

At the end of the long corridor they hung a left. They came into an almost identical hallway. It appeared just as long, and was lined on either side with the same lockers. Every twenty feet or so there was a doorway, each presumably leading into a classroom. One difference was that this corridor had a light at the end. The place did have at least some power.

Halfway to the light, an intense cramp crept into Gabriel's right thigh. He groaned and started to fall. The two people on either side held him up, and he used his other leg to keep himself from falling.

"You don't wanna fall," the man on his left said. "Trust me."

Gabriel believed him. He had no reason to believe that whatever group had brought him here were good people. The whole shooting at their SUV and taking their tires out thing had basically stamped out that possibility.

Somehow, Gabriel managed to stay on his feet. They made it to the light at the end of the hall and came to a wide open atrium with ceilings at least twenty-five feet tall. The men led him left again.

Gabriel could now see the front doors of the school. Through the glass doors, he could see the flagpole and the parking lot. Two armed guards stood at the entrance. They didn't appear to be soldiers or anything—just two normal people. Each guard held a rifle across his chest. Sidearms sat in holsters on their waists.

The men holding Gabriel led him to a door. A plate beside the wooden brown door read: Office.

One of the guards opened the door.

"In we go," the man still holding Gabriel said.

They entered the office.

***

It had been years since Gabriel had been inside the main office of a school. Since he'd spent so much time traveling for work, Katie had typically handled all the parent-teacher conferences and any other formalities that had to do with Sarah and her school. Gabriel hadn't been inside one of these offices since he'd been a senior in high school.

The inside of the office had electricity, which came as a surprise to Gabriel. There had been the lights in the room when he'd woken up, but the rest of the school had seemed absent of power. He wondered how these people had afforded the resources to keep a generator running.

The men led him to the rear of the open office, where they came to a door with no windows. The door was lighter in one spot in the shape of a rectangle. Gabriel guessed that there had once been a nameplate for the school's principal. One of the men knocked on the door. A voice said something from the other side, and then the man opened the door.

A large mahogany desk sat in the middle of the room. Behind the desk was a large bookshelf filled with many books. A man stood in the corner of the office, his back turned to Gabriel.

"This is the man you asked to see, sir," the man holding Gabriel said.

The man in the corner of the room said, "Have a seat."

One of Gabriel's captors moved him in front of a chair and then pushed down on his shoulders, forcing him to sit. Gabriel groaned.

"Leave," the man in the corner of the room said. His voice

was deep and authoritative, his body large and muscular.

Gabriel watched the man in the corner as the other two men exited the room, shutting the door behind them. He was somewhat surprised that they'd left him with his hands unbound. Then he noticed the revolver holstered onto the large man's hip.

The man had a broad backside, and wore a black shirt tucked into matching pants. He had a full head of silver hair, but it was hard to gauge his age from behind. A file cabinet sat in front of where he stood. On top was a small wooden box. The man opened the box, and pulled out a single cigar. He ran it under his nose, then let out a relieved sigh.

"Nothing beats that smell," the man said.

Gabriel didn't say anything as the man reached into his pocket, withdrawing a box of matches. He pressed the cigar between his lips, then struck a match, watching the flame spread from the head before settling into a gentle glow. Pressing the flame against the tip of the cigar, he puffed until it was fully lit. Then he turned around.

He had distinct features, but Gabriel had trouble telling what nationality he might be. He spoke with a Southern accent, but he looked to be of Russian descent. He had a full beard which matched the color of his silver hair. Wrinkles in his face put him at around sixty years old, Gabriel guessed. The tip of the cigar glowed orange, and the man puffed on it, sending a cloud of smoke into the air.

He locked eyes with Gabriel as he made his way over to the desk. The man pulled the chair out from under the desk, sat down, and leaned back, propping his large boots up on the mahogany top. He picked up the cigar again, and then pulled it out of his mouth as he blew the smoke into the air. Leaving the cigar between his fingers, his elbows resting on the armrests of the chair, he finally spoke again.

"You're probably wondering who I am and what you're doing here," the man said.

Gabriel didn't respond.

After a few moments of waiting for a response, the man smiled. "Ah, I see. Going to play the quiet game, Gabriel?" He took another drag off the cigar.

Gabriel wondered how this man knew his name, but he managed to remain silent.

"My name is Nathan Ambrose. The reason that you're here at this place and the reason that you're here in this room are two different things. In time, you'll learn why you're here at the school. I won't spoil that for you. But the reason you're in here talking to me right now is because I see value in you. You and your people seem far more experienced than most others we've picked up. It's got me curious. I'm interested to know where you came from. What y'all've been up to since half the damn world turned into upright corpses."

Gabriel remained silent. Nathan picked his size 13 boots up off of the table, setting them down onto the ground. He took another puff of the cigar, and then set it into a gold ashtray lying on the desk. Resting his elbows on the desk, he leaned in toward Gabriel.

"Where'd you get all those guns?" Nathan asked.

Gabriel put his elbows on his knees, and leaned toward Nathan. From this position, he had trouble lifting his neck toward Ambrose, and he held in a groan to keep from coming off as weak.

"Fuck you," Gabriel said.

Nathan laughed. "No matter. They're our guns now, anyway.

If you're lucky and make it far enough, you might just see them again."

Holding an unflinching stare, Gabriel wondered what Nathan had meant by 'make it far enough'.

The door opened, and the two men who'd brought Gabriel to Nathan reappeared in the room.

Nathan stood up and put his hands on his waist.

Not taking his gaze from Gabriel, he said, "Get this piece of shit outta my sight."

CHAPTER NINE

Jessica sat on a barstool in what had once been a high school science lab. About twenty minutes earlier, some woman claiming to be a nurse had come into the room to check her out. Jessica had pried into the nurse for answers, but the woman hadn't responded. She'd simply run a few checks on Jessica and then left.

Now Jessica was alone. She hadn't seen her friends since being pulled half-conscious out of the SUV. Jessica had been awake when they'd recovered her from the SUV, though just barely. Once they had pulled her out of the mangled vehicle, they'd covered her head with a pillow case. She'd been too disoriented from the accident to even get a look at her captors before they took her vision from her.

Tables filled the room. Fifteen of them—Jessica had counted them three times. Two windows allowed light into the room, though that faded fast as night approached. There had been bars placed over them, making this a perfect holding cell. The large dry erase board at the front of the classroom still had the teacher's last lesson written on it. Jessica ran her hand across the steel-top table in front of her and wondered for a moment what it had been like here when the world had changed. How many students had fallen in this classroom?

Jessica looked up when she heard footsteps coming down the long hallway.

"Hello?" she called out.

The boots stomped over the tile floor outside until they came to a stop at the door.

Jessica stood up, her legs still shaky from the accident, and picked up the barstool she'd been sitting on. She held it up, prepared to use it as a weapon.

The original knob on the door had been replaced with one that locked from the outside. It clicked, and then swung open.

Two men appeared in the doorway. One wore a baseball cap and the other had stringy long hair almost down to his shoulders. Each man carried a shotgun. Jessica wondered if either of the weapons had been stolen from the SUV. She stood there, staring at the men, still ready to swing the stool at them if they came closer. It wasn't like the chair would be a match for the slugs in those guns the men held, though.

"You're gonna want to put that down," Baseball Cap said.

"Go to hell," Jessica spat back.

Baseball Cap sighed and said, "Ma'am, we don't—"

But before Baseball Cap could finish, Long Hair had apparently lost his patience.

Long Hair withdrew something from his side. Jessica's eyes widened as Long Hair fired a taser. The two prongs entered her skin and sent a jolt of electricity through her. Jessica's legs gave out and she fell to her knees.

She leaned over and threw up all over the tile floor. Then she fell forward, right into her own vomit, and passed out.

***

When Jessica's eyes fluttered open again, she was looking up at the ceiling. The tiles above her were moving, yet her legs were not. She was lying on something, and when she looked around, she saw the two men who'd just come into the science lab to get her. Leather held her arms and legs to the surface of the moving table.

Both men looked down, not having noticed she'd woken up. If she'd had the ability to be smarter about it, she may have been able to jump off the cart and run away. Instead, she lay still, focusing on her breathing and blanking everything else out.

Once she had found her composure, she looked around. She was on some kind of cart and that the two men were rolling her through a hallway in the school. Someone, a woman, cried out from one of the rooms they passed, and Jessica lifted her head up. One of the two men quickly pushed her back down onto the cart.

"Stay down," he said.

"Where are you taking me?" Jessica asked.

Neither of the men responded. She heard another scream, but this time the voice was that of a man's.

"Please, where are you—"

"Quiet," Baseball Cap said, "or I'll take off my underwear and stuff it into your mouth."

Jessica gagged at the mere thought of it. She kept her mouth shut.

Long Hair walked away from the cart and opened two double doors ahead of them. This room's ceiling was at least three times as high as the hallway they'd just left. Long tables were arranged throughout the large space, and Jessica noticed a buffet line at the far side of the room. It was the school's cafeteria.

They crossed the room and came to another set of double doors. Baseball Cap coughed and it echoed throughout the vast, open and vacant space. Jessica wondered where everyone else was, and just how many people were here at the school. More than that, how many of them were prisoners like she was?

The men pushed the cart through yet another set of double doors and they were now in the school's gymnasium. Bleachers lined each side of the basketball court and Jessica saw a large Jaguars logo on the wall.

"What've you got for me?"

The voice came from a man on the other side of the gym. Jessica looked over and saw a gangly guy, no younger than 45, standing in front of a door. Above the door was a sign that read: Men's Locker Room.

"We've got one female for processing," Long Hair said. "Her name's Jessica Davies."

Jessica started to ask how the guy knew her name, and then remembered that her ID had been in her bag. Her eyes widened as a more immediate fear came to mind.

Her journal.

Jessica had spent so much time writing in that book and chronicling the past weeks. Now, the book was out of her possession and owned by a group of people who'd taken her prisoner.

"She's a pretty one," Gangly said. "Much prettier than the others." His voice made Jessica beyond uneasy.

"Don't even think about doing anything to her, Bruce," Baseball Cap said. "Unless you want Ambrose down your fuckin' throat."

Bruce chuckled and said, "Now, Lance, you think I'd do anything to her?" Jessica faced him in time to see him morph his face into some kind of disgusting smirk.

Lance shook his head, mumbled something to himself, and then looked down at Jessica. He undid her restraints.

"Get up," Lance said.

Jessica tried to push herself up off the cart, but apparently moved too slowly for the men's liking. Lance and Long Hair reached down and picked her up off the cart. When she landed on her feet, she felt like her knees might buckle beneath her. Bruce took her hands, offering her assistance, but she quickly pulled away.

"Just follow me," Bruce said.

Behind her, the other two men retreated. Bruce headed for the men's locker room door.

Jessica reluctantly followed.

The next word that the gangly, disgusting man said sent a chill down Jessica's spine.

"Strip."

"What?"

"You fucking heard me," Bruce said. "Don't play those games. Take off your fucking clothes."

He reached over and grabbed a fresh pair of latex gloves out of a box sitting on top of the long vanity. After he'd put them on and Jessica still hadn't followed his instructions, he grew impatient.

"Look, we have a procedure here. We can either do it the easy way, or we can do it the hard way." He smiled at her. "Based on the way you've been looking at me, I don't think you wanna do this the hard way." His face had now returned to that grotesque 'fuck me' smirk.

Knowing that she should comply, Jessica went to remove her shirt, but her shaking hands wouldn't cooperate. In this moment of terror, she hated herself for leaving the campground. Hated herself for being jealous. How could she have allowed something so petty to put her in this situation? Part of her wanted to reach for the gun on the man's hip, put a bullet in his head, and then push the gun to her own chin and fire. In the end, she did the smart thing and resisted that urge.

Jessica took three deep breaths, calming herself, and then

reached down to the tail of her shirt and pulled it up. Before her shirt raised over her face, she watched Bruce wrap his tongue around his lips as he continued to stare at her.

After throwing her shirt to the ground, she reached down and began to unbuckle her jeans. As she did this, she kept her eyes to the ground, ignoring his disgusting gaze. Even so, she could feel him still staring at her. She closed her eyes, focusing on her breathing as she pushed her jeans off of her hips. Both the unflattering sports bra and the saggy panties she wore were dirty. She only owned a couple of sets of underwear. With no way to wash them since they'd left the hospital, she just rotated them out every few days. She'd hoped that this would turn Bruce off, but she could still feel his eyes on her and hear his panted breathing.

When her pants had hit the ground, Jessica finally looked up to him again. He was, indeed, still staring at her, his eyes glowing.

"There," she said.

Bruce shook his head. "That ain't strippin'." He pointed to her chest, and then to her midsection. "It's all gotta come off."

Jessica narrowed her eyes and said, "Go to hell."

Bruce took two steps toward Jessica, and she felt her arms shaking again. Her legs quaked, her lips quivered.

"Off," he said.

But Jessica no longer cared. The man could kill her. It would likely be better than being at this place.

She spit in his face.

The smirk went away as Bruce brought the back of his hand to his face and wiped the spittle away. He then used the same side of that hand to strike Jessica across her jaw. She fell back onto the ground and reached for her face. When she pulled her hand away from her lip, there was blood on it. Before she could look back to Bruce, he'd struck her in the back of the head. Jessica fell down onto her stomach.

Then he was on her.

Bruce straddled Jessica's backside and ripped her bra off. Jessica screamed, writhing on the ground, but unable to get his weight off of her. He smacked the back of her head before she could reach back and cover up. Bruce repositioned himself and ripped her panties away from her buttocks. Tears flowed from Jessica's eyes.

Once she was completely naked, Bruce pulled her hair, jerking her head back. He gripped her locks so hard that she felt like they might rip out. Bruce leaned down to her ear.

"Bitch, I told you that you didn't wanna do this the hard way," he said. "Now unless you want this to be much worse, I suggest you let me do what I am ordered to do. Do that, and you might make it out of here in one piece, and just a little less violated. You got it?"

Her eyes flooded with tears, Jessica grumbled the word, "Yes."

Jessica could sense him smiling. "Good." He pulled her head back a little further, to where she thought her throat may rip, and licked her cheek. Then he let her head go, and she'd almost lost all control to where it nearly hit the ground.

She continued to cry, looking down at the concrete floor of the locker room. Enough tears had fallen from her eyes to darken the ground beneath her.

Bruce moaned, and then his non-lubricated, gloved index finger slid into her anus.

It was in that moment that Jessica knew she would kill this man. Whether it meant the end of her own life or not, this disgrace for a human being would die at her hands.

CHAPTER TEN

By the time Bruce finished, Jessica had been stripped, assaulted, put through a full body cavity search, and bathed by the grotesque man. The bath had actually been the most painful part, physically. He'd used a scrub brush that was stained with dirt—likely the grit of other human beings. And he hadn't been gentle, grinding the brush against her sensitive skin. After having been stripped and then searched, her mind had turned numb. She'd accepted what was happening to her. This had allowed her mind to absorb every single moment. And the memories would be as real as the demon she'd seen raised from Will's throat. Memories of every moan that escaped from around Bruce's black tongue between his yellow teeth. Every time he smacked his dry lips. She'd remember every bit of it.

Jessica stood at the front of the locker room, drying off after the rough, cold bath. Bruce had at least allowed her the decency of being able to dry herself. He'd stepped to the other side of the room, removed his gloves, and was jotting a few notes down onto a clipboard.

A knock came at the door, and the two men who'd brought her to this hell pit appeared in the doorway.

"Good to go?" Lance asked.

"Yeah, I'm through with her," Bruce said.

Jessica looked around for her clothes, but couldn't find them. Long Hair must've seen the confusion in her face, because he reached into a bag he held and threw her a garment.

"Where are my clothes?" Jessica asked.

Bruce scoffed, and she felt a splash of spittle hit her bare shoulder. "Those aren't your clothes anymore. Believe me, I'd rather see you walk around in that little sports bra than this."

Jessica dropped open the one piece jumpsuit in her hand, which unrolled like a sleeping bag. It was obviously too big for her, but she doubted if these men cared.

"Put it on and let's go," Lance said.

Jessica turned and started to make her way towards one of the stalls, but a hand reached out and grabbed her. It was Long Hair's.

"Now," he said.

Hanging her head in embarrassment, Jessica dropped the towel onto the ground. She opened the jumpsuit and proceeded to step inside it. As she'd expected, it was indeed at least one size too big. She zipped it up, having felt all six eyes in the room on her the entire time. Once she had it all the way zipped up, the two guards turned.

"Come on," Lance said.

Jessica followed them out the door, walking like a penguin. She still felt a throb in her rectum where Bruce had dug his finger inside of her. It hurt to walk, and she chewed on her lips in just taking the first few steps.

"See ya soon, buttercup," Bruce said. "Hope it was as good for you as it was for me."

Jessica didn't turn around. She kept her eyes closed and choked back tears, trying to focus on happy thoughts to help her put the pain in her buttocks aside.

As the door shut behind her, Bruce's predatory laugh turned into a muffled blur that had become her life.

***

They came to a door in a hallway that was completely

engulfed in darkness. One of the men used a flashlight to guide them. The two men had threatened Jessica several times, to use the taser on her again if she continued to move slowly. She dug deep and fought to ignore the pain.

A door opened and Lance said, "Get in."

Jessica wobbled through the doorway. When she was just barely into the room, the door slammed behind her, leaving her in total darkness.

As the boots stomped down the hallway, Jessica heard something inside the room.

Breathing.

Crying.

"Hello?" Jessica asked.

The crying seemed to stop.

"Jessica? Is that you?" the person said.

Jessica gasped. "Claire?" She followed to where the voice had come from until she and Claire touched hands.

"I was worried that you guys were dead," Claire said as the two women found each other in the dark and hugged. Jessica pulled away.

"You haven't seen the others either?" Jessica asked.

"No," Claire said. "I woke up in some room with other women, and then they took me to some real creepy guy to get a bath. Did they do that to you?"

"Yes," Jessica mumbled. Embarrassed, she opted to keep how the man had violated her to herself. "Did you say there were other women?"

"Yeah," Claire said. "It was a classroom, and there were about six other women in there."

"Did they say anything? Why they were here? Why *we're* here?"

"No. I think they may have been drugged or something."

"What the hell is this place?" Jessica wondered why she'd been put into a room by herself, while Claire had been placed with other supposed prisoners.

"I'm just glad you're here," Claire said. "Maybe that means they'll bring Thomas and Gabriel here, too."

Jessica didn't respond. For some reason, she felt as if that wasn't likely to be the case. She couldn't put a finger on why, but she supposed that if these people had read the stories in her journal, they'd have to realize that putting all four of them together could be a bad idea. In fact, it may have been the exact reason that they'd decided to keep her and Claire away from the other women.

They sat next to each other, absorbing one another's body heat. An hour later, Jessica's half-open eyes caught a glimpse of a beam of light coming from the hallway. Jessica tapped Claire on the arm, as she'd somehow managed to doze off.

"What is it?" Claire asked as Jessica hopped to her feet.

"Someone's coming."

Claire shuffled, standing up. She patted down the front of her coveralls and moved next to Jessica.

The light shined through the window, into Jessica and Claire's eyes. Jessica turned, covering her face with her forearms.

"Turn around and put your hands on the wall," the male voice said.

"What do we do?" Claire whispered.

Reluctantly, Jessica said, "We listen to him."

"Now," the male voice demanded.

Jessica walked over to the wall behind her and put her hands on it, her back to the door. Claire stood beside her, and Jessica faced the ground, closing her eyes.

The door clicked, then opened.

Jessica opened her eyes as the flashlight illuminated the room. She heard something being set on the ground, followed by the same noise just a few moments later.

"I suggest you both get as much rest as you can," the man said. "You can turn around again once I've left the room." He flashed the light over toward them once more, and then the door closed. His heavy boots moved down the hallway, away from the room.

Jessica pushed herself off of the wall and turned around. Neither of the women spoke. She crept to the door, her hands out in front of her. It was impossible to see, and she had trouble gauging how far away from the door she was. But the guard had placed something on the ground, and she was determined to find out what it was.

When Jessica felt like she had come more than halfway to the door, she kneeled down and got on her hands and knees. She crawled until her hand hit the edge of something. It was glass, and had a rounded edge.

"Food," she mumbled to herself.

"Did you say food?" Claire asked. "Please tell me you said food."

Claire started to rush over. Not wanting Claire to step on the food, Jessica quickly turned and said, "Wait." When she did, Jessica lifted her hand and knocked something over. The glass tumbled over, and she heard the liquid pour out onto the ground. Claire stopped.

"Did you just spill water?" Claire asked.

"Don't move," Jessica said.

"How could you spill water? Do you know how thirsty I am?"

Jessica closed her eyes and drew in a deep breath. Of course she knew how thirsty Claire was. Jessica hadn't had a drop of water since some time before the accident. Both of them were starving, and Jessica refused the urge to snap at Claire. She refocused on where she'd found the plate and carefully felt around on the ground more. *Please find another glass of water,* she thought.

Her hand came across a second plate, which gave her hope. She then moved her hand a little further over until she felt the bottom of a glass. She got so excited that she almost knocked it over, and then sighed in relief when she didn't.

"There's another plate and another glass of water down here," Jessica said.

"Thank God."

Jessica reached over and felt around until she found the tipped glass. It was still in tact, and she picked it up.

"We'll each have our own plate of food, but we'll have to split the water," Jessica said. "I'll transfer half into this other glass."

"Please be careful," Claire said.

Jessica went to her knees and touched the two glasses together. With extra care, she tilted the full glass over the lip of the empty one. The liquid poured over, and she allowed it to do so until the glasses felt of equal weight.

"This is all there is," Jessica said. "So be sure to conserve it."

Claire accepted the glass, and then Jessica raised her own to her mouth, taking the smallest of sips. The water refreshed her dry, chapped lips.

Jessica grabbed one of the plates and handed it to Claire. It took a moment for Claire to find the plate and grab it without dropping it. Jessica then took the other plate and sat Indian style on the floor.

"Do you know what it is?" Jessica asked.

"I'm so starving that I don't really care," Claire said.

Jessica pulled the plate up to her nose and sniffed. The food had almost no smell. Even with it right in front of her face, she couldn't identify it in the darkness.

"Beans," Claire said.

Claire shoveled the food into her mouth, the silverware smacking against the plate.

It was a mix of black beans and green beans. Also on the plate was a piece of bread and a slice of American cheese. Jessica ate the food so fast that her once empty stomach now ached. She didn't care. As soon as the plate was clear, she put it down and grabbed the glass of water. She went against her own advice that she had given Claire and downed the glass in seconds. The canned beans had been too salty, leaving her throat with a type of dryness she had never felt.

Moments later, Claire set her plate on the ground. Jessica was somewhat surprised that she had finished her meal before Claire had.

With her stomach hurting and with nothing to do in the darkness, Jessica found herself suddenly tired. She scooted a few feet away from the door, and then laid down on her side.

"Let's try to get some rest," Jessica said.

Within minutes, she was sleeping.

***

Jessica's eyes opened when she heard the door click. Her back was to it, but she didn't move when she heard it start to open. She remained still, steadily controlling her breathing.

Then she heard that perverted, yet familiar moan.

Bruce.

A low beam of light flashed onto the wall that she was facing.

It was just bright enough that he could see, but not so bright that it would have woken Jessica or Claire. Only, Jessica was already awake. But he didn't know that.

He moaned again before he finally spoke.

"I've got you now," he whispered. "And ain't no one gonna be able to stop me. Not you, not Ambrose, and not your friends. Especially the crippled one."

Crippled one? Jessica thought.

But before she could investigate the thought any further, she felt Bruce's warm, stank breath hit the back of her neck. She shuddered. Jessica sensed his tongue was just inches away from her. She remembered what it had felt like when he'd touched her with it before, and feared she might never forget.

Just as she felt that he was about to touch her, Jessica received a lifeline.

"Who's there?" Claire asked.

Bruce's heavy breathing stopped, and he flashed the light towards Claire. When he did this, she screamed.

With no reason to any longer pretend that she was sleeping, Jessica sat up just in time to see Bruce lunge at Claire. He wrapped his hands around her neck, muting her scream. Jessica reached out to pry him away from her, and Bruce backhanded Jessica in the face.

Footsteps raced down the hall as Jessica lay on her belly, her palms flat on the concrete.

"You stupid bitch," Bruce said to Claire. "You lucky fucking bitch. I'm gonna kill you for that."

But before he could hurt her, two armed guards entered the room.

"What the hell are you doing in here, Bruce?" one of the men demanded. Jessica couldn't see the men's faces, as the flashlights they held were much too bright.

Bruce stood. "I was, uh, walking down the hall. I thought I heard one of the girls in here call for help, so I came inside."

"That's bullshit," Claire said. "He—"

"I wasn't fucking talking to you," the man said, flashing the light into Claire's eyes. He looked back to Bruce. "Is that true?"

"Of course it's not true," Bruce said. "Don't listen to her."

The other man spoke now. "Just get your ass out here. Everything seems fine."

The two men left the room and Bruce followed. He turned around to close the door, but before he did, he stood there and stared. Even though Jessica was only looking at his silhouette, she could still feel his eyes raping her.

"Sleep tight," Bruce said.

Neither of the girls did.

CHAPTER ELEVEN

The door to Maureen's house swung open and Will was the first to rush inside. He stopped when he'd made it just a few feet into the living room.

Dylan lay on the table, completely still. The lights above the table had been shut off, and with the sun going down, the room hadn't enough light for Will to see if the boy was breathing or not. The others collected behind him just as Timothy entered the room, drying his hands off with a towel.

"How is he?" Will asked, a tremble in his voice.

"He's going to be fine," Timothy assured him. "He's still out from the anesthetics."

Will felt a hand squeeze his and turned to see Mary Beth looking up at him. He put his other hand out toward Holly and she took it, and then he moved toward the table.

Closer now, Will could see Dylan's stomach moving up and down. He could almost hear the boy's shallow breaths echo through the silent house. What was left of his wounded arm had been wrapped up in a thick bandage reaching almost all the way up to his shoulder. Will imagined what it looked like underneath.

"There was still enough flesh and tissue left for me to close the wound," Timothy said. "It wasn't easy, but he should heal up fine."

"And you didn't find any kind of infection?" Will asked.

"Honestly, it's impossible for me to truly know with the tools I have available here. But Doug and I did our best to clean the wound before I closed it." Nevertheless, Timothy told Will some signs to look for to spot infection, including checking for fever and making sure the wound didn't begin to smell.

Will sighed in relief as he felt Holly squeeze his hand.

"He's very lucky," Timothy said. "Clearly, *someone* is watching over him."

"When will he wake up?" Mary Beth asked, mumbling.

"Hopefully within the next hour or two," Timothy said. "It's hard to know for sure."

"You should all go rest," Doug said. "We just wanted you to see that he was all right."

Mary Beth let go of Will's hand and moved in next to Dylan. She grabbed onto his hand. "I'm not leaving him again."

Doug said, "But, young lady, you should—"

"I'll stay with her," Will said.

Smiling, Doug nodded.

"I'm staying, too," Holly said. "I'm with Mary Beth: I can't leave him again."

Charlie shrugged. "Guess we're all staying."

"Very well," Timothy said. "Maureen, why don't you see if you can gather some blankets for them?"

"Of course," Maureen said, and she headed to another room.

"Is he going to be in pain when he wakes?" Holly asked.

"Some," Timothy said. He reached into his pocket and pulled out a small bottle. He shook it, and the tiny pills inside clanked back and forth in the plastic container. "This will be better than the over-the-counter pain medication you had for him. It should help make him at least somewhat comfortable. He can have two of these shortly after he wakes up. He'll need to eat something with them, so I'll be sure that Maureen has something ready for him."

"Thank you for doing this," Will said. "I can't tell you how much we appreciate it."

"It's no problem," Timothy said. He signaled to the sofa. "Come on, how about we sit down for a little bit?"

"I need to get some fresh air," Charlie said. He looked to Mary Beth. "You wanna go outside with me?"

Frowning, the girl said, "I wanna stay with Dylan."

"Why don't you go outside and play, sweetie?" Holly suggested. "We can let you know if he wakes up."

"All right," Mary Beth said, her eyes glued to the floor.

Charlie took Mary Beth by the hand and they went to the back door. At the same time, Maureen re-entered the room holding blankets and pillows. She set them down on an empty spot on the sofa.

"Thank you," Will said. He'd sat down on the sofa next to Holly, while Timothy had plopped down into the recliner in the corner of the room.

"Anything else I can get y'all?" Maureen asked.

"I think we're good for now," Holly said. "Thank you, again, for your hospitality."

"It's no problem," Maureen said. "If you'll excuse me, I'm going to go upstairs to my room for a while. You folks just feel free to make yourselves at home."

After Maureen climbed the last step of the staircase, Will looked over to Timothy.

"She alone here?"

Taking a sip of water, the doctor said, "Yeah." He wiped his mouth and then sighed. "Her husband died a few years back in Iraq. She had two children. One of them, her son, was taken by the plague. He bit his baby sister."

Holly put her face in her hands. Will said, "Jesus."

"I live two houses over. Her children were the first two that I saw. I tried to help them, but as you know, it was impossible."

"What happened to them?" Holly asked.

Timothy swallowed and took a deep breath. "They're gone." He said it short and flat, signaling he wanted to end the conversation.

"Did everyone who lives here now always live around here?" Will asked.

"Most, yes. We've let in a few stragglers, but for the most part, everyone you'll meet already lived around here. There aren't many of us left, but anyone that is now lives in this cul-de-sac. A few people still live in other parts of the neighborhood, but they don't want anything to do with us. I'm not even sure if they're all still alive. We offered to have them join us early on, but they refused. We keep this cul-de-sac guarded, and we keep to ourselves."

"How far out have you guys gone to explore?" Will asked.

"Not far," Timothy replied.

"But eventually you're going to run out of food," Holly said.

Timothy furrowed his brow. "Let me ask you, how long have you people been out there? How far have you come?"

"We traveled here from Nashville," Will said. "Well, the two of us have."

"Nashville? You made it all the way here from Tennessee, alive?"

Holly frowned. "We've had our fair share of loss." She reached over and grabbed Will's hand.

Will bit his lip, thinking of his parents, of Marcus, and of his own near death.

"Yes," Timothy said. "I suppose we all have."

The front door of the house opened, cutting off the

conversation. Samantha, Timothy's wife, entered first. Behind her was Karl. Timothy stood, and Will and Holly followed.

"Please," Timothy said to his wife, "have my seat."

She waved him off. "It's fine. I'd rather stand, really."

Karl rocked his head toward Dylan. "How is he?"

"Good," Will responded. "The doc here says he's going to be fine."

"That's good," Karl said.

Samantha looked to her husband. "Did you ask them yet?"

Puzzled, Will said, "Ask us what?"

"Damn, Samantha," Timothy said. "The boy hasn't even woken up yet."

"What is she talking about?" Holly asked.

Timothy sunk back down into the chair, sighed, and then spoke.

"I said we have plenty of supplies, but there are a few things we *are* running low on. A few important things."

Will knew where this was going.

"As I said," Timothy continued, "We don't have a lot of experience out there."

"So, in return for you helping Dylan, you want us to go for you?" Will asked.

Timothy nodded. "We won't send you out alone. Karl here will go with you. He's our best scavenger, and he's got the most experience being outside these walls. And we'll send one other person."

Will turned away from Timothy and walked toward the window at the front of the house. Outside, the sun was almost totally hidden. The clouds had cleared out enough to show the moon, which appeared to be only a few days away from being full. He put his hands on his hips and waited to reply.

While Will was tired of being pulled away from their journey in order to help others, the people here had saved Dylan. Without Timothy and Doug, there was a good chance that they'd still be looking for help. That Dylan would be in agonizing pain. Instead, Dylan was safely sleeping, his wound closed. Will glanced back to look at him. While he stared at Dylan, Holly moved to his other side. She grabbed his hand.

"You know what the right thing to do is," she said.

Will looked at her and chuckled as he smiled.

"All right," Will said. He turned around to face Timothy. "Where are we going?"

***

Will had thought he might never drink a cup of coffee ever again. But that wasn't the case.

Maureen had heated up a pot of water and used a French press to provide everyone with a mug. Even young Mary Beth, who'd claimed she'd never had coffee before, took a small cup.

And as the girl took her first sip and scrunched her face, the adults in the group laughed. Regardless, she choked back the drink.

After another couple of sips, Mary Beth said, "It's really not that bad."

"It grows on you," Charlie said, smiling.

"I'm going to head upstairs," Maureen said. "Let me know if you need anything."

"Thank you, darlin'," Timothy said.

"All right," Will said. "So, tell me about where you want us to go."

Timothy cleared his throat and took another sip from his coffee. "Karl, why don't you tell them?"

His palms flat on the table, Karl said, "On one of my first

runs, this would have been a couple of weeks ago, I met someone from another group. They were very cordial and didn't come off as threatening. We only spoke for a few minutes, but they trusted us enough to tell us where they live. Said that if we ever needed anything to come to them, and we could see about making some trades."

Charlie shrugged his shoulders. "But what is it you would need from them?" He looked around. "You guys seem to have just about everything you need here right now."

"They claimed to have a surplus of medical supplies," Samantha said.

"We were already running low on things before you guys showed up on our doorstep needing us to help your child," Timothy said. He said it matter of factly, not out of spite. "We were already planning a run there to see what they've got."

"I would have to think medical supplies would be an awful expensive barter at this point," Will said. "What do you guys have that you can offer them?"

"You'll be taking with you lots of food," Timothy said. "We figure that we're lucky enough here that we have enough good soil in these yards to grow our own. You're also taking a generator and a few weapons."

"You're willing to give up a generator?" Holly asked.

"If they have the right items, yes," Samantha said.

"I've prepared a list," Timothy said. "I would also recommend that you folks be thinking of things that you can trade. If they have pain medications and broad spectrum antibiotics, especially, I'd suggest you be ready to make an offer. The boy is going to need continued attention in order to fully and properly heal. I'd be glad to make you your own list of things to look for."

Holly smiled. "We'd very much appreciate that, thanks."

"It's no problem," Timothy said. "We have a place for you all to stay tonight. I would assume at least one or two of you might want to stay here with Dylan. But if any of you want a bed to sleep in, we have somewhere for you."

"I think I might have to take you up on that," Charlie said. "Not sure when I'll get to sleep in a real bed again."

"I don't want to go," Mary Beth said. "I want to stay with Dylan."

"I'll stay here with Holly and Mary Beth," Will said. Holly looked at him and smiled.

"Very well," Timothy said. He signaled to his wife. "Samantha can show you where you can—"

In the living room, Dylan stirred. He groaned, and moved around on the table. Already on his feet, Will pushed off the wall and went to the boy's side.

Will ran his hand through Dylan's hair. The boy was moving, but had yet to open his eyes.

And when he did, Will cried.

***

For the first few minutes after Dylan woke up, he worked to clear his head of all the fogginess caused by the drugs that had put him under. He tried sitting up a few times, but Timothy urged the boy to remain lying down while he regained his bearings.

Then the boy spoke his first words since coming out of the surgery.

"Am I going to be okay?"

Running his hands through Dylan's hair, Will said, "Yes. Everything's going to be fine. The doctor here took good care of you."

Dylan looked down at the bandage on his arm. "It hurts."

"You are going to experience some pain," Timothy said. "Unfortunately, it's just part of the process. But from what your friends here have told me, you're one strong little boy. I think you're going to be just fine, and you should feel much better in no time."

Will ran his hands through Dylan's hair, and the child couldn't help but continue to look at what was left of his arm. Will felt a tap on his shoulder. It was Timothy.

"Do you mind if I have a few words with you?"

Will shook his head. "Not at all."

Timothy led Will into one of the downstairs bedrooms. It had a twin bed with all the linens neatly made up. On the walls were scenic paintings of flowers and outdoor landscaping. Timothy sat on the edge of the bed and looked up at Will.

"He really is a strong boy," Timothy said.

"Yes, he is."

"But I need to know; what happened to him?"

Will swallowed and stared at Timothy. Even though the doctor had helped Dylan, he wasn't sure how much information he wanted to share. He hadn't met the majority of the people at the camp. If people knew about what was causing the mutations of humans around the world, how would they react?

"He was bit out in the woods," Will said. "I just figured if I amputated the arm, it would keep the disease from spreading."

"That's good thinking," Timothy said. "But I'm still a little bit surprised it worked. The virus must travel very slowly through the blood stream."

Will swallowed, unable to lie anymore.

"Timothy, I—"

He was cut off when the door opened and Samantha entered

the room.

"Oh, I'm sorry," Samantha said.

"It's all right," Will said.

She looked to Timothy, her thumb pointing over her shoulder. "They need you across the street."

"All right," Timothy said. "Be right there."

Samantha exited, and Timothy looked back to Will.

"Finish this conversation later?"

Will smiled. "Sure."

Timothy shook Will's hand, and they exited the room.

That night, Will and Holly slept in a nice, large and clean bed in one of the houses. Dylan had been allowed to come with them, sleeping in the next room in his own bed.

Will didn't bring up the conversation he'd had with Timothy. But he thought about it. Felt bad about it. The rest of the group was exhausted, and he didn't want to burden them with his guilt.

Tonight, they would sleep.

CHAPTER TWELVE

Gabriel awoke the next morning having spent the entire night tossing and turning on the tile floor of an empty classroom. After he had met with Nathan Ambrose, he'd been taken to a classroom with no other people inside. His own suite, he'd thought, morbidly laughing at the notion. Because it was more like solitary confinement. He'd hardly slept a wink. They hadn't given him any blankets or even a pillow. With his body still aching from the accident, he'd known sleeping on a hard floor wouldn't be easy. He'd ended up taking off his coat, folding it in half, and using it to lay his head on. With no sleeves covering his arms, he'd gotten a little cold in the non-powered space, but at least he'd had a place to rest his head. In the absence of sleep, he spent most of the night thinking of his wife and his daughter. And, of course, about Dylan.

Though these men hadn't given him any sort of makeshift bed, they had at least fed him. The dinner served had been chicken noodle soup. Out of a can, no doubt, and cold, but Gabriel hadn't cared. It was nourishment to keep him alive a little longer, for whatever reason they were letting him live.

He wasn't entirely sure whether his internal clock had woken him up, or if it was the boots stomping down the hallway. Gabriel wiped his eyes and tried to get up, but his entire body screamed at him. His back locked up, stiff as a dining room tabletop. The joints in his knees popped with the slightest movement.

A shadow encompassed part of the room, and Gabriel looked

up through the tiny window in the door to see a man standing there. As the door clicked open, Gabriel drew in deep breaths. Having made it from his back to his side, he fought to relax his muscles.

The door swung open, and two armed men walked in. One of them had long, stringy hair, and the other wore a Philadelphia Eagles hat. These were different guards than those who had come and fetched him the day before.

"Get up," Stringy Hair said.

Gabriel groaned. "I'm trying."

Neither of the men apparently had any patience or gave two shits that he'd slept on a hard floor all night. They walked over to Gabriel and picked him up off the ground. His back screamed at him all the way to his feet.

"Can't you at least give me a second to wake up?" Gabriel asked.

"Shut the fuck up and put your hands out," Eagles Hat said. He reached down to his waist and drew forth a pair of handcuffs.

Gabriel complied and stuck out his arms. Eagles Hat wrapped the cuffs around Gabriel's wrists, and tightened them more than they needed to be. The suffocation of his wrists now drew him away from the dull ache in his back.

"Come on," Stringy Hair said.

Stringy Hair walked in front of him while Eagles Hat walked behind. Eagles Hat gave Gabriel a nudge in the form of a light punch to the kidneys just as he started to walk out the door. Gabriel groaned and bit his lip. He wanted to turn and punch the asshole in the face, but he knew it would likely only lead to a beating. He instead took a deep breath and followed Stringy Hair.

Stringy Hair drew a walkie talkie from his hip and said,

"Derek here, and I've got Lance with me. We're on our way."

Sun poured in through the windows, bringing rays of natural light into the hallway. The men led Gabriel down a long corridor, and he wondered if he'd ever see daylight again. Wondered if he'd ever see his family again.

As they came to the end of the corridor, Gabriel swore that he heard something peculiar. It sounded like a loud commotion outside. Derek opened a door and they walked into a small room. It had a staircase leading to the school's second level, as well as a door that led outside.

When Derek opened the door that led outside, the sound Gabriel had heard got much louder.

It sounded like a crowd.

Even though it had only been a day since he'd been outside, Gabriel's eyes had trouble adjusting to the sun's light. He brought his bound hands up to his face to cover his face as the roar of the people got louder and louder.

When his eyes finally adjusted, he saw where the men were leading him.

Across the parking lot was the school's football stadium. The sport must've been a big deal to the school and its town because the stadium looked big enough to house a small college team. Cars were scattered across the parking lot. There were at least fifty of them. At the stadium's entrance, there was a line of about ten people waiting to get inside.

"What the hell is going on?" he asked.

"Shut up," Lance said from behind him.

Only one person remained at the entrance by the time they'd walked across the parking lot. She was a woman, and she stood by the turnstile. Two large boxes lay next to her, each filled. Gabriel noticed some canned food, as well as a couple of boxes of ammunition inside.

"Morning, Stephanie," Derek said.

"Good morning, gentlemen. You're looking nice today."

Lance chuckled. "Likewise, darlin'."

Glancing at Gabriel, Stephanie blushed. "And who might this be?"

"It doesn't matter. Some piece of shit," Lance said.

Stephanie smiled, looking Gabriel up and down. "He sure doesn't look like it."

"All right, well, thanks, Stephanie," Derek said, running his hands through his hair. Gabriel felt a light punch to his kidneys and grimaced.

"Move," Lance said.

Gabriel could feel both Stephanie's and Lance's eyes on him as he stepped through the turnstile. Each staring at him for different reasons. He could hear Lance sigh behind him, and smirked at the thought that he'd made him jealous.

They started the walk around the stadium. Closed concessions stands were to the left. They varied in condition, all looking like they'd been raided. Popcorn machines had been broken and the doors of the beverage coolers had been left open.

They didn't walk far before Derek turned into section 114.

Gabriel followed Derek up the open-air tunnel. At the top, the open football field came into plain view, and Gabriel's eyes widened.

"Oh, my God."

CHAPTER THIRTEEN

When Will woke up, he rolled over to find that Holly no longer lay at his side. After a few minutes of allowing his mind and body to transition from sleep, he swung his legs over the side of the bed and sat up. He dressed, used the restroom, and then headed for the room next door.

The door to Dylan's room was open. The linens were scattered all over the bed, but the boy was nowhere to be seen.

The clanking of pots and pans sounded from the kitchen, and Will heard a laugh.

He walked down the hallway, arriving in the living room. When he looked into the kitchen, he saw Holly looking down at the counter. In the dining room next to the kitchen, Dylan sat at a table large enough to seat six people, leaning over a bowl with a spoon in his hand. The boy looked up at Will and smiled. Holly looked over to Dylan, and followed his gaze to Will.

"It worked," Holly said, smiling.

"What?" Will asked.

"I was kinda banging those pots and pans around on purpose, hoping that it might wake you."

"Gee, thanks," Will said, returning a crooked smile. "It's not like I need sleep."

Lumbering toward the dining room table, Will scratched the scruff on his face and ran his hand through his hair. He had shaved while at the cabin, but the hair on his face had already returned to the annoying itchy stage of growing a beard.

Placing his hand on Dylan's back, Will asked, "How you doin' this morning?"

Dylan kept his head buried in his fruity cereal, which he was eating with water. "I'm okay," he mumbled.

"He's hungry," Holly said.

"Where's Mary Beth?"

"Still sleeping," Dylan said, with cereal stuffed in his mouth.

Will walked into the kitchen and kissed her. Staying leaned in near her ear, he asked, "How's he really doing?"

She pulled away and looked him in the face. "I think he's in a little bit of pain, but it's better than yesterday. He woke up hungry, and I think he'll be in a better mood once he's done eating."

Will looked back over his shoulder. "Cereal and water?" He sounded disgusted.

Dylan looked over to him and shrugged. "Hey, I actually like it."

Will smiled. "Well, that's good, I guess."

Holly took Will by the hand and pulled him to the far end of the kitchen. Standing in the corner, she asked, "When are you guys leaving?"

Shaking his head, Will said, "I'm not sure. I've gotta go check with Charlie and Karl here in a little bit and see."

"You have to go, don't you?"

Will sighed. "Yeah." He looked over his shoulder at Dylan, who was eating the last few bites of his watered-down cereal. "If it wasn't for Karl, Laurie, Doug, and Timothy, I'm not sure he'd be here."

Holly moved her hair from in front of her eyes, and wouldn't look at Will.

"Hey," Will said, pushing her chin up. "Everything's going to be fine. We aren't going far."

"But what if those people you guys are going to see aren't... good?"

"I trust Karl's sense of that sort of thing," Will said. "The way he handled the situation with us showed me a lot. He was extra cautious and didn't allow his guard to come down too quickly."

"Can I have some more?"

Will turned around to Dylan, who was looking at him and Holly, his bowl now empty in front of him. Will smiled.

"Of course, buddy."

He turned back and kissed Holly once more. "Everything's going to be okay."

Will opened the cabinets until he found a bowl, and then grabbed the box of cereal and walked over to the table. He set the box in the middle of the table and took a seat across from Dylan.

"I've gotta try this."

Dylan poured himself another bowl, then handed the box to Will. Will topped it off with water from a pitcher, and dipped the spoon in for the first bite. He scrunched his face as if he'd just eaten something sour.

Dylan laughed. "That bad, huh?"

"Just gonna take a little bit of adjusting."

Will sat and ate with Dylan. They talked mostly about Dylan's favorite comic book characters. Holly stood and watched from the kitchen, absorbing the moment.

For Will, it was a welcome distraction. It pulled his mind away from thinking about going back into the world.

***

About half an hour after Will and Dylan finished breakfast, Laurie stopped by and asked Will if he could be ready to leave in twenty minutes. Will said he could, and that he would meet Karl outside.

Twenty minutes passed, and Will stood in the foyer with Holly. Her face was pale, her arms crossed over her chest.

"We shouldn't be gone too long," Will said. "Hopefully just a couple of hours. Maybe less."

"All right," Holly said. She sounded almost disconnected.

Dylan and Mary Beth approached them from the living room.

"Take care of them," Will told Dylan, speaking of Holly and Mary Beth. "Can you do that for me?"

"Of course," Dylan said.

Will smiled and hugged the boy, whose single arm held Will tight. He kissed Mary Beth on the cheek, then went back to Holly.

"Timothy is supposed to come by soon and change out his bandage," Will said.

"Mm-hmm," Holly mumbled.

"Hey, look at me."

Holly lifted her head to look into Will's eyes.

"We'll be fine, okay?"

"I just worry about you going out there with people we barely know," Holly said. "They haven't seen the things we've seen."

"Charlie will be with me," Will said, trying to reassure her. "We'll make it back. All of us."

Knowing that his words would do little to comfort her, he simply leaned in and kissed her on the forehead. The only thing that would ease her emotions would be for him to live up to the words and to actually come back to this house.

***

As they exited the neighborhood, Karl pointed out the houses which he knew had survivors in them. He showed them one house where a family of four was. Another where a man lived on his own, having lost his family at some point after The Fall. An elderly couple lived in another home.

"And you said that you tried to help these people?" Charlie asked Karl.

"Sure have," Karl said. "They all have their own reasons for not wanting to join us. The elderly couple told Timothy they're just waiting for everything to pass over, comparing this situation to Ebola or Anthrax. That the government will find a cure for all this and that everything will be okay soon."

"Exactly how far away is this place?" Will asked.

"As long as we don't hit any resistance, I think we should be there in only about fifteen minutes."

"How are you sure that we can trust these people?" Charlie asked.

Karl laughed. "I'm not. Why the hell do you think I brought y'all long? You think I was really gonna go check out this place with only Spencer back there?"

Spencer was the other person from the campground who Timothy had chosen to ride along with them. He'd been out on a couple of runs with Karl before, and had apparently proven that he could handle himself. He was also one of the few people at the camp who had experience firing guns, having grown up in a home where his parents owned them. He was now in his early 30s and had come to the camp in a way similar to that of Will and the others. He had lived in an apartment complex not too far away from the neighborhood, and had made his way over to the houses at some point after The Fall.

A few miles down the road, Karl hit the brakes. Will looked up from double-checking that his handgun was loaded.

Trees lined either side of the road. Every fifty to a hundred yards was another driveway. The houses out here were older, ranch-style homes, each sitting on several acres of land.

Fifty yards ahead was a herd of Empties—six of the creatures. They spanned the width of the road, making it impassable.

"Shit," Karl said.

"It's all right," Will said. "This happened quite often to us out on the open roads. We'll have to get out and take care of them."

Karl reached between the seats and grabbed his pistol. He'd started to check that it was loaded when Will reached over and grabbed onto his wrist.

"If we can, we need to try and use melee weapons. Guns will be far too noisy, and we need to try and conserve ammo. If there's other creatures or any people in the area, firing guns will surely bring them out."

"You mean we've gotta get close to 'em?" Spencer asked. "No way, man."

Great, Will thought. He said, "Charlie and I will go first, and we'll try to spread them out. I'll try to get a couple of them to follow me to the right, and Charlie, you take the left. If we can each draw a couple of them, that'll make things easier for the two of you."

Spencer slapped Karl's shoulder. "We should just shoot 'em, man. Shoot 'em, jump back in the car, and get the hell out of here."

"No," Will demanded. "Don't fire unless you absolutely have to."

Karl peeked over his shoulder. "Listen to them, Spence. They've spent a lot more time out here than we have."

As Will checked his handgun again for the umpteenth time to make sure it was loaded, he felt a tap on his shoulder. It was Charlie, handing him the same machete he'd used to sever

Dylan's arm. Will accepted the weapon, examining the blade. Charlie had taken the liberty of wiping it clean of Dylan's blood, though the blade had been forever tainted with a crimson stain.

The other weapons had all been scoured from garages in the cul-de-sac. Charlie and Spencer each held an ax while Karl wielded a large knife.

"That going to work for you?" Will asked, looking at the knife.

"I'll be fine," Karl said.

"Want to trade?" In truth, Will would have loved to pass the machete off to someone else after what he'd had to do to Dylan with it, and he'd killed plenty of Empties with a knife.

Shaking his head, Karl said, "Really, I'll be fine."

"All right." Will looked back to Charlie. "Ready?"

Charlie nodded. "Let's go."

Sitting behind the driver's seat, Charlie exited the vehicle just before Will.

The creatures had made it a mere twenty-five yards, cutting the distance to the van in half. A narrow shoulder and shallow ditch divided the trees from the road. The next driveway was past the pack of Empties. Will wondered if he could drive the creatures down into the ditch as he started to make his way for it.

"Come on, you bastards," Will said, waving his arms with the machete in one hand.

"Hey, ugly," Charlie said, pointing at the creatures nearest him. "Yeah, you. Come on!"

With that, four of the creatures headed toward Will and two toward Charlie. The plan worked. But when Will glanced back to the van, Karl had remained frozen in the front seat, and Spencer was still in the back.

"Come on!" he yelled, waving toward the van.

The first creature slipped as its feet left the pavement, and it rolled down into the ditch. The second and third kept their footing, and the fourth fell like the first. Under Will's feet, the ground was still muddy from rain, and he found it hard to keep his own footing. In front of him, the Empties seemed to be having a similar problem. Will stopped moving backward, readying himself to attack.

The Empty leading the way came within a few yards of Will. He almost slipped again, but managed to rear back and swing the machete. He connected with the thing's neck before it could bring its arms up to block the blow. It fell forward, and when Will tried to move back, he found that his feet had stuck into the mud. The body slammed into him with enough force to knock him back. Will fell down, the back of his head slamming into the muddy soil.

Above him, the other standing creature snarled, and aimed for Will's exposed stomach. Will pointed the machete blade straight up, and the Empty fell on it like a stake. The blade entered under the thing's chin and came out through the top of its skull. Will lost his grip of the machete handle, and the butt-end of it landed next to him. The Empty's entire weight fell down onto the blade. It made a sick slurping sound as its head slid all the way down to the handle. The rest of the creature's body fell on Will, pinning him down.

"Shit," Will said, looking up.

The other creatures had made it to their feet, and were creeping toward Will. They seemed to have no trouble with the sopping ground beneath them.

Will yelled, "Help!" He tried to look over toward Charlie, but he couldn't see over the top of the ditch.

The two beasts, both having been stout males in their living days, were now only a few yards away from Will. He tried to push the weight of the Empty off of him, but it proved impossible. The creature was too heavy, and the butt-end of the machete had sunk into the mud, holding the beast in place. He'd made some progress in pushing the creature off of him when one of the other Empties piled on. Now he had the weight of two creatures on him.

With the slain Empty as the only barrier between them, the live creature chomped its jaws, trying to find any piece of Will's flesh that it could. Will squirmed, trying to keep clear of the Empty's decrepit teeth. Its saliva dripped down onto Will's arm, and Will continued to call out for help.

A loud bang sounded through the air, followed by another. After the second, the standing Empty fell backward, blood shooting out of the side of its skull. The Empty in his face screamed, and then another shot went off, this bullet sinking into the side of its head. Blood splashed down onto Will's face, and he turned his head, closing his eyes. When he looked up again, he saw Spencer standing over him, a gun in his hand. A thin cloud of smoke floated from the barrel.

Charlie appeared at the edge of the road and dropped the ax.

"Shit," Charlie said. He shuffled down into the ditch and pushed the top Empty off of Will, then helped Will move the other. He extended his hand to his friend, who accepted it. "You all right, man?"

Will pulled away from Charlie and hurried out of the ditch, coming face to face with Spencer.

"What the fuck is your problem?"

"Get the hell out of my face," Spencer said. "You said not to use the gun unless I had to. By the looks of you down there, I think I needed to use it. You should be thanking me."

"Yes," Will said. "Thank you. Thanks a lot for taking your sweet ass time in getting out of the van."

"Fuck you."

Will swiped the gun out of his hand and aimed it at his forehead. Spencer raised his arms.

"Whoa, what the fuck, dude?"

Karl raised his own weapon, aiming it at Will.

"Whoa, whoa, hold on," Charlie said, raising his hands up toward Karl.

"He needs to put his gun down," Karl said, speaking to Charlie of Will.

"No," Will said. "You need to listen to me, and listen good. Timothy asked me to come here with you all. He did that for a reason. Because I have the most experience out of any of us out here in the world since all this shit started happening. Now, if you're not going to do what I say, we're going to have a problem."

"You're not in charge," Spencer said.

"You're wrong," Will said. "When it comes to how we handle these monsters, I *am* in charge."

"Let's all just cool it," Charlie said. "Will, come on."

"Karl, if you aren't going to side with me on this, then you may as well just drive us right back to that house and let us be on our merry-fucking-way."

Karl bit his lip. He kept his gun fixed on Will for another moment before finally dropping his arm.

"Good," Will said. He refocused his attention on Spencer. "Now, don't pull that shit again. Got it?"

Shaking, Spencer nodded.

"All right." Will lowered the gun. He clicked the safety on, then took the gun by the barrel and handed it back over to Spencer.

Spencer looked surprised that Will would hand him the gun back, but Will did so anyway as a sign of trust and as a way of saying it was time to move on. Spencer accepted the gun, and slipped it back into its holster on his waist.

"Now, let's get the hell out of here." Will moved past Spencer and loaded back into the passenger seat of the van.

In two minutes, they were back on their way.

CHAPTER FOURTEEN

The blood stains spread across the football field were most apparent where the fading chalk lines remained. The field was empty now, but it looked like a battle of nations had taken place there.

A chain link fence standing about eight feet tall lined the perimeter of the field. Part of it looked like it had been there when the football field had been used as a sporting arena. The rest of it looked like it had been built more recently.

After zoning out for a period of time, a punch to the spine alerted Gabriel. He clutched his back.

"Move," Lance commanded.

Derek walked down the aluminum stairs and stopped at a row of seats six rows away from where other people were sitting. He moved to a seat in the center of the empty row and Gabriel followed.

After Derek took a seat, he said, "Leave an empty between us. I don't need you all up on me while we sit here."

Gabriel did as he was asked, leaving a vacant seat between himself and Derek. Fortunately, Lance had the same idea, and left an empty seat to Gabriel's opposite side.

"I don't need your queer ass all on top of my shit, either," Lance said, adjusting his hat on his head.

Likewise, Gabriel thought.

Only about a hundred people were in the crowd. Half of them sat on the side of the stadium Gabriel was on while the other half sat on the opposite side of the field. Guards had been stationed around the outside of the fence. About every twenty-five feet or so, a person stood with a rifle in their hands. Most of the guards were men, but some were women, each facing the field and not the crowd.

Everyone in the stands stood as they erupted into applause. Gabriel looked around, confused as to what they were yelling for.

"Stand, you piece of shit," Lance said, grabbing onto Gabriel.

With Lance pulling him to his feet, Gabriel stood. He looked down to the field, trying to figure out what everyone was clapping and cheering about. He saw nothing of interest, and was further confused. When he looked over to Derek to follow his gaze, he finally realized what all the commotion was about.

At the far end of the field, a smaller set of bleachers sat under the scoreboard. Gabriel assumed this was where the band would have played during the football games. Today, there was no band. Instead, a muscular, gray haired man waved to the crowd as he made his way to his seat.

Nathan Ambrose.

Surrounded by a small entourage, he stood in front of his seat, continuing to wave as the people on either side of him clapped. What the hell was so special about this guy? Gabriel wasn't sure, but found himself suddenly more intrigued with finding out.

Ambrose put out his arms, signaling everyone to sit down. As everyone abided, Gabriel nestled back into his own seat and worked to get comfortable. For the first time since Gabriel had emerged from the inside of the school, everyone in the crowd had gone silent. They all turned to look toward a building on the opposite end of the stadium from where Ambrose sat.

A man emerged from the building.

He was young, maybe in his early 30s. Many in the crowd stood up and cheered as he walked toward the field. Instead of reacting to the cheers with excitement, the guy looked scared. Confused. Hand-drawn across the front of his white t-shirt was the number 12. Gabriel found himself in his own state of confusion. What was he about to see?

The crowd calmed down for just a moment as Number 12 came to a stop at the five yard line. Then they began shouting again as another man walked out from the field-house. While this guy also looked scared, he walked onto the field with more confidence than the other man had. He stood slightly taller than his counterpart, with the number 32 drawn in permanent marker across the front of his own white t-shirt. Number 32 walked out onto the field and stopped next to Number 12. The two men looked at each other for just a moment, then focused to the bandstands where Ambrose had stood up again.

Everyone fell silent. They focused their attention on Ambrose, who held a revolver in his hand.

One of the armed guards walked away from the goal post which stood in the end zone near Ambrose. An ax hung from the uprights. Gabriel hadn't noticed it before. Gabriel's mind started to spin as he put together the pieces of what was about to happen. He glanced down to the two men on the field, who were both now positioned in a sprinter's lunge. Gabriel looked back up to Ambrose, who pointed the revolver to the sky.

He fired.

The crowed erupted.

Both of the men on the field took off in a full-on sprint. Number 12 ran out to an early lead, but only by about a half-a-car length. By the time they reached the fifty, the two men were in a dead heat.

When they reached the other thirty-yard line, Number 32 body checked the smaller man. Number 12 lost his footing, flying horizontally into the air before slamming down onto the ground. He fell on his side and his head bounced off of the turf. Part of the crowd roared in excitement while the rest filled with a collective sigh. Gabriel thought the blow to the head may have knocked Number 12 out cold, but the competitor grabbed at his side.

Number 32 laughed as he looked behind him and saw Number 12 writhing in pain near the thirty-yard line. With the competition over, Number 32 slowed his sprint to a light jog. He reached the goal post at the back of the end zone and grabbed the ax with ease.

At this point, Gabriel expected Number 32 to run thirty yards back and bury the ax into his counterpart.

But it didn't happen.

Instead, the crowd went silent, and only the roar of an engine could be heard.

Everyone in the bleachers leaned down and looked toward the noise. Number 32 glanced that way, too, and then started to jog back toward the fifty yard line. He passed by Number 12 without paying him any mind.

At the corner of the field, in the direction everyone stared, a group of guards swung open the chain link fence.

An 15-foot box truck drove through the opening, and the crowd erupted again. The doors and side windows of the truck were covered with metal panels. A similar sheet of metal had been placed over the windshield. Only, this one had a small window cut out of it, allowing the driver to look out.

The truck moved to the middle of the end zone, and then the driver cut the wheel. He parked the truck at around the eight yard line, its rear bumper facing the center of the field.

Four men dressed in full, restrictive body armor made of steel wobbled out onto the field. They moved toward the truck. The suits they wore reminded Gabriel of homemade costumes from a renaissance fair. Three of the men were armed while one was not.

The four guards arrived at the back of the truck, and the unarmed guard put his hand on the handle of the sliding back door. The armed men each aimed their weapons toward the back of the truck as he unlatched the door and pushed it up. As soon as he pushed, he pulled the truck's loading ramp out and then darted away from the vehicle.

Gabriel watched what came out of the truck, and he understood the game now.

One after another, Empties spilled out of the back of the truck. The four guards moved in a semi-circle, distancing themselves from the creatures while keeping their weapons aimed at them.

When all the Empties had vacated the box truck, one of the guards fired a single shot into the air. The brake lights faded as the truck raced off the field. Gabriel counted at least fifteen Empties. The four guards moved as fast as they could in the armor, running around the back of the horde. Each of the humans made it out of the arena unscathed, and another guard shut and locked the gate.

Only the horde of Empties, an armed Number 32, and a still injured Number 12 remained on the field.

The crowd stood and cheered.

Number 12 had managed to make it back up to his feet, but stood with a bend in his torso as he held his side. He massaged his ribs to try and comfort them. His counterpart stood ten yards back from him in a battle stance, the ax firmly in his hands.

The horde, no longer distracted with the guards, focused on the two men remaining on the field. The Empties lumbered toward them.

Number 12 yelled out and started to limp toward the fence. He turned toward the side of the stadium in which Gabriel sat, and most of the crowd booed as he tried to get away. He looked terrified, his jaw moving up and down as he cried out. Tears ran down his face.

The guards along the perimeter of the fence raised their weapons, aiming them at Number 12.

Gabriel had been completely entranced by the situation until an elbow jabbed his shoulder. He looked up to see Lance cupping his hands around his mouth and booing. On the field, Number 12 stopped twenty yards from the fence.

"What's going on?" Gabriel asked.

Lance waved Gabriel off.

"They're making him stay and fight," Derek said. "If he tries to run away, the guards will shoot him in the legs and leave him to get eaten." He laughed. "It's fucking awesome."

Gabriel swallowed. He scanned the crowd. Apparently, everyone else thought it was awesome, too. Everyone except for poor Number 12, struggling to even stay on his feet.

"What the hell is this?" Gabriel finally asked.

Before Derek could answer, the crowd came to life in excitement. Gabriel looked out onto the field and saw Number 32 sprinting toward one of the Empties. It was standing just out in front of the rest of the horde. Number 32 swung the ax and decapitated the beast.

Everyone cheered as the blood sprayed onto the turf.

Number 32 readied the ax again, and then took a second swing. The blade of the ax buried into his target's shoulder, and he had trouble pulling it out of the Empty. He yelled out, unable to withdraw the weapon just as the thing started to lunge at him. Number 32 evaded the beast and kicked it in the back, sending it to the ground. Without hesitation, Number 32 drew the ax from the fallen creature's shoulder. He lifted the ax over his head and crushed the stumbled Empty's skull before it could stand back up. With the rest of the group hovering toward him, he retreated fifteen yards, allowing himself time to catch his breath.

Number 12 had finally turned to face the creatures, and part of the group had broken off to walk toward him. He had no weapon, and found himself torn between trying to appease the guards and fight the Empties by hand, or taking his chance with trying to outrun them. With either option, he seemed destined to die, barring a miracle.

That miracle came in the form of a fatal mistake by the arrogant Number 32.

Again, a single Empty had separated itself from the rest of the group. Number 32 saw a golden opportunity to thin the herd, and ran towards the creature with the ax on his shoulder. This, of course, drew a fury from the crowd. Even Ambrose stood and smiled, clapping his hands and raising a fist into the air.

Number 32 struck the creature in the neck, sending the blade halfway through its flesh. When he went to pull the ax out, though, he did so with too much excitement, and he threw the weapon fifteen yards behind him.

The crowd gasped.

He turned to go after the weapon. Everything seemed to go into slow motion. Gabriel watched as the man's foot turned onto its side as his ankle twisted around. He fell face first onto the turf and screamed in agony. His hand immediately went to his injured joint.

Number 32 tried to stand, but it was too late.

The first Empty reached him and attacked. Number 32 tried to fend the creature off, but then another Empty came, followed by another. The creatures swarmed him.

The last memory of Number 32 Gabriel would have was his hand reaching through a gap in the horde. Then it, too, disappeared.

Many in the crowd cheered while others either booed or were silent. Looks of surprise and awe covered their faces. Much of the crowd now shouted at Number 12. An opportunity had arisen for him. He eyed the fallen ax as patrons shouted "Go!" and "Grab it!"

Number 12 ran. He wobbled like a penguin, still holding his side. He seemed to have received a new-found energy with the lifeline he'd been thrown.

He made it to the ax without any of the Empties turning their focus away from the body of Number 32. Each was too busy trying to pull off the flesh of the fallen competitor.

The crowd went ballistic when Number 12 grabbed the ax.

Now armed, Number 12 looked even more mortified than before. Running was no longer an option. He was the only human alive on the field, and he'd have to take on these creatures by himself if he wanted to walk off. From the information Gabriel had gathered, if he failed to fight, he would die by the hands of humans.

Number 12 crept over toward the horde while the crowd continued to scream at him. Either by adrenaline or the sheer will to live, Number 12 swung the ax and connected with one of the creatures. The ax cut all the way through the back of its skull, shaving off the top of the Empty's head. The creature fell to the ground, and the others lifted their heads from the carcass of Number 32.

Even from up in the stands and across the field, Gabriel could see the man shaking.

The ax fell from Number 12's hands, and he turned and ran.

The crowd booed, yelling at him to "Stop being a pussy!" and to "Stand and fight!"

Again, the guards on the fence's outer perimeter raised their weapons.

Number 12 made it to the chain link fence, the horde of Empties still halfway across the field. He held onto the fence and shook it, pleading to be let out. A guard on the other side pointed and yelled at him. Number 12 didn't seem to be listening, as he continued to negotiate an exit from the sickening contest.

The guard turned away from Number 12 and looked up to the bleachers where Ambrose sat.

Ambrose, standing now, simply nodded to the guard.

The guard backed a few feet away from the fence and raised his weapon.

Number 12's eyes went as wide as oranges. He turned and ran back toward the end zone near the field-house. The guard, having stuck the barrel of the rifle through a gap in the chain link, followed Number 12 in his sights. If Number 12 had been smart, he would've swerved, making himself a moving target. Instead, the guard fired, and the bullet bit into the remaining competitor's calf like a rabid dog. Blood spewed from his leg, and he fell to the turf, face planting at about the twenty-five yard line.

Once again, the crowd cheered. Some even laughed.

One of those someones was Ambrose. Gabriel stared over at the gray haired man, who smiled from ear to ear and clapped. He looked down to the guard and gave him two thumbs up. The guard, as if he were nearing the end of a Broadway show, took a bow.

The horde snarled, lumbering toward the fallen competitor. Number 12 lay on the ground, holding the back of his leg and crying. Not just screaming came from him, but tears swimming down his face.

And as the horde reached him, Gabriel turned away.

The crowd erupted.

CHAPTER FIFTEEN

For the rest of the short drive, everyone in the vehicle remained silent. The quiet remained until Karl pointed ahead and spoke.

"There," he said. "That's the landmark."

Ahead was a two-way stop. Karl came to a complete stop and pointed to a tree that was a short distance away from the red sign.

In the middle of the tree were three words carved into the bark with a knife: 'Come For Us'.

"Come for us?" Spencer asked, curious.

"God," Charlie replied.

Spencer still looked confused.

"They are asking God to come for them. To get them out of this nightmare," Charlie clarified.

Spencer sat back in his seat.

As Karl made a right turn, he said, "Should be not far down this road."

He drove until he came to the entrance of a neighborhood. Much like the place Karl and Spencer had been staying, it was a gated community. The location was far enough off the beaten path to where few people would find it without knowing it was there. The road inclined, and at the top of the hill, they arrived at a gate.

"This is definitely it," Karl said.

Two guards sat perched on makeshift crows' nests to either end of the gate. One of the men held an assault rifle while the other appeared to only have a pistol.

"Stop," a strong female voice called out. It came from a loudspeaker, and it hadn't come from either of the guards stationed up high.

Karl brought the van to a complete stop, and Will looked around for the person speaking to them.

"Shut off your vehicle and throw your keys on the dashboard," the voice said. "Then keep your hands on the wheel. Everyone else in the vehicle, please put your hands behind your head."

"What is this?" Spencer asked, frustrated. "Where the hell did you bring us, Karl?"

"They're just being cautious," Will said, raising his hands to behind his head. "Now, just do as they ask."

Karl turned the key in the ignition, killing the engine. He tossed the keys up on the dash, then set his hands on the wheel. Everyone else in the vehicle followed the instructions, placing their hands behind their heads. The guards up top kept their weapons fixed on the van, and the woman behind the voice still had yet to show herself.

On either side of the road, there was grass for about ten yards before a line of trees started. There'd been trees along the road for the entire drive, so these woods likely went back several hundred yards. Will heard a rustling, and looked over toward it.

Out of the trees walked a woman holding at her side a megaphone. Three men carrying heavier artillery appeared behind her. The woman wore a military style jacket, faded green with the front open, with a tattered thermal shirt underneath. She had a dark complexion with oily black hair and dark brown eyes. She approached the van with little hesitation or worry. Arriving at the passenger side front door, she opened it.

"Are you armed?" she asked Will.

"Yes," Will said. "We all are."

She looked Will up and down. He'd used a towel to wipe most of the blood and matter off of his face and from his hair, but his outfit was still covered in body fluid.

"What happened?"

"We had a run-in while on the way here," Will said.

"Human?" she asked.

Will shook his head.

The woman scanned everyone else in the vehicle. Then she focused her attention to the rear compartment where the group had placed all the things they meant to barter.

"Why are you here?" she asked.

"I met Adam while out on the road," Karl said. "We met at a gas station. He gave me directions and said that you all would be willing to do some trading. We have a list of things we need, and we've come with items to trade."

The woman glanced into each of their faces, not moving from her cold stare. The three guards behind her remained with their weapons crossed over their chests, not aimed at the van.

"We'll need your ammo. You can keep the guns."

Before Will could say anything, Spencer leaned into the front seat and said, "No way, man."

"Shut up," Karl yelled.

Taken back, Spencer faded into the back seat.

"Give them your ammunition," Karl said, speaking to all three men in the car.

Will hesitated, trying to read the woman. She held a cold stare on Karl, but shifted it to Will.

Charlie handed both his and Spencer's ammo through the window. Karl followed suit.

"Do it, Will," Charlie said to Will.

Will sighed, and turned his bullets over to the woman.

Still staring at Will, the woman shouted, "Let them in." She backed away from the van.

The gate opened, and Karl swiped the keys off the dash. The engine roared to life and he pulled forward through the entrance.

There was almost a quarter-mile stretch of pavement between the gate and any houses. The land leading into the neighborhood had once been decked out with beautiful landscaping, but flowers in the median had died off and the bushes along the curb were now unkempt.

When they reached the first house on the corner, there were another two men waiting on them. Neither man held a weapon, but each had a pistol affixed to their side, and one of the men also had a large knife on his hip. Karl rolled down his window as he pulled up beside the two men.

"What's your business here?" the man with the large knife asked.

"Here to see Adam and hoping to do some trading."

The man looked into the van, scanning the faces of the four people inside before shifting his gaze to the items in the back.

"All right," the man said. "Go up the road and take a right onto Calvin. You'll see a group of people outside, and Adam's place is 345."

"Thanks," Karl said.

The man tapped on the window seal and backed away from the van.

The houses they passed appeared empty and no one stood outside. Strangely, it looked like this neighborhood had seen little action. Either nothing had happened here, or the survivors living in the area had done a good job of cleaning up.

Karl hung a right on Calvin.

Several people loitered in the street and yards, turning to watch the van approach as it came around the corner.

Spencer said, "I don't like this."

"It'll be fine," Charlie said.

"How do you know, man?"

"No, he's right," Will said. "If they wanted to kill us, they could've already."

Karl pulled the vehicle forward, and everyone outside just stared at them. He drove until he had no choice but to stop, as no one in the road had moved. He saw the number '345' posted on a mailbox behind the group.

"Hang here," Karl said. He stepped out of the vehicle and approached the group.

"This just doesn't feel right, man," Spencer said again.

Even though Will had said it was fine, he had his own doubts. He wished that he hadn't agreed to turn over his weapons at the gate. In fact, it seemed like a really stupid decision in this moment.

Karl walked up to the group and spoke to a man. They shook hands, and the man thumbed over his shoulder toward 345 Calvin Street—Adam's house. The man shouted at someone else, and a teenage boy hurried through Adam's yard and knocked on his door.

The door opened, and a man appeared in the doorway. They spoke for a moment, and then the man looked over the teen's shoulder and waved at Karl. The two men met halfway across Adam's yard, and it was as if they'd known each other since grade school. They hugged, shook hands, and chatted for a moment before Karl looked back and waved to the van.

"I guess we're safe to get out," Charlie said.

Will opened his door and stepped out of the vehicle. The air had a cool tinge to it, and the breeze blew down the center of the open street. He shut his door and, when he turned to face the group, everyone in the street stared at him. He glanced to the houses, and the eyes of people standing in the yards and on porches stared him down. Standing still, he looked down at his clothes. They were covered in blood. He had wiped his face off as best he could, but could still feel the dirt and dried blood on his cheeks and in his hair.

He found a cloud on the horizon to focus on, looking past the crowd. Even so, he could still feel all their eyes on him as he approached Adam's house.

***

There was a half-bath located on the first floor of Adam's home. He allowed Will to use it to clean himself up, providing him with a couple of hand towels. The house had no running water, but Adam had been kind enough to give him a couple of bottled waters to rinse off with. Will wondered if he would have to pay for the bottles later in a trade.

A vanilla-scented candle illuminated the space. Will got as much of the crud out of his hair as he could, and then he used the remaining water to clean off his face. As he looked in the mirror, even in the dim light he could see how much he'd aged in such a short period of time. The stubble on his face would grow thicker, which would help keep him warm in the oncoming winter. New lines had formed on his face. The dark ones under his eyes didn't wipe away with the blood and dirt.

Once he'd used all the water, Will dried off his face with the second towel, blew out the candle, and exited the half-bath.

The door opened up to the living room, where Charlie, Karl,

and Spencer sat on a long, three-piece sofa. Adam sat across the room in a recliner, gesturing with several hand motions as he spoke. He was tall, around six-foot-three, and was balding on top. Like Will, he had a new beard growing in, though Adam's was a little more mature. He wore a hooded sweatshirt with a hole in the front pocket. He looked over to Will and smiled.

"Feel better?" Adam asked.

"Much," Will said. "Thank you."

"Karl here was telling me what happened. You're really lucky."

You don't know the half of it, Will thought, chuckling. "Yeah, I was."

"Please, have a seat," Karl said, signaling toward another chair on the other side of the room.

Will went to the chair and eased into it. A fresh bottle of water sat on a nearby table, and Will opened the top and took a swig.

"Thanks," Will said, pointing the top of the water bottle toward Adam.

"Not a problem," Adam replied.

"You guys have been here since people fell?" Charlie asked.

Finishing his own sip of water, Adam nodded. "Pretty much everyone who lives here now was here before. We have a couple of stragglers, but we're so hidden back here that we haven't had to worry about much. The population in this area is dense. This was the first of several subdivisions being developed in these parts, but then, well..."

"Yeah," Charlie said.

"We've met a few other people when we've ventured out into the world. No one since we met you," Adam said, signaling toward Karl. "We're pretty well stocked here, so we've been fortunate enough not to have to leave too often. But from what I've heard, we've been pretty lucky."

"How many people fell?" Will asked.

"Seven," Adam said.

Will's eyes widened. "That's it? You guys made out very well. When it happened, I was the only person alive where I was. I had to kill more than seven to get out, and that was in a 50,000 square foot building."

"I'm sorry to hear that," Karl said. "We do know that we're very fortunate. The truth is, this neighborhood isn't even finished, so there weren't a lot of folks here to begin with. And the construction was a blessing in itself. We've got enough lumber to last us maybe twelve winters." He took another swig of water. "With that, maybe we should get down to business."

"Oh, yeah," Karl said. He reached into his pocket and pulled out a folded piece of paper. He opened it and handed it over to Adam.

Adam leaned over and grabbed a set of reading glasses from a table next to him. He put them on, and then looked at the note.

"Hmm," he mumbled.

"What?" Will asked.

"You guys sure need a lot of medical supplies," he said.

"Do you have them?" Will asked.

He continued scanning the list for a sec, and then nodded. "Yeah, I believe we have most of this. We were able to raid a pharmacy up the road right after everything happened. So we have quite a few prescriptions. I can tell you that these aren't going to be cheap."

"That's fine," Will said sharply.

Adam looked up from the paper and lowered his glasses down his nose. He eyed Will for a moment curiously.

"You got a painkiller addiction or something?"

Charlie butted in. "We have a badly injured child with us. He's resting in a house back with Karl's group. Those painkillers and antibiotics are for him."

"Must be a pretty serious injury," Karl said.

Will's attitude had changed on a dime. What had once been a pleasant conversation was now just annoying him. He hated negotiations. Especially now, when bartering over supplies could mean the difference between life and death. Seeing that Will was becoming frustrated, Charlie took the liberty of explaining to Karl what had happened to Dylan. When he finished, Adam's expression soured.

"Jesus Christ," he said. He rubbed his forehead, sinking back into the recliner.

"We need those things so that he can recover," Will said. "Without them, he's going to be in a lot of constant pain, and we could risk infection."

"All right," Adam said. He pushed himself out of the chair and stood. "Let's go see what you've got to trade."

***

Outside, many of the same people still loitered. A small group of adults stood in the middle of the road, circled around three children playing with a jump rope. One child stood at either end while the third jumped. They counted with each leap, and the girl jumping had just passed twenty skips.

Karl led the others across the yard, down to the van. He opened the back doors and Adam peeked inside. Again, he used his reading glasses to get a better look at everything.

Ignoring all the canned food, Adam put his hands on the generator.

"It work?" he asked, looking back.

"Sure does," Karl said. "Just needs gasoline."

Adam looked inside the van again, and began rummaging through the weapons. He put his hands on a shotgun. "Do you have any shells to go with this Remington?"

"Your gatekeepers took all the ammunition, but we've got it. There's also a few other things in that box next to the generator."

Karl picked up the box and looked inside to see two knives and a pistol.

"All right," Adam said. "So are you willing to part with all of it?"

"All of it?" Spencer asked, sounding surprised.

"What are we going to get in return?" Karl asked.

"You're not actually considering this, are you?" Spencer asked Karl. "We just brought all this so that they'd have options. Now you wanna give it all away?"

"You'll get everything on your list. Since you have a hurt child, I'll throw in extra quantities on the stuff that he needs."

"We have some things we can trade," Will said.

Adam shook his head. "Just consider them a gift from me."

"Can you throw in a little bit of lumber for us? Just anything you might have that we could fit in here and take with us." Karl pointed his head toward the generator. "She runs like a champ. And I'm sure it's going to be worth a hell of a lot more than what we're asking, the further into this mess we all get."

Adam considered it for a moment, and then he stuck his hand out. "You've got a deal."

Spencer grabbed Karl by the shoulder and turned him towards himself. "You can't do this."

Ignoring Spencer, Karl turned back to Adam. "Show me the items that we're asking for, and then you've got a deal."

Smiling, Adam shook Karl's hand and said, "Fair enough."

"I can't fucking believe this," Spencer said. He shook his head and stepped away from the van, walking down the street in the direction from which they'd come.

"You sure we got a deal?" Adam asked, still gripping Karl's hand.

"Yeah," Karl said. "He'll be fine."

Will stepped in as the two men broke their handshake and said, "Thank you." He offered his own hand and Adam took it.

"I had a son of my own," Adam said. "He and his mother died in a car accident six years ago. I would've done anything to save him."

"I'm so sorry," Will said.

Adam shook his head. "It's fine, really. Honestly not sure if I could deal with him living in this world. In a strange way, what happened to him might have been better."

It stunned Will to hear the comment, but he decided not to reply.

"Come on," Adam said. "Let's go get your things."

***

They finished the trade by helping Adam carry the generator into one of the nearby yards. As promised, he had been able to provide them with all the medications and supplies on their list. With everything loaded, they set the generator down next to the weaponry they'd traded away. Karl had also brought a small selection of canned goods, but Adam had told him the guns, ammunition, and generator would be enough payment.

Will extended his hand to Adam. "Thank you, again."

Accepting the handshake, Adam said, "It's no problem. You just take care of that boy, you hear?"

"Will do."

Will, Charlie, and Karl were ready to head back, but Spencer had yet to return.

"Where the hell could he have run off to?" Charlie asked.

Sighing in frustration, Karl said, "I'll go find him."

"No," Will said. "Stay here and have the van ready to go. I'll go find him."

"All right," Karl said.

Will left the van and headed down the street. He passed residents along the way, exchanging waves. Everyone smiled now as opposed to just staring. It probably helped that Will had cleaned himself up and no longer looked like he'd spent his entire day slaughtering cattle.

When he reached the end of the road, he came to trees. To his left was the exit out of the neighborhood. And to his right was a chain link fence, stretched across the road, and several lots where houses were supposed to have been under construction. He'd started to go left to see if Spencer had headed back toward the fence when he heard a scream straight ahead. It had come from the trees.

Will turned back and saw residents looking down the street toward him. The doors of the van were open, and Charlie and Karl were among the eyes staring his way.

The human scream sounded again, prompting Will to look back toward the trees.

Without hesitation, he raced into the woods.

The fact that he was unarmed didn't escape him, but he chased after the cry anyway. He sprinted as fast as he could, pushing away branches, stomping over twigs, and nearly tripping over a stray log. The human scream came again, bouncing off the woods all around him.

Will ran for another thirty yards or so before he came to a fence. Vines had found their way through the openings, gripping the steel. He heard the scream again, this time coming from his right. He followed for a few hundred feet until he came to an opening. It was just big enough for someone of Will's size to walk straight through to the other side. He squatted down and noticed the fresh blood dripping off the chain link.

"Oh, shit," he mumbled.

"Help!"

The voice came from behind him, and Will turned back toward the woods. He ran again, but he didn't have to go far to find the source of the human cries.

A large group of Empties, perhaps around twenty, or maybe two dozen, were gathered around a tree. They were about fifteen yards from where Will stood. Hanging from the tree like an exhausted gymnast was Spencer. He hung from a long branch, its end almost touching the ground under the weight, his arms extended. The creatures stood under him, his feet just out of reach from their dead grasps. He managed to look up and make eye contact with Will just before Will concealed himself behind a nearby tree.

"Help! Will, help me!"

Will stood against the tree, his eyes closed, trying to come up with a strategy. All the while, Spencer continued to cry a desperate plea for Will to help him.

Drawing in a deep breath, Will opened his eyes and shifted from behind the tree. He walked five yards and stopped. Spencer continued to cry out, and he shook the branch as he writhed. Will waved at him with both arms, trying to get him to calm down. The branch bounced with every single movement that Spencer made. It looked to Will as if it might not hold up much longer if Spencer kept tugging on it.

Continuing to wave his arms, but looking down at the

Empties now, Will yelled, "Hey! Over here!"

The creatures lowered their hands and turned in unison. They snarled, and the creature that Will was focused on tilted its head, as if curious. It led the pack in lumbering toward Will, who stepped backward slowly, so as to not trip and fall.

"That's it," Will said. "Come on, you ugly bastards."

The monsters continued toward Will. In the tree, Spencer's expression had stretched into a smile.

"Yes!" Spencer yelled. "Fuck yes! Get the fuck outta here, you ugly cunts!"

The tail of the horde had almost cleared the space under Spencer when he yelled again. The Empties looked back to Spencer, dangling in the tree.

"What? No!" Spencer cried.

"Spencer, shut the fuck up!" Will yelled.

But Spencer apparently didn't hear him, or at least didn't heed the advice. He continued to bawl. Most of the horde turned away from Will and moved back under Spencer. As each creature made their way under his feet and reached for him again, Spencer writhed more. Will looked up to see that the branch was close to faltering under the pressure.

"Spencer, you've gotta stop moving. That branch is gonna br —"

The crack of the branch echoed through the forest, even overshadowing the Empties' hungry howls. Spencer fell to the ground, still holding the branch. He landed on his feet, but immediately screamed and fell down. His screams now were those of agonizing pain. Through a gap in the horde, Will could see Spencer rolling on his back and holding onto his ankle. He imagined the ankle rolling like that of a basketball player's, coming down awkwardly from a rebound attempt.

Spencer screamed one more time, and then the Empties piled on top of him, and the cries faded. Will, still backing away from about five Empties who'd remained focused on him, turned away from the gruesome scene. He looked back for a brief second before he cut through the woods and ran back to the neighborhood.

CHAPTER SIXTEEN

When Will emerged from the trees, Charlie was waiting on him.

"I was just coming to look for you," Charlie said. "What the hell happened?"

Working to catch his breath, Will thumbed over his shoulder. "There's a group of Empties in there. There's a hole in the fence and they must've come through. They got Spencer."

"Shit," Charlie said.

Adam jogged up from behind Charlie with three people, one of which was the woman who had greeted them at the gate.

"What's the matter?" Adam asked.

Will told them about the Empties in the woods, and Adam raised his eyebrows, mouth wide in disbelief.

"They killed your man?" he asked.

Will nodded. "I don't know why he didn't just outrun them and come back. He either panicked, or they ended up surrounding him somehow."

"I'm so sorry," Adam said.

"He shouldn't have run off," Charlie said.

Before answering, Will said to Adam, "You're going to have to fix that fence once you take care of the herd. There's about twenty of them. You have plenty of artillery, right?"

Adam furrowed his brow. "You aren't staying to help?"

Will shook his head. "I'm sorry, but no. We have to get back to our own group and get the medications to Dylan."

Karl ran up behind them. "What happened?"

The woman nudged Adam on the shoulder. "It's fine, we can handle it. Let them go."

"Handle what?" Karl asked. "And go? We can't leave without Spencer. Where is he?"

Charlie looked to Will, then pulled Karl aside to explain to him what had happened. Will extended his hand to Adam.

"Thank you," Will said.

Accepting Will's hand, Adam said, "I hope the boy ends up all right."

Will smiled and nodded. "I think he will."

When he heard the faint snarls, Will turned around to look back into the trees. The creatures weren't yet visible, but they sounded like they were close. Will hurried over to Charlie.

"And he's sure he's dead?" Karl was asking Charlie as Will approached. Karl then directed the question at Will.

"I'm sorry," Will said. "We need to get out of here."

As they ran toward the van, the woman and Adam shouted orders at the other survivors. Many of them were already armed, and others raced to find weapons. Others, women and children mostly, scurried away from the scene entirely, though many of the women held weapons and were ready to fight. Will, Charlie, and Karl found themselves running against a small wave of individuals as they headed back to the van. They loaded inside, this time lighter by one person and a generator. Karl's hands shook on the wheel.

"You need me to drive?" Will asked.

"No," Karl said, shaking his head. "I'll be fine."

One of the guards who had been perched up high at the fence waited for the van as it approached. The gate opened, and he saluted Will and the others as they passed by.

And as Karl drove through the gate, a fury of gunshots rang

out behind them.

***

Each time Will looked over to Karl, he seemed to be gripping the steering wheel tighter. Will noticed sweat glistening off its leather covering. He thought about trying to speak with Karl about what had happened, but then he thought back to friends and family he'd lost over the past few weeks, and how he had wanted to just be left alone.

The silence gave Will time to reflect on what had happened. He felt guilty about leaving the survivors to handle the horde on their own—especially when they'd had so little experience dealing with Empties. But after losing Spencer, the risk of staying had elevated. Going home light one person would be grueling enough, and Will knew he needed to get the supplies they'd obtained back to Timothy. Most of all, to Dylan.

Playing over and over again in his head was the scene with Spencer. Surrounded by trees on the ride home, he couldn't help but think about Spencer's face as the branch broke, sending him to the ground and, inevitably, his death. It replayed in his mind in slow-motion, especially the terror in Spencer's face as his hands had let go. Then, when they passed the place where they'd stopped to fight the small group of Empties on the way to trade for supplies, Will held back tears. Even though he'd been frustrated with both Spencer and Karl for the way they'd frozen inside the van, Spencer had still saved Will's life. That same sour attitude Spencer had displayed then was the exact thing that had killed him barely even an hour later. The whole thing was sad, but Will had to remind himself there was nothing more he could've done to save the man.

On the way home, they had no physical encounters with any Empties. Within only twenty minutes, they were back.

A few people who Will didn't recognize were there to greet them when they arrived. One of the people, a woman in her forties, called Timothy's name. Others began gathering outside.

Will stepped out of the van. When he looked over the hood, he saw Holly on the porch of the house they'd been staying in, a grin stretched across her face. She shuffled down the steps and ran to him, and he picked her up and hugged her. When they were finished, she stepped back, moving the hair out of her face, and looked back at him.

"What happened?" she asked.

Even though he'd been able to clear most the grime off his face and out of his hair, Will had forgotten that his shirt still displayed the aftermath of their encounter with the small pack of Empties on the road.

"We had a run-in with a small pack," Will replied. "No big deal."

"Were you guys able to trade with them?"

Will nodded.

Charlie stepped out of the back seat, holding some of the medical supplies in his hands. He hugged Holly, and Will turned around as Timothy approached.

"Did you get everything off the list?" Timothy asked.

Will handed the list back to Timothy. Everything had been scratched off, telling him that it had all been obtained.

"We had to trade just about everything we took with us, but we got everything you needed."

"This should last us a long time," Timothy said. "I'd like to give you some for the boy."

Waving his hand, Will said, "When Adam heard the story about what happened to Dylan, he offered to give us a small supply. It should be enough to get Dylan through until he heals."

They shook hands. Timothy said, "Thank you for going."

"It's no problem. Thank you for all the care and hospitality you've shown us."

When Timothy looked over to Karl, he scrunched his face in confusion. "Where's Spencer?"

Karl put his hands on his hips and he shook his head.

"Shit," Timothy mumbled, looking down to the ground.

Will explained to Timothy what had happened. How Spencer had become upset when they had agreed to unload everything they'd brought with them. How he'd then wandered off, and what had happened when Will found him.

When Will finished, Timothy fell silent.

"Did he have any family here?"

"No," Timothy said. "Thank God, too, because I'm not sure I could go through that."

"I'm sorry," Will said, his hand on Timothy's shoulder. He glanced over to the house and saw Dylan and Mary Beth standing on the front porch. Will patted Timothy on the back, then moved past him and headed up the yard.

Dylan smiled, looking the happiest he'd been since his arm had been amputated. Will leaned down and hugged Mary Beth first, then Dylan. Dylan's single arm wrapped around Will's side, patting him.

"I'm glad you're back," Dylan said.

"Me, too, buddy." Will pulled away and observed the dressing on Dylan's arm. "How's it feeling?"

Shrugging, Dylan said, "A little sore, but a lot better."

"Well, we got you some medicine that should help out a lot, all right?"

Will turned around to face the gathering crowd in the street. Timothy had his head in his palm and he appeared to be crying now. The same was true with Karl. Charlie and Holly headed up the yard as others poured into the street.

"Come on," Will said, putting his hand on Dylan's shoulder. "Let's go inside."

***

When Will and Holly finished packing, they joined Charlie and the kids in the living room of the house.

"You guys ready?" Charlie asked.

"Yeah," Will said. "Let's get out of here."

When they walked outside, a small contingency awaited them. This group included Timothy, Samantha, Doug and Maureen. Others who Will recognized but had not met kept their distance. Will placed his hand in the middle of Dylan's back, urging him down the stairs first. They met Timothy and the others on the sidewalk.

"Are you sure you don't want to stay?" Timothy asked.

"We appreciate the offer, but we can't. We need to get to Roanoke."

"Why?" Samantha asked. "The boy would be safe here. You're really welcome to stay."

Will considered the question for a moment, but then said, "We have to get there to see a friend."

"We understand," Timothy said.

Will used his head to signal Timothy away from the others. They met in the middle of the yard, a good fifteen yards from earshot of the group.

"Thank you, again, for helping out with Dylan," Will said. "I'm not really sure what would've happened if not for your help."

"It's no problem. You all are good people. I'm glad that we could help and that we were able to meet you. And thank you for helping us out, as well."

"I'm sorry again about Spencer."

Timothy shrugged. "That's the unfortunate world that we now live in." He sighed and said, "Sadly, I doubt he will be the last."

Will thought of everyone he'd lost, and simply nodded in agreement. He shifted his bag to the front, where he could reach into it. He opened the front pocket and pulled out an envelope. After looking down at it for a moment, slapping it into his palm, Will handed the envelope to Timothy.

"When we're gone, please read this." Timothy accepted the envelope. "It is for your eyes only unless you choose to share it with others. That's up to you. I'm sorry that I didn't have the chance to talk to you about this in person, but this letter should explain a lot."

Timothy furrowed his brow. "What's in the letter?"

"The truth," Will replied. "Or at least as much as we've learned about it."

Timothy looked as if he wanted to ask another question, but Will cut him off.

"Please, just wait until we're gone, and read it. Things are going to seem quite unreal. Hopefully you've gained my trust enough to where you can believe that everything I have written here is true. It should help you and your people understand this world a little bit more and help you to survive."

Licking his lips, Timothy stared down at the letter, and then back up at Will. He looked as if he had so many questions. Will knew that he would have many more once he read about Samuel drawing the demon out of him, but he'd tried his best in the letter to answer any questions Samuel or the others might have after reading it.

Timothy smiled and said, "All right." He extended his hand once more, and Will shook it. This time, Timothy pulled him in for a hug. They embraced, and Will pulled away and patted him on the shoulder, then walked to the SUV.

Holly, Charlie, and Dylan were already inside when Will approached. He shook hands with Doug and Samantha, then hugged Maureen, thanking her for all of her hospitality.

As Will loaded into the SUV, Timothy called after him and he turned.

"You know where we are if you change your mind," Timothy said.

Will smiled and nodded. He loaded into the SUV, and they were headed North again, back on the open roads.

CHAPTER SEVENTEEN

The scene played over and over again in Gabriel's head. Everything from watching the two men walk out onto the field, as the crowd cheered at them as if they were animals, to both of the competitors' lives ending in such a horrific way. They'd been eaten alive, and no one in the crowd aside from Gabriel had seemed to give a damn. Gabriel had always told himself that if he were in a position where getting eaten by an Empty was a certainty, he'd take as many of the bastards out as he could, before using the last bullet on himself. But neither of these men had been given that choice.

Worst of all, Gabriel now knew why he was here. What he didn't know was why he'd been given his own space, or why Ambrose had opted to take a one-on-one meeting with him. Gabriel was just a pawn in Ambrose's sick game—a gladiator slave like in ancient Rome. What Gabriel had seen was the form of entertainment in a lawless land. Nothing more. And, now, he was part of the game.

Back in his room, Gabriel sat on top of a desk, a sharp hunger in his stomach. He remained alone, still turning to thoughts of his family, to Dylan, and wondering what had come of Jessica, Thomas, and Claire. He'd looked for them at the stadium, but hadn't spotted them in the crowd. He thought that perhaps they'd been in attendance, but placed in a spot where they'd been unable to locate Gabriel or each other.

Someone approached, and Gabriel didn't even bother to get up off the desk. If these people were coming for him, so be it.

The sound stopped in front of the door, and the handle clicked. His elbow resting on his knees, Gabriel didn't look toward the door as it opened. But out of the corner of his eye, he could see that Philadelphia Eagles hat.

"Come on," Lance said.

Gabriel snorted. "What? You gonna drag me out there and let me prance around in front of all those fucking psychopaths?"

Lance made a move toward Gabriel, but was held back by the guard with long hair.

"Derek, let me go," Lance said.

"You insane, Lance? You really think laying a hand on this douche is gonna be worth it when you have to explain it to Ambrose?"

Gabriel finally looked over and found amusement in looking at Lance's face. His cheeks had turned beet-red, and his eyes looked like they might explode from their sockets. He breathed like he'd just sprinted two hundred yards.

Lance's mouth curved into a malevolent smile.

"It's all right," Lance said. "You got plenty comin' to you, you piece of shit."

Derek stepped in front of his counterpart and said to Gabriel, "Come on. Mr. Ambrose wants to see you."

Gabriel drew in a deep breath, and then he stood.

***

They led Gabriel outside and, for the first time, he was able to see the front part of the school. It looked to be out in the middle of nowhere, as no major roads appeared to be nearby. There was no sign of any other buildings or even any residential establishments. Trees lined the perimeter of the property. Seeing's how the school appeared to sit out on its own, he was surprised at just how big it was. The sign out front confirmed it was a high school. From the size of it, he guessed that the senior class of this year might have had nearly 300 students.

The two guards led Gabriel down a sidewalk. Up ahead, he saw the group's gray haired leader, sitting on a large concrete slab near the school's entrance. A flagpole rose from the middle of the structure, reaching thirty feet into the sky. It had been built as a large bench which the likes of thirty or forty students could have sat on. Nathan Ambrose sat on the second level of the bench, his back facing Gabriel. Smoke rose from the front side of him, spreading into the air to form a cloud. Once they had almost reached Ambrose, he turned around.

Ten feet away from Ambrose, Derek stopped, and Lance came around next to Gabriel's other side. Ambrose motioned to the bench beside him.

"Have a seat, Gabriel," Ambrose said.

Nathan drew the last drag from his cigar, then ground the tip into the concrete before flicking it away.

"How'd you sleep?" Ambrose asked.

Gabriel snorted. "How do you think? You ever slept on a tile floor with no pillow or blanket?"

Ambrose laughed. "Well, if you comply, there's a chance you may not have to sleep on that tile floor again."

Gabriel didn't respond.

"I spent last night reading your girl's diary," Ambrose said. "Well, not *your* girl per se, but your friend, Jessica."

That's how they know my name, Gabriel thought.

Ambrose stood up, and groaned as he stretched. He stepped off the concrete bench, onto the ground.

"Walk with me."

Gabriel joined Nathan at his side. Nathan glanced over to the two guards, and signaled for them to hang back.

Ambrose put his hands behind his back as they started to stroll down the sidewalk.

"You folks have been through a lot," Nathan began.

"You could say that," Gabriel said.

"You guys seemed to have a really good thing going for you at that hospital, and then also at those cabins. You were with other people. Why'd you leave?"

"I guess you could say that we had a different agenda," Gabriel said.

"I see," Ambrose said. "Headed to D.C.?"

Gabriel didn't respond.

"That's what I figured. A lot of the people we've picked up were headed to D.C. They all think they are going to find some kind of refuge there." Ambrose chuckled. "Yeah, right. You're dumb as hell if you think you're going to find that there."

"How do you know?" Gabriel asked.

"You think we haven't been there? The government has fallen apart, Mr. Alexander. Washington is just as broken as anywhere else in the country. You're not going to find peace there."

Gabriel hesitated. He thought to tell Ambrose about the real reason he needed to get to the D.C. area, but decided against it. The less Nathan knew about him, the better. And at this point, Ambrose already knew too much.

"Not exactly feeling like I'm gonna find peace here, either," Gabriel said.

Ambrose smiled. "That, you will not. But, you can make things a lot easier on yourself if you want."

"And how is that?"

"You agree to do as I say. For at least a time, I own you, Mr. Alexander. That is the case whether you like it or not, and whether you want to believe it or not. The sooner you accept that, the better a chance you have of living at least a little bit longer."

Gabriel stopped and turned to face Ambrose. Lance started to come forward as if he might lunge at Gabriel, but Nathan stopped him with a raised palm, never allowing his eyes to leave Gabriel's. The dull stench of dozens of cigars drowned out Nathan's face. His yellow teeth flashed through his cunning smile. Years of tobacco abuse were settled into his stained, gray mustache.

"Fuck you," Gabriel said.

Without hesitation, Lance leaned forward and punched Gabriel, landing a jab to his cheek. Gabriel fell backward onto the ground. Lance straddled Gabriel, bringing his hand back to throw another punch. Gabriel heard a click, and Lance froze, slowly looking back.

Ambrose pointed a revolver at Lance's face, who lifted the bill of his hat so that he could see easier.

"I suggest you get up, Lance," Ambrose said.

"Boss, what are you—"

Ambrose fired. The bullet blew into the concrete sidewalk, narrowly missing Lance.

"I swear to Christ, I won't waste another bullet. The next one goes right between your goddamn eyes, so you better get the fuck up, right now."

Without looking back toward Gabriel, Lance stood. Just as he made it to his feet, Ambrose grabbed him by the collar of his shirt and slammed the butt-end of the revolver into his nose. Gabriel heard the crunch and saw a splash of blood spray from the side of Lance's face. The Eagles hat fell off of his head as he cried out, doubling over to hold his nose.

Ambrose looked down to Gabriel, who still lay on the ground holding his own face.

"We'll see who does all the fucking around here." Ambrose looked at Derek. "Get Mr. Alexander back to his room, and then take your fairy friend here over to medical to get that nose checked out."

Ambrose put on a pair of sunglasses, took one last look at Gabriel, and then walked away.

Lance cussed Gabriel all the way back to his room. If it hadn't been for the pain in his own face, Gabriel might have laughed, and especially since he knew that Lance couldn't touch him. Instead, he chose to ignore him all together.

Derek uncuffed Gabriel, pushed him into the classroom, and locked the door.

A bowl of soup lay on one of the desks. It was in a small Styrofoam bowl, and had a plastic spoon inside it. Gabriel took the spoon and shoveled the first scoop into his mouth. It was cold and bland, but he didn't care.

As Gabriel ate, he reflected more on what he'd seen earlier in the day and what Ambrose had told him. He wondered what exactly Nathan had in store for him, and more importantly, what it had to do with the sadistic spectacle on the football field. He hoped that, if they were going to throw him out onto that field, he'd be served a real meal first. Gabriel didn't see a scenario in which he would survive if he hardly had enough energy to stay on his feet.

He wondered, again, where Jessica, Thomas, and Claire were, and if they were okay.

All these things raced through his mind until he fell asleep on the floor.

CHAPTER EIGHTEEN

Sometime, in what Jessica guessed was the middle of the day, people marched down the hall toward her and Claire's room. Jessica sat on top of a desk while Claire stood up from the floor. She cowered, stepping back into the corner of the room, her arms across her chest, trying to keep herself warm.

"Just stay calm," Jessica said.

A familiar face appeared in the window, and Jessica hopped off the desk. The two guards, Lance and Derek, appeared in the doorway, each holding a rifle. Derek reached down to his belt, grabbed a set of handcuffs, and threw them to Jessica.

"Put these on." He looked over to Claire, who'd slid down the wall and now sat down in the corner of the room. "And you, get over here."

Jessica held the handcuffs in her hands, staring at them.

"Did you hear me?" Derek asked.

"Where are you taking us?" Jessica asked in return.

In the corner, Claire started to cry. Lance, who Jessica had learned was the more ill-tempered of the two guards, let out a frustrated sigh and marched over to where Claire had sunk onto the tile floor.

"Please, don't hurt her," Jessica said. "She's just scared."

Lance apparently hadn't heard Jessica or just didn't care—likely the latter. He bent over in the corner and yanked Claire off of the ground, pulling her up by the baggy shoulders of her jumpsuit. She fought it, bucking like a spoiled toddler, until Lance slammed her into the wall.

"Bitch, if you don't stop this fuckin' horse shit right now, I'm gonna be draggin' your ass out of here unconscious. You got that?"

Claire nodded, unable to control her sniffling. Lance cuffed her, then grabbed her by the back of her jumpsuit and led her over to the door.

When Jessica turned around again, Derek was just a couple of feet from her.

"I suggest you put those on like I asked, and that you don't ask anymore questions."

Jessica put on the handcuffs.

The two guards led Jessica and Claire down a familiar path. Jessica remembered the cafetorium from when she'd been taken to the disgusting man, Bruce, for processing. She pleaded in her head that she wouldn't be returning to him now. There were few places they could take her now that would be more terrifying than looking into his predatory eyes again.

Then the doors to the gymnasium opened, and she saw such a place.

***

Not being forced in or pulled by either of the guards, Jessica stopped in the doorway and simply looked. Her brain lagged behind her eyes, and she couldn't exactly process what she was seeing.

Spread across the gymnasium floor, a group of around ten other women stood in pairs. They almost identical jumpsuits to what Jessica and Claire wore, and each held a different weapon in their hands, none of which were firearms. Most of the women had blood on their faces, and they all appeared to have stains on the front of their jumpsuits. Two men stood guard on either wall, each holding their own weapons

—assault rifles. Another man walked back and forth with his hands behind his back as he shouted instructions at the women.

Derek grabbed onto Jessica's arm, pulling her attention away from the scene.

"Well, you're not just here to watch," Derek said. "Get your ass in here."

As Jessica and Claire walked into the gymnasium, the man in charge stopped shouting at the women. Everyone watched the two new women enter.

"We've got some new trainees for you, Stanley," Lance said.

"Excellent," Stanley said. He looked over to two of the women next to him. Pointing to a blonde, he said, "You, go with her." He was directing her to Claire. This meant Jessica would be paired with the other woman. She was a redhead who stood two inches taller than Jessica and appeared to be twenty pounds heavier.

Stanley approached Jessica. He grabbed her arms and squeezed, then smiled.

"We've got a strong one here."

"Why am I here?" Jessica asked.

Stanley stepped out of the way, and Derek removed the handcuffs from Jessica's wrists. Stanley turned around and linked his hands behind his back.

"Why are you here, you ask?" Stanley answered. He snorted, then turned back, glancing back and forth between Jessica and Claire. "You're here to learn how to fight."

"For what?" Jessica asked.

Stanley smiled, and then turned around. "Ladies, why don't you show these newcomers what we do here?"

Jessica looked over to the redhead standing across from her. She pinned the woman at ten years her senior. Her hands trembled on the staff that she held, and fear filled her eyes. Jessica winced when she felt a sting in her calf, and turned to a smirking Lance, holding a staff in his hand.

"Here you go, darlin'," Lance said.

Jessica accepted the staff, then turned to face the redhead.

"Ready?" Stanley asked. He looked back and forth between the two women, and then brought his hand down in a chopping motion. "Fight!"

Redhead seemed startled after the command, as if Jessica would come lunging at her. But Jessica didn't. Instead, she glanced over to Stanley and dropped the staff down to the ground. Stanley smiled, and then looked over to Redhead. He nodded toward Jessica.

Redhead froze. "Y-you want me to still fight? She's defenseless."

"That's her goddam problem," Stanley said. "Fight!"

Jessica held her ground. She simply sneered at Stanley, standing her ground. Impatient, Stanley marched over to Redhead.

"22," he said, calling Redhead by a number. "If you don't fight right now, I swear to Christ that you're going to regret it."

22 looked to Jessica again, and clenched her eyes shut. She drew in a deep breath, then stepped toward Jessica.

"I'm sorry."

She swung the staff, cracking Jessica in the ribs. Jessica doubled over, and then 22 grunted and struck Jessica in her knee. Jessica fell to the ground, moaning as she rolled on her side and grabbed her knee. 22 backed up, wiping a tear from her eye. Stanley grabbed her by the collar.

"Don't fucking cry! When you're out there with those beasts, you won't be crying. You won't be remorseful when you knock them down. No mercy!"

Stanley then bent over and picked Jessica up. She still held her knee, and did her best to keep weight off of it as Stanley lifted her up.

"You ready to quit being a fucking hero, or do you want me to have her take your other knee out?"

Jessica breathed heavily, but kept herself from crying. Her knee ached, and she felt her rib scream at her with each breath she took. Stanley picked the staff up and put it back into her free hand. She used her other hand to massage her side, where her rib ached. She wanted nothing more than to swing the staff as hard as she could and break it over the top of Stanley's head. But she thought better of it, looking past him to remember the armed guards standing against the wall. One move toward him, and she'd be dead

Stanley lifted her head by the chin. "You will do this. You will complete your training." He turned away.

Jessica stood up straight. When she looked over, she saw Claire, who was crying, holding a staff in her own hands. She stood square with the blonde that Stanley had paired her with.

"Now, let's try this again," Stanley said. "All together now. Let us see what you're made of."

A new focus appeared in Jessica's eyes. She collected every emotion she'd usually pour onto paper, determined to use it as fuel. Every ounce of pain and sorrow.

Stanley raised his hand, and then brought it down in the chopping motion again. "Go!"

This time, Jessica didn't hesitate. She lunged at 22, who was taken aback by Jessica's sudden surge. Only, Jessica didn't see the face of the aged redhead. Instead, she saw the face of Bruce as an Empty. She swung the staff, which 22 blocked with her own. But Jessica quickly struck again, connecting with 22's knee. Much like Jessica had before, 22 doubled over and held her leg. Jessica raised the staff over her head, ready to bring a final blow down onto the back of 22's skull. She looked over to Stanley, who smiled uncontrollably. Jessica waited, expecting him to give her the signal to finish 22, which she would not do. But it never came. Instead, he clapped his hands.

"Good," Stanley said.

Jessica looked back down to 22, who cried through glassy eyes. She'd fallen onto the ground now, grabbing at her knee. Jessica felt a sudden feeling of remorse. She'd let this man get into her head, and had hurt someone who didn't seem to deserve it. What the hell was going on here?

Stanley snorted. "You're all a bunch of filthy whores. Hit the showers."

***

Jessica had fully expected further patronizing and humiliation in the shower, but the captors had allowed the prisoners at least some dignity. Instead of the male guards inside the bathroom, gawking over the slave women while they bathed, four female guards had been assigned to the locker room. Each guard stood armed with an assault rifle, and none of the quartet seemed to have any remorse for the beaten women.

Her palms against the shower wall, Jessica stared down at the drain as a sea of red passed under her feet. The showers were open, each woman standing mere feet from each other, and the blood flowed off the other women's bodies, creating a river that disappeared into the pipes underneath them. Jessica couldn't bring herself to look up, into the faces of these other women. She so desperately wanted to ask them why they were here, but they'd been forbidden to speak to one another. Talking once would constitute a warning; talking twice would lead to corporal punishment. Jessica abided, assuming she'd understand in time why she was in this prison.

The guards informed the women when their shower was over, and Jessica pulled the lever over to shut off her showerhead. When she turned around, a towel hit her in the face. She caught it before it fell, and when she pulled the towel away, Bruce stood in front of her with that same perverted smirk on his face. His eyes did not look into hers, instead looking up and down her naked body. Jessica quickly covered herself, and Bruce's eyes moved up to meet hers. He chuckled.

"That's all right. I got me enough of a look to think about you later." He wrapped his tongue around his lips and Jessica looked away.

One of the guards rolled a cart toward the women, fresh sets of coveralls sat stacked on top of it.

"Get dressed and we'll file out," one of the guards said.

Jessica picked one of the garments up and the guard grabbed onto her wrist.

"You're number 41," the guard said. She picked up the coveralls with the number 41 on them and handed them to Jessica.

The coveralls included a set of undergarments. The faded sports bra fit snug on Jessica, pinching slightly into her back. The panties sat baggy on her hips. She put the coveralls on next, all while ignoring the creep's eyes that she knew were surely looking her up and down. To help block him out, she closed her eyes and tried to think of the mornings before school which she'd used to spend down by the pond near her house. While thinking of this, she wondered if she'd ever see such a thing again. Would she ever even set foot outside again?

"All right, ladies, let's move out," one of the female guards said. Two of the guards led the women out, while the other two followed behind the women.

"See you later."

The voice was that of Bruce, and Jessica pinched her eyes shut and refused to turn around.

When they reentered the gymnasium, Lance and Derek—the two guards who'd brought Jessica and Claire from their room—stood with their arms crossed.

"We'll take these two," Derek said. He grabbed Jessica while Lance stepped to a few women behind Jessica and gathered Claire.

"What's so special about us?" Claire asked.

"No questions," Lance said. He cuffed Claire's hands while Derek did the same with Jessica's.

They waited until the other women had been taken out of the gym, and then till a few more moments had passed.

"All right, let's go," Derek said.

The two men led Jessica and Claire toward the same door that the other women had been taken out through. On the other side of the door, Jessica could hear the stern voice of a man giving directions. It sounded like Stanley.

Derek pushed open the door, and Jessica focused her eyes, opening them wide.

Another group of prisoners, these all men, came walking toward the gymnasium. They wore similar garments to what the women had on; only, these were a slate gray instead of orange. Armed male guards flanked the men, and it had indeed been Stanley that she'd heard barking orders.

When Jessica saw who anchored the tail of the line, she gasped.

Thomas had one eye open, the other swollen shut. More shockingly, he rode in a wheelchair. Jessica thought back to the accident, and how Thomas must've been tossed around the inside of the SUV. She could only assume that he had been badly injured in the accident, or that they just didn't have the proper medical staff present to help him.

Yet, it was much worse than she'd thought.

"Thomas?" Claire said, seeing her brother. "Oh my God!"

Thomas' left leg was missing. Completely gone from just above the knee.

When Claire tried to run to her brother, Lance held her back.

"Stay back," Lance demanded.

"Please, he's my brother."

"I don't care if it's Elvis Fucking Presley walking by, you're not going near him."

"Claire?" Thomas asked.

Crying, Claire again tried to go to Thomas. She came within just a few feet, when Lance pulled her back and backhanded her across the face.

"You son of a bitch!" Thomas said.

As soon as the words left his mouth, a guard behind Thomas clubbed him in the back of the head with the butt-end of a rifle. He slumped over in the chair.

Derek and Lance pulled the two women with haste through the cafetorium now. Claire cried, yelling her brother's name.

This can't be real, Jessica thought. *I'm in hell.*

CHAPTER NINETEEN

Thirty miles outside of Roanoke, Will pulled over at a gas station. They had tried to stop at the previous two exits, but had seen too many Empties loitering around. When they arrived at this one, the gas station looked like it had been closed long before The Fall. The grass had grown up around it and been left unkempt. Parts of the roof were falling apart, and the price of gas was displayed as being $1.09. But no creatures loitered around the area.

Will stopped under the shelter of the gas pumps and put the SUV in park.

"The place doesn't look entirely empty," Charlie said from the passenger seat. "We should take a look just in case."

"Agreed," Will said. "I'll check the pumps for gas, even though I'm sure they're long dry. Never know, though." He looked to Holly in the back seat. Her eyes were half-open, and she had an arm around each of the children, their heads nestled into her chest as they slept. "We'll scope it out real quick, all right?" She nodded.

Charlie picked up a shotgun off of the floorboard and he and Will exited the vehicle.

"Let me just check this pump real quick and then I can go inside with you," Will told Charlie. He drew his knife and cut the rubber hose open.

"Damn," he said under his breath.

"Anything?" Charlie asked.

Will shook his head. He replaced the pump and the cap, and

joined Charlie at the front door of the shop. The inside was barely visible through the dust-covered windows. Will cupped his hands around the side of his head and tried to look inside anyway. He noticed some shelves and the front counter, but the place looked mostly empty. He was surprised to see all the windows in tact.

"Hard to believe no one at least tried to check this place out," Charlie said.

"Must've seen the gas prices and figured it wouldn't be worth the time."

Will pulled on the door handle and it didn't budge. He looked over to Charlie, glancing down at the shotgun in his hands and shrugging. Receiving the message, Charlie smiled. He pulled back and used the butt of the weapon to slam it into the front door. The glass cracked, but didn't shatter.

"Hit it like a man," Will said, smiling.

"Fucker," Charlie said. He pulled back further and grunted as he drove the butt into the door again, hitting the same spot. This time, the glass shattered. He looked over to Will. "That 'man' enough for you?"

They both chuckled as Will reached inside and unlocked the door, swinging it open.

As they entered the building, a cloud of dust rose from the concrete floors. The tile floors had been stripped in over half the store, revealing the concrete underneath. Will covered his face and coughed as he inhaled the age-old grit. Once it settled, he pulled his hand away and rubbed his eyes. The shelving remained, as he'd seen from the outside through the window— still neatly placed, forming four aisles. The displays on the wall behind the front counter had been torn away, except for the plastic display case that had once held cigarettes. It was there, but empty.

"Not looking like we're going to find much," Charlie said.

"Let's look around anyway."

Will walked down each aisle, checking the shelves for anything, but found nothing. At the back of the store were two restrooms. The doors were open, and Will saw nothing in the women's room, and only a single roll of damp toilet paper in the men's. The floor was wet, and he looked up to find a ceiling tile showing water damage.

A third door near the bathrooms was ajar and had a plate across the front that read: 'Employees Only'. Will pushed it open and then jumped back when he heard something rustle inside. He looked down, and two rats scurried by his feet. These weren't little home mice, but rats, each nearly the size of a shoe box.

"Scared they'll bite?" Charlie asked. When Will turned to face him, he smiled.

"Not a big fan of rats," Will said. He started to peek inside the room again, and then added, "Or snakes."

The natural light from the sun didn't reach to the back of the store, making it nearly impossible to see inside the room. Will opened the door as wide as it would go, and Charlie moved out of the way, taking his shadow with him.

Inside, all Will could make out were some cleaning supplies: various chemicals, a mop, and two brooms. One thing he did see that could be of use was a flashlight, so he picked it up. Sliding his finger over the power switch, he noted that the plastic clicked, but didn't power on.

"At least we've got some batteries for it in the SUV," Charlie said. "We can at least put some in and see if it works."

"Yeah, well, doesn't look like we're gonna find anything else in here."

They walked back outside, only having salvaged a flashlight from inside. The sky had darkened, not only because the day was fading, but also because of an oncoming storm. Holly opened the door as Will and Charlie exited the store.

"Find anything?" she asked.

Will held up the flashlight. "Just this."

"That's all?"

"The place is dirty and it's empty, but it seems pretty safe," Will said. "We should consider camping out here for the night."

"We're only thirty miles from Roanoke," Charlie said, seeming confused.

"Yeah, but look at the sky. Not only is it going to be night soon, but it looks like a storm is coming. Roanoke isn't a small town. We don't know what it's gonna be like there or how many Empties we're going to run into. We should play it safe and go into town tomorrow. At this point, I'm not sure getting there tonight will do us much good."

"Yeah," Charlie said. "You're right. We don't even know where we're going. Going to be hard enough to find that preacher in the daytime."

Will looked to Holly. "The kids can have my share of blankets. For all I care, I'll sleep sitting up."

"You and I can cuddle up together with a blanket and give Dylan and Mary Beth the rest," Holly said.

Possibly at the sound of his name, Dylan poked his head out of the SUV. He appeared to still be half-asleep, but managed to form his mouth into a smile toward Will.

"We're staying here tonight?" the boy asked.

"We are. It's not the Double Tree, but we'll have shelter over our heads and be out of this rain."

"I think there's enough garbage in there to get a fire going, too," Charlie said.

"Good call," Will said. "Let's go ahead and grab our things so we can head inside."

By the time they'd gathered all their gear and headed inside, it had started to rain. It only drizzled at first. Then thunder roared, and with it came harder rain. Water leaked through the ceiling in the bathroom, but after inspecting the rest of the place, they saw that that appeared to be the only leak. Charlie found a plastic bucket inside the supply closet and placed it under the leak.

With the rain came the birth of night, and Holly lit two candles that had been parting gifts from Maureen. The vanilla scent helped to mask the dank odor of the mold in the walls, and the light helped the group rummage through their things. Charlie took one of the candles and went back to the supply closet, returning with another bucket. It was old and made of metal, not plastic like the other had been. Will went over to one of the display shelves on the floor and tried removing parts from it with his hands.

"Watch out," Charlie said.

Will stepped to the side and Charlie came forward, leg raised, and kicked the display over. The crash echoed through the tiny space and pieces of the wooden display broke away from it. Charlie bent over and picked up two pieces, and held them up for Will to see. Will smiled and shook his head.

Will lined the bottom of the bucket with paper before putting the wooden pieces inside. Holly struck a match and dropped it into the bucket. The first one dwindled out, but the second match lit the paper and, within moments, had caught the wood on fire.

Holly blew out the candles.

Will said, "We'll just add a little wood and paper to this every now and then and it should stay lit. Hopefully, it'll also help keep any rats away." He found a spot against the front counter, a short distance away from where they had set up camp in the middle of the store. Charlie lay on his back, and Holly had the medical bag in her hands.

"How are you feeling?" Holly asked Dylan.

"I'm okay right now."

"Are you in any pain?"

He shook his head.

"Good," Holly said. "Then we will save this medicine for now. If you start to hurt, just tell one of us, okay?"

"Okay."

Holly put down the bag and then crawled on all fours over to Will. In other times, this may have turned him on. But considering the present company in the room, he simply smiled and lifted his arm so that she could snuggle in under it.

Charlie shifted his view from the ceiling to Will and Holly. He stared for a moment, frowning, and then looked away.

"Everything okay, man?" Will asked.

"I'm good. Just missing D." That was Charlie's nickname for his late wife who'd been lost during The Fall.

Will looked to Holly and then withdrew his arm from around her.

"I'm sorry," Will said.

Charlie looked over again. "It's all right. You guys keep cuddling and stay warm, seriously. I'm gonna miss her whether I see you two being affectionate or not."

In the moment, it felt awkward to Will. Holly's eyes said that she agreed, so they stayed apart for the time being, just sitting next to each other. Holly changed the subject.

"How are we going to find this preacher we're looking for? You said yourself that Roanoke isn't a small town; it's a city. It could be like trying to find a needle in a haystack. We don't even know what church he's supposed to be at."

Looking down at his shoes, Will said, "You're just gonna laugh if I answer."

"What? Why would I laugh? Do you have an idea how we're going to find him?"

"I don't think we'll have to look," Will said.

"What do you mean?" Charlie asked, curious now.

"I think we're supposed to find him," Will said. "Everything is lining up perfectly for us. We meet Samuel, he saves my life by performing a freaking exorcism, and then we get to Father Bryant moments before he dies. You don't think that's all for a reason?"

"It's all amazing," Holly said. "But how does that help us in Roanoke?"

Still looking down, Will smiled and laughed. He shook his head, and then he looked up at Holly.

"Because I think God will lead us to him."

CHAPTER TWENTY

It was, Gabriel guessed, midway through the next day before the guards came to retrieve him. He'd only seen another human once that day, when a guard had brought him food. With no natural light coming into the room, it had been hard for Gabriel to determine what time of day it was. He'd used his normal sleeping patterns as best he could, knowing what time of the morning his biological clock usually woke him, and using that to guess the time.

The door opened, and both Lance and Derek appeared in the doorway. Derek had the same neutral look on his face that he'd carried with him each other time Gabriel had seen him. Conversely, Lance looked like a rabid dog, ready to rip Gabriel's throat out. Though he looked angry, a bandage now covering his nose, part of him also looked exhilarated; there was a slight glow in his eyes, perhaps.

"Up," Derek said.

Gabriel sighed and stood up from the desk. Knowing what would come next, he extended his arms, offering to let the men cuff him. Lance stepped forward with the handcuffs while Derek remained ready with the rifle. Gabriel wondered if Lance would try and provoke him to make a move, giving Derek a reason to use the weapon in his hands. But it didn't happen.

As Lance cuffed Gabriel, he said, "Boy, you're in for a treat today."

They led Gabriel down the hall, following the same path they'd taken him along when he'd been forced to watch the atrocities on the football field. He assumed he was heading back out there now. Was Ambrose trying to intimidate him? Threatening him with the possibility that he might send him out into the sick and twisted game?

They exited the building through the exit in the stairwell.

Outside, the sun worked to peek through clouds in the sky. The asphalt had darkened, signaling that it had recently rained. Though the sun had soaked up any standing water, except that gathered in cracks and dips in the concrete. The air carried with it a humid breath, though an Autumn breeze still attempted to blow through.

Unlike before, Gabriel didn't hear a commotion coming from the football field. There was no woman standing at the gate, accepting canned currency to get inside the stadium. Even so, death was in the air. Gabriel could not only smell it, but he could feel it.

Derek and Lance pulled Gabriel through the front gate. As they walked down the tunnel, the field became visible. As Gabriel had expected from the silence, the seats were empty. Four armed guards stood down by the fence, just below where Gabriel had entered the stadium.

"Go," Lance said, nudging Gabriel forward.

Gabriel walked down the stairs and he swallowed the dryness in his throat as he looked down to the end zone at his left.

Parked on the five yard line was the armored box truck that had unloaded the Empty competitors onto the field during the game. Two guards stood at the back of the truck.

Enough sweat seeped from Gabriel's pores that he felt like he might have been able to slide right out of the handcuffs if they hadn't been essentially welded to his wrists. A bead of perspiration dripped down the side of his face, tickling and irritating him.

When they reached the first row of seats, Derek said, "Stop."

Gabriel stopped, and looked back.

"Take a seat," Derek said, pointing to the first row.

The four armed guards stood with their backs against the wall, facing Gabriel. He sat, elbows on his knees, staring into the eyes of each one of them. While each of the men, and the one woman, appeared tough, he could see the fear settled deep in their eyes.

"We're here," Derek said into a two-way radio.

Gabriel stared into the eyes of the guards for a few more moments before he saw a figure in the near distance beyond them. The figure of the man walking through the end zone, down to his right, was unmistakable.

Ambrose.

As per usual, Ambrose had a cigar pressed tight between his lips. The tip glowed bright orange, and the smoke polluted the air. The closer Ambrose got, the more the smell of cigar stirred with the rot in the air, which permeated from the battlefield below.

Ambrose approached the fence and the guards didn't turn to face him.

"Good to see you again, Mr. Alexander," Ambrose said.

His back stiff, Gabriel sat up straight. He nodded toward the truck. "Let me take a guess what you got for me in there. I'll only need one."

Ambrose pulled the cigar from his mouth and pushed a thick cloud into the air. "I told you that things could be much easier for you if you'd take my side. But you didn't seem to wanna listen yesterday."

"I listened."

Nathan chuckled. "Saying 'fuck you' didn't exactly tell me that you understood what I was trying to do for you."

"I don't give a shit what you're trying to do for me," Gabriel said. "What I give a shit about is where my friends are, and how the fuck I get out of this hellhole."

"Oh, you won't be getting out, of that I can assure you," Ambrose said. "But if you had just listened to me to begin with, your stay here could've been so much more pleasant." Ambrose put the cigar between his lips again, inhaled deep, and snapped his fingers toward Derek.

"All right," Derek said, speaking into the radio. "Let 'em out."

One of the guards at the rear of the truck gave a thumbs up, and then said something to his mate. The other guard backed up, while the one with the radio opened the back of the truck. He pulled the ramp down, and then backed up ten feet from the truck.

Gabriel waited, fully expecting to see a mob of Empties spill out of the truck. Instead, only two walked out. He chuckled.

"You think just two of those things are going to be able to kill me?" Gabriel asked. "You can throw me out there with these cuffs on, and I'll still have no problem taking those fuckers down."

Ambrose smiled and drew in another long, deep inhale of his cigar. He pulled it from his mouth, looked at Gabriel, and shook his head.

"They aren't for you."

Gabriel turned when he heard feet stomping on the steel floor of the grandstands behind him. Two guards led Jessica and Claire to the front row of seats, one section over from Gabriel. He looked back to Ambrose.

"Please," Gabriel said. "Take me. Don't send them down

there."

Ambrose smiled. He flicked the butt of his cigar onto the ground. As he stomped it out, he said, "Mr. Alexander, you really need to learn some patience."

Jessica and Claire stared over at Gabriel as the guards forced them to sit. The two armed people instructed the two women not to speak to Gabriel, to which they abided. It hurt Gabriel to see Jessica. She looked tired and malnourished. Her eyes had sunk into her head, and her face had developed cracks that hadn't existed before. She looked far more exhausted than Gabriel felt. She looked defeated.

Ambrose nodded to Derek again, who picked up the two-way radio and said, "Okay, we're ready."

Ambrose turned back toward the field-house, and Gabriel stared beyond him. Behind Gabriel, Lance chuckled, but Gabriel didn't turn around.

Through the open fence at the back of the end zone, two men appeared. One sat in a wheelchair, and the other, another guard, pushed the wheelchair out onto the field. The man in the wheelchair was missing one of his legs, and something about him looked familiar.

In the next section over, Claire cried out. Gabriel looked over at her and saw she was mumbling something, but he couldn't make out what. Then Jessica made eye contact with Gabriel, and mouthed one word. His eyes widened as he looked back out onto the field.

"Thomas?"

The chair stopped on the fifteen yard line, and Gabriel could now make out his face. It was Thomas. *He must've lost his leg in the accident*, Gabriel thought.

"Nathan," Gabriel said. "You can't—"

An open palm smacked Gabriel in the side of his head, boxing his ear.

"Shut the fuck up," Lance said. "And when you address him, it's 'Mr. Ambrose'."

"Just enjoy the private show, Mr. Alexander," Ambrose said.

***

Thomas breathed heavily. The sun shined into his eyes, blinding him. He looked into the stands, using his hand as a visor. He saw the small contingent of people who sat on the front row bleachers, and he immediately recognized his sister, sitting near Jessica. He shifted his gaze to the other side of the field, and he thought his heart stopped.

A box truck raced off the field, trailed by two of the creatures. Once the truck had driven to the other side of the gate, a guard closed and locked the chain link fence. He then gave a thumbs up toward Thomas. The guard standing behind Thomas blew a referee's whistle. The high-pitched squeal rang into Thomas' ears. He looked back and saw the guard waving to the opposite end of the field. The noise caught the attention of the beasts, and they trudged toward Thomas.

"What the fuck?" Thomas asked.

The guard stepped away from the chair, smiling. Thomas swung at him and the man laughed as the attempted blow didn't come close.

"Good luck," the guard said.

"You fucking cowards," Thomas said. He writhed in his chair, almost tipping it over.

"Be careful there, squirt," the guard said. "I'm not helping you up if you fall out of that chair." He pulled a knife from his waist and looked at it for just a moment.

Thomas stared at the weapon like it was a porterhouse steak.

He was as desperate for that knife as he was for food, and he could feel the inside of his mouth water.

"Fetch, doggy." The guard reared back and threw the knife as far as he could, toward the two oncoming creatures. He laughed and said, "Good luck." Then he turned, and jogged off the football field.

The sun reflected off the steel blade, the knife lying twenty yards in front of Thomas. He circled his lips with his tongue, gripped the wheels of the chair, and pushed.

Even if he'd had more experience in a wheelchair, he wasn't sure if he'd have been able to make it to the knife in time. The turf made it difficult enough for him to move, an attempt that was made even more so by the rain that had soaked the grass. It had made it thick and soggy. He'd only progressed five yards, and the monsters continued to encroach upon his space.

In the stands, he heard his sister scream. He looked up just as a man slapped her across the face. She slumped in her seat, and the man who'd struck her pointed and shouted in her face.

"Son of a bitch," Thomas said.

This sight seemed to give him new life. He bit his bottom lip hard enough to draw blood and pushed at the wheels of the chair as fast as he could. At first, they just spun in place, sunken down in the mud. He lunged the weight of his entire body forward, and the chair moved.

By the time he reached the knife, the Empties stood only fifteen yards from it. Thomas pushed himself up onto his foot, which slid from under him. He fell, landing on his side in the grass. The fall didn't hurt, but he felt a burn in his side. He rolled over and touched his ribs. Raising his hand to his face, Thomas saw the blood and realized he'd fallen on the knife. It had cut his side. He grabbed the weapon and pushed himself up to his foot just as the creatures' shadows passed over him.

The first one lunged at him, pushing him back into the chair. It toppled backward, he with it. Fortunately, the Empty fell beside the chair and didn't fall back with Thomas.

Thomas' head hit the turf as he fell back. He now sat in the chair, facing the sky. As he started to try and roll onto his side, the second beast appeared. It stumbled over the chair and fell on top of him.

Raising the knife, Thomas caught the creature, but only in the chest. This didn't seem to faze it, as the Empty swung at Thomas, snapping its jaw. Thomas kept the knife lodged in the creature's chest, using it as leverage to keep its mouth away from his face. But as the knife dug deeper into the rotted flesh, the Empty snarled and moved closer to Thomas' face.

Thomas withdrew one hand from the knife's handle and grabbed the creature by the throat. He then pulled the knife out and jammed it into its temple.

The Empty fell limp, leaving its weight on top of Thomas.

And that's when the other creature lunged on top of him.

***

Seconds after the Empty had made it to its feet, Gabriel turned at the sound of a human scream.

"No!" Claire cried. She writhed in her seat, trying to break free from her handcuffs.

One of the guards shouted at Claire, trying to get her to calm down. Gabriel heard a shallow laugh behind him. He turned, and saw Lance staring over at Claire. His mouth had formed into a huge smile, and he continued to giggle at the sight of Claire and what was happening on the field.

Gabriel jumped to his feet, and in an instant he was over the top of his seat. It happened so fast that Lance hadn't had time to process it. Catching Lance off guard, a handcuffed Gabriel slammed his forehead into Lance's already injured nose. Blood spewed from his nostrils and he fell backward, crying out.

Gabriel smiled as he watched Lance clutch his nose and cry out in pain.

"Son of a bitch," Derek said.

Then an object hit Gabriel upside the head, and he was out cold.

CHAPTER TWENTY-ONE

A bang on the outside glass, combined with a guttural howl, woke Will. The scream was not human; it came from an Empty. Will grabbed his pistol as he sat up; he had laid it on the ground next to him before he'd gone to sleep. Holly awoke at the same time, crying out as she shot up.

An Empty stood outside, banging and spitting on the glass. It didn't have the sense to reach in through the broken front door and open it. When he realized the creature was outside, Will sighed in relief and lowered the gun.

"Damn," Charlie said. Holly's scream had woken him and both the children up.

Will slipped his gun into its holster and squatted. He opened the bag holding their other weapons and pulled out the machete.

As Will walked over to the exit, the Empty moved down the length of the window toward the door. Its palms lay flat, leaving a trail of blood on the glass. When it arrived at the door, it reached its hand through the opening Charlie had made with the shotgun. Will stepped away, avoiding the thing's grasp. The creature waved its hand, trying to grab Will. He raised the blade overhead and swung the machete down with enough force to severe the Empty's arm.

When the arm hit the ground, he found himself having a flashback. He was in the woods. Dylan was screaming. Mary Beth and Holly were crying. It felt as if he was at the tree stump again, amputating Dylan's arm. On the ground, the creature's fingers wiggled. The hand opened and closed a couple of times, and then it stopped moving. The creature was unfazed by the missing limb, still pointing the nub of its arm at the hole in the door.

Will opened the door.

Before the Empty could break the barrier of the entrance, Will shoved the machete up through its chin. The other end of the blade came out the top of the thing's skull, and its body fell limp. Will pushed forward, forcing the lifeless creature down onto its back. He let go of the handle and the Empty's head cracked on the concrete. He stepped on its chest and bent down to grab the handle. As he pulled up, the creature's neck cracked. It must've fractured after its fall, and the slight move of the machete, still lodged through its skull, finished snapping its neck. The sound and the feeling of pulling the blade out never became an easier experience. No matter how many times he did it.

Will stepped out into the parking lot to make sure there were no other creatures around. There weren't. The rain had stopped some time during the night, leaving puddles scattered around the parking lot. But the sun coming out would soon dry them. With not a cloud in the sky, the day would be a good one for travel.

"Will!"

The voice was Holly's, and Will turned and ran back inside, jumping over the fallen Empty.

Dylan lay on the ground, hyperventilating. Holly was over him, and Charlie stood across the room, hugging Mary Beth.

"Holly, give him some air," Will said.

After a few moments, Dylan breathed easier. Will kneeled down to him.

"It's all right, buddy. Just close your eyes and breathe."

Dylan did as directed, shutting his eyes and drawing in long, deep breaths.

Will stood up and pulled Holly aside. "What happened?"

Crying and shaking her head, Holly said, "I don't know. He just kinda had this blank stare on his face after you cut that thing's arm off. He wouldn't take his eyes off the arm after it fell on the ground. Then he just fell down and started breathing fast. That's when I called for you."

"P.T.S.D.," Charlie said.

Holly looked confused.

"Post-Traumatic Stress Disorder," Will clarified. "He saw the Empty's arm fall off, and he had a flashback." He looked back over his shoulder to the arm still lying on the ground. Then he said to Charlie, "Come on, let's go clean it up."

Charlie ran to the storage room and came back with a box of latex gloves.

"Better than nothing," he said, pulling a pair out and handing the box over to Will.

Will picked up the creature's arm, wanting to get it out of Dylan's sight. He walked around the side of the building and threw it on the ground. He'd dispose of it out back in a bit, but he wanted to help Charlie move the body first.

When he arrived back at the front of the building, Charlie was standing at the top of the Empty's head.

"You get the legs," Charlie said.

Will kneeled down and grabbed the Empty under its legs. It was hard to distinguish the thing's age, though it had definitely been a male in its living days. But it was too far decomposed to tell how old the man had been. Based on its condition, Will figured its reanimation must've come early on. It had likely survived this long due to the scarce traffic in the area.

As they moved the creature around the side of the building, Will did his best to look away and ignore its face. The machete's blade had shot straight through its skull and mangled what was left of it, leaving the top of its head open like a blooming flower. Charlie gagged.

"Don't look at it," Will said.

"I'm trying not to," Charlie replied. "You're not seeing what I'm seeing. You did a fucking number on this thing."

"Let's just take it all the way to the back."

They walked down the side of the building until they reached the open parking lot in the rear. Shrubs lined the back of the property, and beyond them was nothing but undeveloped land.

Looking off in the distance, Will said, "Go to the curb and let's see if we can toss this thing in the shrubs."

Will startled when he almost lost his grip on his end because the weight changed after Charlie had almost dropped it. He looked up at Charlie and followed his gaze.

Together, they dropped the body.

In the middle of the back lot was a stack of bodies. There were six of them, all tangled together and stacked on top of one another like a small pyramid. Another ten feet past the stack was a single body, lying on its back. The man's arms lay spread like an angel's wings, and a handgun lay next to his right hand. A pool of blood had dried around what remained of his head. Several hundred flies hovered around the bodies.

Will covered his mouth, and Charlie looked off into the shrubs at the back of the property and vomited. The smell was unbearable. The bodies had been lying out here for an unknown amount of time, exposed to all the elements: the sun, the rain, rabid animals. Will had smelled something strange inside the convenience store the night before, but passed it off as something inside the store.

Will covered his mouth and nose and grabbed Charlie by the arm. They fled the scene, rushing back to the front of the building.

***

Even though Holly noticed something was off, Will and Charlie managed to keep what they'd seen behind the building to themselves. Holly and the children had no reason to know what they'd seen. Instead, Will and Charlie simply went back inside and told everyone it was time to leave. They packed up the SUV and left the gas station behind.

Will drove again, and Charlie sat in the front seat. Holly held her normal position in the back with the two children. Even after the incident with the Empty back at the gas station, Dylan was having his best day since before the accident. He and Mary Beth played a game where they'd try to spot certain words on billboards. They laughed together. Will was happy.

They passed a sign that told them they were now only seventeen miles from Roanoke. The scenery had started to become more urban. They began to drive by exits where there were more restaurants and retail stores. Likewise, they also came across more Empties.

"How are we going to find him?" Charlie asked.

Having answered the question in a way before that threw Charlie and Holly off guard, Will kept silent. He focused on the road, watching the scenery shift as the sun came up.

"Will, I know you said that 'God will show us the way', but come on, man. We gotta start thinking seriously about how we're gonna find this Bartman. Otherwise, this whole trip is just going to be a waste."

"Maybe we can find a phonebook or something at a gas

station," Holly suggested.

"Yeah, I looked for one last night and didn't see one," Charlie said. "But that's likely going to be about our only shot, unless we run into some locals or something. And we know how dangerous that can be."

"Then we should try to stop at a gas station somewhere."

Will slammed on the brakes. Charlie shot forward, the seatbelt catching him before his head hit the dash. Holly and the two children yelped in the back, and Will felt Mary Beth's hands slam into the back of his seat. Charlie, leaning over, put his hands up.

"What the hell?"

"Will, what's your problem?" Holly asked, frustration in her voice.

Will pointed to something.

After a moment, Charlie said, "Son of a bitch." There was silence for a few seconds, and then he scoffed and laughed.

A billboard sat off to the side of the road, and on it was a man with his hands raised to the sky. An exaggerated smile stretched across his plump face. He wore a suit with a purple shirt underneath, and the little hair he did have on the top of his head was more salt than pepper. The man's photo was aligned to the left of the billboard, and the rest of the sign read:

Ministry of Life Church

Pastor Philip Bartman

Take Exit 143, Mountain View Road, 9 Miles Ahead

Then, in big letters, was a single verse from the Bible.

Now I tell you before it comes, that when it does come to pass, you may believe that I am He. - John 13:19

Will faced Charlie, then glanced back at Holly.

"I think we've been shown the way."

CHAPTER TWENTY-TWO

Gabriel Alexander opens his eyes, and the sun instantly blinds him. He tries to shade his face with his hand, but realizes he can't. His hands are bound to the armrests of a wheelchair. He tries to wiggle them free, but it's useless. He scans his surroundings, and finds he is familiar with where he is. The green turf still appears so alive while so much of the world is dead. From what he can tell, the stands are clear, and he is the only one around.

Then he hears them.

Though he can't see the source through the sun's blinding light, the snarls of the Empties are unmistakable.

He thinks he can, perhaps, get onto his feet and run away, even though he is strapped to the chair.

That's when he looks down to the ground and notices both his legs are gone. Each leg has been severed mid-thigh.

Gabriel screams.

He writhes in the chair, trying to break free. He rumbles the chair so hard that it tips over.

Falling down on his side positions him to where the top of the stadium blocks out the sun. No longer blinded, Gabriel can see the Empties lumbering along, twenty-five yards away from him.

One of the creatures has long auburn hair and wears a flowered sun dress. It looks to have been around Gabriel's age when it was possessed.

The other creature is nearly half the size of the other, and was also a female when it breathed. It wears a t-shirt with a unicorn on it, and a pair of purple tights.

Two things strike Gabriel as strange.

One is that neither Empty has any blood on it. He would've assumed that they would have consumed their share of flesh by now.

The other is that, the closer the two creatures get to him, the more familiar they become.

It is when they cut their original distance in half that it hits Gabriel.

These two creatures are his wife and his daughter.

Tears slide down the sides of Gabriel's face, falling onto the blades of grass he lays on. Katie and Sarah—his babies; he has failed them.

"No," he cries. "Please, God, no."

But it's too late.

As he bathes in his failure as both a husband and a father, a certain peculiar calm falls over Gabriel.

He will soon be free. He will soon join them on the other side. Perhaps not right away, but eventually, when their bodies are released. But are their souls already standing in an afterlife waiting for him? Of that, he is unsure. He thinks he will be waiting, but hopefully, not long.

Just five yards away now, he looks at his wife.

"I love you."

He looks down to his beautiful daughter, staring into her empty eyes.

"Baby."

They snarl as he closes his eyes.

Gabriel's wife and daughter fall on him.

Gabriel awoke in a cold sweat. While the room was dark, there were candles lit along the walls. He lay flat on a table, and when he went to wipe the sweat from his brow, he found he was unable to move his hands. He was strapped to the surface.

"Nice of you to join us."

Gabriel looked over to see Ambrose sitting in a chair. From what Gabriel could tell, they were the only two people in the room.

Gabriel tried again to break free.

"You're wasting your energy," Ambrose said. "Now, let's just relax and talk a bit."

"Why the fuck do I wanna talk to you? You killed one of my friends."

"And if you don't want the others to end up the same way, I suggest you listen."

Gabriel tried to break free again, and then he finally gave in. He relaxed, lying flat on his back and looking at the ceiling. The aroma from the candles helped calm him, and he closed his eyes and breathed in and out deeply.

Ambrose struck a match, and brought it to the cigar hanging out of his mouth.

"Don't fucking smoke in here," Gabriel said. He didn't present it as a question.

Nathan snorted, waved the match in the air, and slipped the fresh cigar back into his pocket.

"Why?" Gabriel asked. "Why did you have to kill him?"

"I'm not so sure we saw the same thing," Ambrose said. "Your friend had the same opportunity that all our other competitors have."

Gabriel looked up and said, "Bullshit."

"See it how you want, Mr. Alexander, but I killed no one. And

I won't allow you to throw such accusations my way."

Gabriel rested his head on the flat, hard surface again. "What do you want?"

Ambrose stood up and circled the room as he spoke, his boots clicking on the hard floor. "I think that we can help each other, Gabriel. You want to stay alive. And I need a champion gladiator."

"What the hell are you talking about?"

"These games we play aren't just for fun, Mr. Alexander. The people you saw cheering in the stands weren't just doing so because they wanted to. They were gambling."

Gabriel scoffed. "Gambling? What the hell good is money anymore?"

Ambrose stopped next to Gabriel and stared down at him, smiling. "Not money. We use food and ammunition as currency."

Gabriel then thought back to when he'd walked into the stadium. He had noticed the box beside the ticket collector that had been filled with canned food and ammunition.

"And what do I have to do with your gambling ring?"

"You, Mr. Alexander," Ambrose said, "could be my guaranteed winning ticket. I see something in you. Something strong. I read about it in that journal. You've been out in the world, fighting these things one at a time. You're strong, the strongest I've seen."

"You just let a stronger man die," Gabriel said.

"Considering he had but one foot to stand on, I seriously doubt that."

"Doesn't matter," Gabriel said.

"No, it doesn't. Now, are you ready to listen, or not?"

Gabriel stared up at Ambrose, and didn't say a word.

"Good," Ambrose said. He paced back and forth in the same line, a distance of only about ten feet beside Gabriel. "I know that the chances of you dying if I trot you out onto that field are much less than other competitors that we've had. The others are weak. Most of them have given up, including your friend Thomas. He lost his family, and he gave up. I could see it in his eyes, whether you want to believe it or not.

"You, Gabriel, are quite the opposite. You've kept moving forward, and you can't lose hope. To lose hope would mean to give up on your family, to assume that they are gone." Ambrose waved his index finger. "You haven't done that. And I don't think you will."

Gabriel still didn't respond; he only continued to listen.

"I want you to fight for me, to be my main attraction. We'll put you up against the other fighters, and they will be favored, but you will win. Hopefully, most of the crowd will bet against you, because they do not know you yet. We'll take advantage of that for as long as we can."

"And then?" Gabriel asked.

Ambrose shrugged. "And then we let you go. You and both your friends."

"And why am I supposed to trust you?"

Ambrose smiled and moved closer to Gabriel. "Son, I don't think you have much of a choice."

Though he didn't want to admit it, Ambrose was right. Gabriel didn't have much of a choice. He'd seen what Ambrose was willing to do, as Gabriel had watched Thomas die. Ambrose could claim all day long that they'd had nothing to do with that, but that was bullshit and Gabriel knew it. Gabriel knew that going along with Nathan's plan was likely his only chance of survival.

"If I agree to do this, I want to make sure a couple of things happen," Gabriel said.

"You're not exactly in a place to make demands," Ambrose said.

"I want to be put with Jessica and Claire in the same room. I want to know that they're safe. I've seen a lot of sick fucks around here, and I don't want anything happening to those girls."

"And how am I supposed to feel safe with the three of you being together?" Ambrose asked.

Gabriel chuckled and tried to lift his arms. "You kidding me? We have no firearms, and it's apparently quite easy for you to restrain me whenever you want."

Ambrose put his hands on his hips, and then he nodded. "All right. You've got a deal."

"I also want a decent meal for us, and beds," Gabriel said. "I think it's the least you can do for a guy that's gonna earn you a whole lot of goddamn food and firearms."

Ambrose snorted, but he nodded again.

"All right, so, when do I start?"

Nathan Ambrose walked to the door and knocked three times. The door swung open, and two guards—not the same two assholes who'd been handling Gabriel before—entered the room and unfastened the leather straps around Gabriel's wrists and ankles. With the straps loose, Gabriel sat up slowly, so as to not throw his back out. He could already feel the dull ache near the small of his back. Though it hurt, he managed to make it upright, and he sat with his legs over the side of the table. He massaged his wrists and drew circles with his toes, the joints in his ankles popping. After he'd only been comforting his wrists for a moment, one of the guards grabbed his hands and cuffed them.

"Are you serious?" Gabriel asked, looking to Ambrose.

Ambrose shook his head. "Don't flatter yourself. Just because we made a couple of deals doesn't mean you're not still a prisoner here."

The two guards stood Gabriel up, and Gabriel asked, "Where am I going?"

Leaving the room and walking into the hall, Ambrose turned back.

"Training."

***

If Claire hadn't been given a drug to make her fall asleep, Jessica presumed that the woman would have still been crying. Instead, Claire lay silent, strapped to a gurney that two of the guards had affixed her to.

It had to have been two hours since they'd watched Thomas die on the football field. Jessica hadn't known Thomas long, but he'd become a friend, and she was sick of watching her friends die. Many questions ran through her head. Why had they taken them out there to see that happen? Was it just some kind of cruel, torturous joke? And why had Gabriel been separated from them?

Sitting against the wall with her arms folded over her knees, Jessica looked toward the door when she heard footsteps from down the hall. The door clicked, then swung open, and Lance and Derek entered the room. Derek walked over to Claire, first checking her pulse. Then he grabbed on to the back of the stretcher. Lance moved to the middle of the room and looked down at Jessica.

"On your feet."

"And where are you taking us now?" Jessica asked.

Lance gritted his teeth. "Not another goddamn peep out of your mouth."

Jessica pushed herself up off the ground. She stretched her arms out forward, not wanting Lance to have to touch her, and he cuffed her wrists.

"All right, let's move," Derek said. He pushed Claire, still unconscious, out of the room first.

Lance waved Jessica in front of him, and then fell in line behind her as she exited the room.

All Jessica could do was guess where they were taking her and Claire. She wondered if she might be headed for another one of those training sessions. If Claire would go to some kind of medical area to be tended to, or just to an empty room where she could start to wake up.

Jessica learned quickly that they weren't heading to another training session. Where they should've gone one way at the end of the hall, Derek turned the other.

They walked down another hallway like the one that Jessica and Claire had already been living in. Classrooms lined either side, with rows of lockers installed into the walls between each of the doors. They stopped at one of the rooms. As with their previous room, the knob had been swapped out on the door to one that locked from the outside only. Derek unlocked the door and pushed it open. Jessica looked down at Claire. Her eyes were still closed, and her stomach gently rose and fell. Derek moved back behind the stretcher and pushed Claire into the room.

The classroom was almost identical to the one that Claire and Jessica had previously stayed in. Only, there was one big difference: the cot and two air mattresses sitting in the center of the space. Jessica's eyes widened upon seeing this. She stopped in the doorway, somewhat in awe, and then felt a nudge urging her forward.

"Inside," Lance said.

Jessica entered, and asked, "Is this our new room?"

"Not cozy enough for you?" Lance responded.

Shaking her head, Jessica said, "No, it's not that. I just don't understand why we're suddenly being moved and given beds."

"Because it's what the boss wanted," Derek said. He locked the wheels on the gurney and made his way toward the door.

Jessica furrowed her brow. "Who is the third bed for?"

"Someone will be bringing you a meal soon," Derek said, ignoring Jessica's question.

As Lance pulled the door shut, he poked his head through the crack and said, "Sweet dreams."

CHAPTER TWENTY-THREE

The dull ache in Gabriel's back had begun to vanquish about the time he entered the cafetorium. The guards led him toward a set of double doors on the other side of the large, open room. As Gabriel moved closer to the door, he began hearing shouting and grunting from the other side.

One of the guards opened the door, and the man behind Gabriel pushed him into the gymnasium.

"Jesus," Gabriel mumbled.

Four pairs of men stood in the room, all engaged in combat with each other. Some of them held simple, blunt-force weapons, while others wore thinly padded gloves on their hands. Each of them wore a similar garment to Gabriel's coveralls, and each man had at least a little blood on their front. In fact, most of the men had blood on their faces, as well. Two guards stood on either wall. Each of them were armed with AR's, and they kept their eyes squarely on the combat.

Pacing back and forth in the room was one more man. His hands behind his back, he shouted at the competitors.

One of the trainees fell to his hands and knees, and when he didn't get back up right away, the shouting man paced over to him.

"You better get on your fucking feet right now," the man in charge said.

Gabriel noticed the fallen man's shoulders bouncing up and down, and he stayed on the ground.

"Are you crying?" Shouting Man asked. He laughed. "You've

gotta be fucking kidding me."

He kicked the fallen man in the gut, and the trainee toppled over, clutching his stomach.

"You've got till the count of three to get up, son."

The trainee remained on all fours. "Please," he mumbled.

"One."

The trainee didn't move, and Shouting Man drew a gun from his hip.

"Two."

The shouting man cocked the gun, and upon hearing the click, the trainee started to his feet.

"Please, I'm getting up," the trainee said.

The trainee stood, and the shouting man grabbed him by the collar. He held him within inches of his nose, and shoved the gun under the trainee's chin.

"You pull that shit again, son, and I'll blow your goddamn brains out. Or maybe I'll shoot you in the gut, let you die slowly, and turn you into one of the munchers outside," Shouting Man laughed. He pushed the trainee back towards the man that he had been sparring with, and then turned and faced Gabriel.

"I see you brought me some new meat," the man said to the guards.

"We did," one of the guards said. "This is the one that Ambrose was talking about."

"Perfect," the man said. He looked to Gabriel. "My name's Stanley. But you'll refer to me as Mr. Cochran." Stanley looked Gabriel up and down, and chuckled. "Not sure why Ambrose thinks you're so great, but I guess we'll find out soon enough."

Stanley walked over to one of the trainees. He was a thin man with sandy blonde hair who appeared to be in his mid-30s.

"Go have a seat," Stanley said to the man. "It's your lucky

day, and you get a break since we have odd numbers."

The trainee looked to Gabriel as he walked over to the wall. His face was that of a man defeated.

"All right, you're up," Stanley said, looking at Gabriel.

Before Gabriel could take a step, the guard nudged him forward. Gabriel turned back and scowled at the guard, but then he walked to the spot where Stanley waited.

"Turn around," Stanley said. He pulled a large, black marker out of his pocket.

Gabriel did as he was told, and faced his back to Stanley. He felt something poke his back, which he could only assume was the marker.

"All right," Stanley said, and Gabriel turned around to face him again. "You're now, simply, Number 91."

"Couldn't at least let me pick?" Gabriel asked.

Stanley smirked. "Just get ready to show us what you've got."

Gabriel faced his opponent. The trainee opposite him stood about a half-foot taller than he himself did. He was a slender black man who appeared to be in his mid-20s, his eyes glazed over with fear. Cuts marked various parts of his face, some of them only minutes old. Blood seeped out of the new cuts, dripping down onto his coveralls. Gabriel didn't know if he'd ever learn this man's name, or if he'd only know him as Number 54.

Number 54 licked his lips and stood ready for his confrontation with Gabriel. Something tapped Gabriel on the back of his leg, and he turned to see Stanley handing him a bo-staff. Gabriel accepted the weapon.

"Good luck," Stanley said.

Again, Gabriel faced Number 54, who looked like he knew about as much about handling a bo-staff as he did about using a tampon. Gabriel readied himself, not having any idea how to use the weapon, though it didn't matter. Gabriel had the will to survive, the push to keep going and to never lose. Number 54 would be no exception.

"Everyone, ready?" Stanley asked. He had his hand raised in the air.

Gabriel bent his knees and tightened his grip on the staff.

Bringing his hand down in a chopping motion, Stanley yelled, "Go!"

Number 54 didn't hesitate. He immediately went on the offensive, coming at Gabriel and swinging the staff. It caught Gabriel somewhat by surprise. As far as he knew, they were all prisoners here. He'd figured that they'd somewhat look out for each other. *Apparently not*, he thought. Gabriel ducked the initial swing. When he finally swung, Number 54 blocked it, and then turned around. The two men went back and forth, clanking the sticks against each other. Though Gabriel had never used a staff, the weapon felt comfortable in his hands. Fortunately, he'd been correct about his opponent's lack of experience with the weapon.

But 54 connected the first blow, striking Gabriel on the knuckles. Gabriel yanked his hand away and waved it in the air, feeling as if, at least, one of his fingers had been broken. Trying to take advantage, 54 swung again, going for the kill-shot. But Gabriel reacted, ducking the swing. The miss turned 54 around and Gabriel gripped his staff as best he could with the hurt hand. He jammed the butt-end of it into a disoriented 54's ribs.

Number 54 doubled over and clutched the place on his side where the staff had struck him. Gabriel then brought the staff down across 54's back, and the man tumbled down to all fours.

Gabriel's attention moved away from his opponent when he

heard clapping. He looked over to see Stanley slapping his hands together, a smile on his face.

"Good," Stanley said. "Now, finish him."

Gabriel looked down to 54, who remained on all fours, one hand still massaging his rib. He glanced up to Gabriel, his eyes filled, reflecting the look of a man drawing his final breaths. He clinched his eyes shut, and looked back down to the court. Under his breath, he murmured something—perhaps a prayer.

Continuing to stare at Stanley, Gabriel dropped the staff.

Stanley scrunched his face in anger. "You better pick that up right now and finish him off." When Gabriel turned away and reached down to offer his hand to 54, Stanley approached him and grabbed him by the collar. "You pathetic son of a bitch."

The back of Stanley's hand struck Gabriel across his cheek, grazing his nose, which was still sore from the auto accident. Gabriel clenched his fist. When he turned to counter Stanley's attack, he paused after hearing rifles click from each side of the room. He looked up and saw the guards aiming directly at his chest, and he froze.

With the defense of four armed guards, Stanley intruded into Gabriel's personal space.

"When you're in here, you'll do as I say," Stanley said. "I could give two shits what Ambrose thinks of you, and what the reason is he thinks that you're special. This here is my house. If I say to bark like a dog, you'll bark. If I say to stand on one leg, then onto one you'll go. And if I tell you to finish your opponent, then goddamn, you will strike him down. You hear me?"

Gabriel glared at Stanley and his mind wandered. He wanted to do nothing more than to grab the man's head and twist it like a bottle cap. But would it be worth it? Killing this man would serve a short-term need, but it would also end his own life. And he'd die not knowing whether his wife and daughter were out there somewhere, waiting.

Gabriel nodded. "I've got it."

"I've got it, *sir*."

Again, Gabriel waited, sneering at Stanley. Growing impatient, Stanley grabbed him again by the collar, and he reared back his fist. Gabriel flinched, awaiting the blow. But instead of the sound of Stanley grunting and throwing a punch, the door opened.

"What the hell is going on here?"

Gabriel opened his eyes and looked over toward the door. Entering the gymnasium, with Lance and Derek at his side, was Ambrose.

The grip on Gabriel became nonexistent as Stanley let him go and stood up straight, facing Nathan Ambrose.

"Just going over some training, sir," Stanley said.

'Don't give a shit what Ambrose thinks', my ass, thought Gabriel.

Ambrose approached the two men. It was as if the rest of the people in the room had vanished. When he reached the men, Ambrose looked Gabriel up and down. He took Gabriel by the chin and turned his head. A bruise had begun to form where Stanley's hand had struck him, and a trickle of blood dripped from Gabriel's nose. Ambrose let go.

"You roughing him up?" Ambrose asked Stanley.

"No, sir, I wasn't 'roughing him up'. I was toughening him up."

"I see," Ambrose said. He put his hand on Stanley's shoulder and said, "Good work."

Stanley smiled. "Thank you."

Ambrose patted Stanley on the shoulder. He turned halfway

around then before ramming his fist into the trainer's stomach. Stanley doubled over, and Ambrose grabbed the trainer's shirt and stood him up straight.

"I told you to put him through a training session," Ambrose said. "I didn't tell you to hit him. If I'd wanted you to rough him up, I'd have told you to do so."

"Yes, sir."

Ambrose backhanded Stanley and said, "Don't talk."

Stanley nodded.

"Now," Ambrose said. "You're going to tell Mr. Alexander that you're sorry, and then you're going to send everyone to the showers. Is that clear?"

Again, Stanley nodded. Ambrose let him go.

His hands still on his stomach, Stanley said to Gabriel, "I-I'm sorry."

Gabriel nodded, using his forearm to apply pressure to his bleeding nose. He felt no remorse for the asshole trainer, but he also didn't appreciate the bullshit sympathy from Ambrose. He still didn't know why Ambrose thought he was so special. Surely at least some of these other men standing in the room had had to survive out in the world after it had gone to shit.

"Everyone, hit the showers."

Gabriel had turned to head to the showers when a hand on his shoulder stopped him. He turned back to Ambrose.

"Have a good night, Gabriel. Because tomorrow, you're up."

He patted Gabriel on the shoulder, then headed for the door.

After Ambrose had turned to leave, Lance made eye contact with Gabriel. The man in the hat smiled and winked, and Gabriel knew he had to be cackling on the inside.

And all Gabriel could think was that every one of these men was going to die. Even if that meant he had to go down himself to see it happen.

***

After a shower, two guards led Gabriel back to his room. The time in the shower had been awkward when it should have been one of his more enjoyable experiences while stuck in the prison. The entire time, he had not only felt Stanley's eyes on him, but many of the other prisoners'. They'd likely been wondering why Gabriel had been given special treatment.

Halfway back to his room, he realized the guards were leading him the wrong way. He noticed when they took a left down one hallway when he could've sworn they should've taken a right. He was just about to say something when one of the guards went to a door and unlocked it. Feet shuffled on the other side.

The door swung open, and two silhouettes faced him from the middle of the dark room. His eyes veered from the shapes and drew to the beds on the floor. He sighed, thankful that he'd have somewhere to sleep.

"Gabriel?"

The female voice came from inside the room. When the figure moved closer to the door, Jessica's face appeared in the light.

Gabriel smiled and hurried into the room.

Her hands unbound, Jessica wrapped her arms around Gabriel. He leaned into her, his wrists still bound by steel cuffs. Looking over Jessica's shoulder, Gabriel noticed Claire, now sitting down on one of the beds.

"Break it up and give me your hands, 91," one of the guards said.

Gabriel turned to face the guard, who unlocked the cuffs. He then retreated from the room, and shut and locked the door behind him, leaving Gabriel, Jessica, and Claire in darkness.

Alone now, Gabriel focused his attention on Claire. He went to her, leaning down to hug her.

"I'm so sorry," Gabriel said. Though he couldn't see her, it made no difference. She sniffled, and he could feel how wet her face was from crying as it ran up against his own. She didn't respond with words. Gabriel held the embrace for several moments before letting go. Claire lay down on her side and curled up, signaling she wanted to be left alone.

Gabriel and Jessica went to the other end of the room and hugged again.

"Do you know what that was all about down at the football field?" Jessica asked. She kept her voice low, so as to not upset Claire even further.

Taking Jessica's hand, Gabriel led her into the corner of the room, away from earshot of Claire. "Was that the only time you two have been outside?"

Jessica nodded.

Gabriel massaged his forehead. "Shit."

"What?"

Whispering, Gabriel explained to Jessica what he'd seen when they'd first taken him to the football field. How there was a crowd, and how people had gambled on the hopeless human prisoners and the Empties. He tried to give her every detail, even though most of what he'd seen had been so inhumane and explicit that he found it hard to believe any of it had been real as he recalled the events out loud.

Jessica covered her mouth, and Gabriel allowed her to process everything she'd just heard.

After a brief moment, she asked, "Why are they keeping us separate from everyone else?"

"Because Ambrose, the guy who's in charge, he has your journal. Apparently, he's read it and thinks that we're special because of all the stuff we've been through. In particular, he has this obsession with me."

Jessica's eyes remained wide in surprise. Gabriel felt the temptation to ask her just what the hell she'd written in that book, but he shrugged it off. At this point, did it really matter? Because of that journal, they seemed to have a slight advantage over the others.

Jessica sat down against the wall and Gabriel joined her. It felt so good to be around a familiar face again, especially after having seen what had happened to Thomas.

Her head against the wall, Jessica looked over to Gabriel. "What are we gonna do?"

Gabriel stared at her. He grabbed her by the hand.

"We're going to fight."

CHAPTER TWENTY-FOUR

Exit 143 was just on the outskirts of Roanoke. Another sign for Ministry of Life Church confirmed that this was the right exit. While this sign didn't feature Philip Bartman's picture, it did display the same apocalyptic verse from the Book of John. It also told Will he needed to take a right at the end of the exit ramp.

There were several more Empties around than they'd been used to seeing. Gas stations and strip malls stood on either side of the four-lane road. Creatures moved around in the various parking lots. Many Empties loitered in the road, as well, but Will had plenty of space to maneuver around them.

"I haven't seen this many in a while," Holly said.

"This is why we've got to stay away from cities," Charlie said.

That statement made Will think about Gabriel. If the outskirts of Roanoke were this bad, how crowded with creatures would Washington D.C. be? He pushed aside the thought.

Just over a mile down the road, they came to the church.

Ministry of Life Church wouldn't be considered a mega-church by Will's standards, but it wasn't your back-roads, single-room sanctuary, either. A construction site was on one side of the church while trees were on the other. Will stopped the SUV when the church came into view.

While there were no creatures in the immediate vicinity, a large group crowded around the front door of the church. There was somewhere in the range of twenty to thirty of them. From where they sat in the street, Will could hear the creatures snarling and howling as they beat on the front door.

"How are we supposed to get in there?" Charlie asked.

"I don't want to go anywhere near that place," Mary Beth said from the back seat, a tremble in her voice.

Holly pulled Mary Beth in tight and ran her hands through the girl's hair. "You're not, sweetie. Don't worry."

Will knew they hadn't come this far to just turn around without checking the church to see if Bartman was there. They had to come up with a plan to get inside. He scanned the area, noticing something behind a nearby fast food restaurant. He turned into the parking lot and drove behind the building.

The construction site acted as a deep valley between the restaurant and the church. A guard rail lined the rear of the property, safeguarding it from the steep hill on the other side. An exposed drain pipe stretched from behind the restaurant, across the construction, and to the back of the church. An Empty was on its knees near the guard rail, digging into the remains of a small animal. It looked up at Will when he parked the SUV.

"Hand me the machete," Will told Holly. Within a moment, the weapon was in his hands. "Stay here, and cover the kids' eyes."

The Empty had stood by the time Will approached it. He wasted no time, taking only a single swing to decapitate it.

Will peeked over the guard rail and eyed the opening of the drainage pipe at the bottom of the slope. He turned and got back into the driver's seat.

"That drainage pipe opens up just on the other side of this hill," Will said. "It's big enough to crouch down and walk through. That's our ticket over to the church. It'll lead us to the rear of the parking lot and we can find a back door to enter through."

"So, what's your plan?" Charlie asked.

"You and I will go. Holly can stay here with the kids and keep this thing running until we get back."

"No," Holly said.

Will looked back to her, and saw determination in her face.

"I want to go with you."

Will shook his head. "You need to stay here and be with the children. If something happens, I want you to be here."

"If something happens, I want Charlie to be here. Let me go with you."

Will considered this for a moment. He and Holly had been through many situations together, and he could trust having her at his side. Also, she was right. If something happened near the SUV, Charlie had proven himself to be calmer than her in situations that required it. He would be able to handle it and keep the children safe.

Will nodded. "All right. You come, and Charlie will stay."

"I don't want either of you to go," Mary Beth said.

"Sweetie, this is something we have to do," Holly said. "There might be a man inside there that has some very important answers for us."

"But what if you get hurt?"

"They won't," Dylan said. "Don't worry, they'll come back."

Mary Beth wiped her and eyes and nodded, and Dylan wrapped his arm around her. Holly smiled, running her hand through Dylan's hair.

Will pulled the SUV a few feet away from the restaurant's drive-thru menu, hiding it from any Empties or people who might pass by on the main road. He stepped around to the back and opened the cargo door, grabbing a shotgun for Holly and a rifle for himself. He collected ammo for each, plus extra bullets for their handguns. He'd shut the door halfway before he opened it again and grabbed another handgun and two flashlights.

Holly stepped out of the back seat and Will poked his head in through the door to Dylan. He wrapped his hand around the barrel of the last pistol he'd grabbed and then offered it to the boy.

"You know what to do," Will said. "Only fire this if you have to. Charlie will tell you if he needs your help, all right? Other than that, let him handle it. Hopefully, you won't have to use it."

Dylan accepted the weapon.

"Leave it beside you. You don't have to cock it. All you've gotta do is click the safety off on the side there. See it?" Dylan signaled that he did. He then leaned toward Will and wrapped his arm around him.

"Please come back."

Will ran his hand up and down the boy's back. "We will. Don't worry. Just take care of Mary Beth."

Dylan pulled back and placed his hand over the weapon, leaving it sitting on the seat. Will got out of the SUV and met Holly and Charlie at the front of it.

"Be ready to start this thing and roll out when we get back."

"Will do," Charlie said. "I'll be sure to take a look around each side of the building every now and then to make sure nothing, or no one, is coming."

Will shook Charlie's hand. "Keep them safe."

"You guys just hurry up and get back here."

Will turned and put his hand on Holly's shoulder. "You ready?"

She took his hand and they started toward the guard rail. They were sure to look down the side of the building to make sure nothing was coming or saw them, and then they hopped over the rail.

When they reached the entrance to the tunnel, Will clicked on his flashlight first. Holly followed by turning on hers.

The drain pipe ran straight, and they could see the sun peeking out on the other side. Everything in between was dark, except for a short distance in front of them. Not surprisingly, the pipe's concrete bottom was damp from the rain.

"It looks like the pipe comes out just on the other side of the church," Will said.

"All right, lead the way."

Will entered the pipe first, ducking down, his feet splashing the water underneath them. Will had never been inside of a drainage pipe, and it smelled just about as foul as he'd imagined. They hadn't gone far when a squeal echoed through the concealed space. Holly startled, signaled by the water splashing under her feet and her yelp. Will pointed the flashlight down and watched as two rats passed by. He hated rats. Not quite as much as he despised snakes, but rats still disgusted him. But he kept his cool.

"It's okay, just keep moving."

They did, and the sulfuric smell seemed to worsen, the further along they moved into the tunnel. It became strong and foul enough to where he pulled his shirt collar up over his nose. Additionally, he heard more vermin ahead, squeaking like a dog's play toy. Behind him, Holly coughed.

"What is that?" Holly asked, her voice muffled under her own shirt.

Will was about to respond when his light shined on two rats standing in the middle of their path. Will shifted the flashlight's beam further up, and then turned, coughing.

"What is it?" Holly asked, the squealing rats now just feet in front of them.

"You don't want to know," Will said.

He stepped to the side so she could see, and Holly flashed her light onto the ground.

A body the width of the pipe lay in front of them, making the way impassable without stepping over it. Its flesh had been picked to the bone. The entrails spread out around the immediate area of the body, and a small pack of rats was chewing on them. The body was so far gone that it was impossible to tell if it had been a man or a woman. Or if it had died human, or ever turned Empty.

The corpse went dark again as Holly turned and vomited. The noise startled at least a couple of the rats, and Will jumped as they ran by his feet.

"We've gotta walk over it," Will said.

"I'm not stepping over that," Holly said. "Let's turn around and find another way."

"Holly, this tunnel is the safest way."

"What if that thing was Empty before it died? Or even if one bit it? How do we know these rats can't hurt us if they bite us?"

"It's not a virus, Holly. I think if the rats had been affected, then they would've come after us by now. Just be careful stepping over them."

Behind him, Holly breathed deeply. Will didn't like the idea of passing over the body any more than she did, but he drew in a deep breath and shined the light down toward it.

Five rats still remained, crowded around the body and chewing what was left of it. Will eased forward, keeping the light trained on the pack of vermin. As he approached the body, his boot stomped on something soft. It squished under his feet, amplified by the puddle of water. He coughed, bringing his arm over his mouth, but kept moving. He convinced himself that what he'd stepped on wasn't remains of the dead.

It was inevitable they were going to have to step on at least part of the body to pass. Its remains had scattered enough to where it would be impossible to jump, and the low ceiling would have made that difficult anyway. When Will stepped forward, his boot buried into an unidentifiable part of the thing's body, and it took everything for him not to puke. He skipped forward and moved past the corpse.

On the other side, he turned around and offered Holly light.

"You got this, it's a piece of cake."

He could barely see her face in the reflection of the light, but could see in her eyes that she was terrified. The rats continued to eat, and the sound of them chewing reverberated between their squeals. Will reached out his hand.

"Come on, sweetie. Just come forward and grab my hand for balance."

Holly finally moved forward, stopping right before the body. She was breathing heavy now, almost hyperventilating.

"You got this," Will said.

Lifting her leg to take a step, Holly reached out her arm toward Will. Her boot made a disgusting smashing sound as it landed on the body. Will could sense her being about to cry as she froze.

"Come on, you're almost there."

Holly took another step, but she slipped. Will dropped the flashlight and lunged forward, grabbing onto her by hooking his arms under hers and catching her before she fell. On the ground, the rats screamed, and so did Holly.

"It's biting me," Holly wailed.

Will pulled her clear of the body, and then noticed she still had the light in her grasps. He took it and shined it down on her leg. A rat had grabbed onto her and Will kicked it off, sending it flying through the air. The squeals of the rats faded until they became nonexistent.

"Let me look," Will said. He kneeled down and lifted her pant leg, flashing the light on her skin. "I don't see anything. It looks like it may have just gotten your pants." He could see where the teeth had punctured her pant leg.

Will stood up and hugged Holly, kissing her on the forehead. "You did great."

He shined the light onto the ground and noticed that his flashlight had fallen right in the middle of the dead body. They had a few others back at the SUV, so he decided to leave it. The one flashlight would get them to the church.

They continued on and reached the end of the tunnel within just a couple of minutes. While he could hear the herd howling and scratching at the front of the building, Will didn't hear any Empties in the immediate area outside the pipe's exit. Regardless, he stepped into the open first, and directed Holly to await his signal.

As he'd guessed, the pipe opened up into woods. The trees stood close together, shading him from the sun. He scanned the area and found no Empties. Looking back, he saw a short, but steep hill leading up to the parking lot of Ministry of Life Church. Once they reached the top, they'd just have to step over a guard rail, like at the restaurant.

"All right, come on," he told Holly.

They climbed to the top of the hill on all fours. Three-quarters of the way up, Will showed his palm to Holly.

"Hold on," he whispered.

Will climbed the rest of the way up the hill, staying low and out of sight. When he reached the top, he peeked through the metal guard rail and scanned the parking lot. The building was about twenty yards away. He saw the remains of four bodies lying on the concrete, two of which were being picked apart by crows. A few cars remained abandoned in parking spots. But from what Will could see, no Empties hung around the rear lot. He looked back to Holly and waved her the rest of the way up the hill.

He pointed to a door on the corner of the building.

"That's the door we need to try to enter through," Will said.

"All right," Holly said.

"Just follow right behind me."

Will rose to his knees and then hopped over the guard rail in one fluid movement. He crouched down so as not to be seen just in case any creatures or people were around that he had missed. He crossed the parking lot and Holly followed. In the road, he saw a small group of Empties passing by. Will ducked down beside an abandoned vehicle before the creatures discovered him. Holly joined him, sitting down with her back against the side panel of the sedan.

"Did they see you?" Will asked.

"Don't think so," Holly said. "I don't think they looked over here."

"Let's just give them a second to pass; then we'll go to the door."

They allowed the demons time to limp out of view, and then Will said, "All right, I think we can—"

Inside the vehicle, something slammed against the glass and snarled. Will's heart skipped. He rolled away from the sedan onto his back, drawing his pistol and pointing it at the window. An Empty banged on the glass, its dead mouth wide open. It was in the back seat, and appeared to have been no older than twelve years old when it had been alive.

"Shit," Holly mumbled, staring up at it.

The thing's pale eyes looked down at them, and it continued to howl.

Will grabbed Holly's hand. "Come on, let's go."

Holly's eyes didn't leave the creature as they made the short trip over to the door. It followed them as far as it could, crawling up into the rear window and banging on it. Holly kept looking back until Will physically turned her head toward him.

"I need you to focus," Will said, cupping her face in his hands. She nodded, her head shaking in fear.

The entrance sank into the building by a few feet, giving them shallow walls on either side to hide behind. Will grabbed the handle of the glass door and pulled. It clicked, not budging.

Holly peeked around the corner.

"They're coming," she said.

Will looked around the wall and saw part of the horde from the front door now heading toward them.

"He must've gotten their attention," Will said, speaking of the former boy in the car.

"What are we gonna do?"

Will holstered his handgun and pulled the rifle off his shoulder. "Stand back. Keep an eye on them, and have the shotgun ready. Don't shoot unless you have to. It only looks like part of that group is headed back here."

Will went to the door, reared the gun back over his shoulder, and slammed the butt of the weapon into the glass. Nothing happened. The rifle seemed to just bounce off the glass. He continued to hit it, harder with each blow.

"Hurry!" Holly shouted.

Will kept hitting the glass until it finally cracked. It only took three blows after that for it to shatter, and Will reached inside and unlocked the door. As he opened it, Holly pulled the trigger, taking down an Empty that had made it to within ten yards of her. She hit it in the body, knocking it backward and onto the ground, but not killing it.

"Come on!" Will yelled. He grabbed Holly by the arm and led her through the door.

Inside, they came into a room with another door. This door was wood with a silver handle. If it didn't open, they'd be trapped in the tiny room, and they'd be dead.

Holly shot again, taking down another one of the creatures who stood at the exterior door.

Will pushed down the handle.

The door opened.

He grabbed Holly again and pulled her through.

Once inside, Will slammed the door shut and locked it behind them. He looked around the room and saw a wooden table big enough to seat eight people.

"Help me move that against the door," Will said.

They each got behind the table and pushed. It was heavier than Will had imagined. They moved the table in front of the door, and then Will fell to the ground, catching his breath.

Outside, the Empties banged against the door.

"That should hold them," he said, breathing heavily.

Holly went down to her knees and covered her face. She cried, having trouble catching her breath.

Will slid over to her and wrapped his arms around her. "It's okay, we're safe. Just calm down. We're okay." He ran his hand up and down her back, working to calm her down. After several moments, her breaths moved further apart. She pulled away from him, sniffled, and wiped her eyes.

"You good?" Will asked, placing his hands on her shoulders.

Her eyes closed, she nodded.

With the banging and howling continuing behind them, Will looked around the room, trying to assess where they were. The room had large windows high on the walls, which brought in enough sunlight for them to see by. Other than that, there was no light. Tables sat at intervals, every few feet throughout the large room.

"I think we're in a dining hall," Will said.

Holly began working her way to her feet, and Will reached down and offered her a hand, which she accepted.

The tears nearly gone, Holly said, "Well, it's a beautiful church."

"It looks like an empty church."

"Maybe," Holly said. "But we're here, so there's only one way for us to find out."

"Just stay close to me," Will said. "Keep your shotgun on your back. If we run into any people, we don't want to scare them. Just keep your hand near your sidearm."

They moved with caution through the room. The light coming in through the windows lit the entire space. Holly kept her flashlight handy in case she needed to point it into any dark corners.

"Hello?" Will called. His voice echoed through the hollow room, its ceilings as high as the church itself.

Large double doors were closed on the far end of the dining area. They were taller than average doors, and a sign on the wall beside them read: 'Sanctuary'. Will looked back to Holly and signaled toward the doors. He moved in front of one door, and Holly stood in front of the other.

"You open it, and I'll go in first," Will whispered.

"All right."

"On '3'."

Holly counted down in an almost nonexistent voice, and then swung the door open.

Will went through.

The sanctuary of the church was large, able to seat several hundred people. It had an ancient feel to it, though the church couldn't have been more than a decade old. Will loosened the grip on his sidearm as he stood just inside the entrance, looking around the massive room. The door from the dining hall had brought him to the side of the large worship area. Like the previous space, the sanctuary was well-lit by the sun. Oversized stained glass windows had been built into the wall, letting in plenty of light.

At the front of the sanctuary, sitting on the front pew, was one man. He wore a priest's robe, and sat with his elbows on his knees, his hands clasped together.

After several moments of Will not moving, the man raised his head. He waited before he finally glanced in Will's direction. Behind Will, Holly had entered the sanctuary, standing at his side. The man turned to face Will and Holly, and a smile formed on his face.

"Please, come in."

CHAPTER TWENTY-FIVE

"Are you Father Bartman?" Will asked. The preacher looked like the man they'd seen on the billboard, except years older.

The priest stood. "I am. Who asks?"

Will raised his hands in the air to show that he meant no harm. "My name's Will, and this is Holly. Father Bryant told us to come see you."

"Father Bryant?" Bartman asked. "He is alive?"

Will shook his head. "He died soon after we met him, but he told us that you could give us some answers."

"Answers?" Bartman scoffed.

They reached the front row of the church, opposite the aisle of Father Bartman, and stopped.

"Are you here alone?" Holly asked.

"Do you mean to rob me?"

"No," Will said. "Like I said, we're just hoping for some answers. We've come a long way to see you."

"And why did Bryant tell you that I could help you?"

Will removed his rifle from his back, which caused Bartman to jump. But when Will tossed it onto the ground, the preacher seemed to settle down. Will pulled out his sidearm and threw it down, as well. He removed his jacket as he approached the preacher. Will came within just a couple of feet of Bartman, and then he rolled up his shirt sleeve.

"He told me you could help me with this."

The scar on Will's arm had healed some. It was a much darker shade of pink than the rest of his arm, and the places where the teeth had sunk in were still obvious. Bartman looked down at the wound and then met eyes with Will again, his mouth open.

"You were bit." He presented it as fact, not question.

"I was," Will said. "But another preacher, a man by the name of Samuel; he healed me." There was a pause as Bartman seemed to process what Will was trying to tell him. Will said, "He drew the demon out of me."

Bartman brought his hand to his mouth and mumbled something to himself. He took two steps back, glancing back and forth between the scar on Will's arm and Will's eyes.

"It's true," Bartman said. "It's really true."

"So you *do* know about this demon plague?" Holly asked.

Bartman, still shaken, nodded. "Yes. Yes, I do."

"When Samuel pulled the demon out of me, he said some sort of prayer. It wasn't in English; in fact, I'm not sure what language he spoke. But we need to know what it is."

"Please, help us," Holly said.

"This Samuel, he was speaking in tongues. That is why you didn't know the language."

"Do you know what it was?"

"He believed in the lost text," Bartman said.

Holly wrinkled her brow. "Lost text?"

"There's no single prayer that is said to exorcise these spirits," Bartman said. "This isn't like a witch's spell. It has far more to do with the heart of the one performing the exorcism than it does with the specific prayer that's spoken. That language you heard, that's the language of the Lord."

"Are you trying to say that he was speaking the word of God?" Holly asked.

"As I said, if you don't believe, it is trivial."

Will pointed down to his arm. "Are you questioning whether I believe?"

"That you believe now? No. You have received possibly the most shocking of spiritual awakenings since the Lord's tomb was discovered empty, three days after the crucifixion. But what you believe up here," he pointed to his head, "is a far cry from what you feel in here." He tapped his chest with his fist.

"So you can't help us?" Holly asked.

"What is it that you want exactly? If I were to give you the information that you want, what would you do with it?"

Will said, "If we could get this information to Washington, then we might be able to find a way to stop it."

Bartman stepped forward and put his hand on Will's shoulder. "Son, there is no stopping this. This isn't some concoction that can be mixed and put into a needle for the government to pass around."

"You don't know that," Will said, shaking his head. "You don't know if this can be stopped or not. I'm living proof that it can be, be that on a small scale."

"How do you figure we will be able to convince, not only an entire nation, but the whole world, to believe? We have been trying that for centuries. It's done nothing but caused wars, political ramblings, and social debates. We were never 'One Nation Under God', and He knows that. Now, we pay for our sins. We must pay for how we have treated the world, the Son, and His word."

Will threw the preacher's hand off of his shoulder. "Bullshit! You may have the only key to end this, and you're still lost in your own piss pile of religious jargon."

"Will," Holly said sharply.

The preacher looked to Holly and sighed. "And this is why I

cannot help you."

Holly stepped in front of Will. "Father Bartman, please, anything you can do to help us. We have children with us, and one of them was bit, as well."

Bringing his hand to his mouth and biting his finger, Bartman said, "And he did not turn? How is that so?"

Holly told Bartman about Dylan's incident in the woods. And how, in an act of desperation, Will had amputated the boy's arm and stopped the possession.

"This is talked about only sparingly in the text," Bartman said. "The only way a human can become possessed is for the demon to ride into the brain. And the only way to destroy it, as I'm sure you have found by now, is to sever the connection of brain and body." He cleared his throat. "These spirits move slower through the body than you might imagine. It is foreign to them, and they must acquaint themselves with the vessel once they arrive. That is why you were able to save the boy. You acted quickly and demolished the demon's route to the brain."

"See, you can help us," Holly said.

The preacher sighed. "With certain things, perhaps. But it is impossible for me to teach you how to expel the beasts once they have taken root. This can only be done by one who is pure, and of the cloth. Are you that?"

Holly blushed. Will shook his head, still frustrated.

"Thus, that, I cannot share."

"Then come with us," Holly said.

Clasping his hands behind his back, Bartman strolled down the center aisle. He moved toward the church's main entrance, where the creatures continued to howl outside. Will had somehow managed to blank out the sound while they spoke to Bartman, but now it was clear. The preacher stopped when he arrived halfway to the entrance.

He spread his arms out like an angel spreading its wings. It was like Christ himself on the cross as he spun around.

"I cannot leave my congregation—my children. Don't you hear them?"

He's gone crazy being in here alone, Will thought.

"Eventually, they will make it in here," Will said. "And if these so-called exorcisms are performed like the one that was done on me, you'll never even heal one of them before they pounce on you."

"Then that is His will."

"And you should know," Holly said. "We entered through the kitchen and some of the creatures left the front of the building and chased after us. They could bust inside at any minute."

Bartman smiled. "Then, as I said, it shall be my time. I will not leave my congregation."

And with that, Will saw no hope. Bartman would not leave. He wasn't going to share any other information with them. What he had told them had further helped them understand things they already knew, and it *was* valuable, but Will knew there was no hope that Bartman would ever explain to them how to perform the exorcisms. And after considerable thought, Will understood.

Will looked over to Holly. "Come on, let's get out of here."

They turned their backs to Bartman and searched for a door to lead them back outside.

When Will turned around to ask the preacher about the best way out of the church, he was surprised to see Bartman standing only feet away from the church's front entrance.

"Father," Will said. The banging outside continued. Will shouted louder, trying to get the preacher's attention over the commotion.

Bartman lowered his wings and grasped on to the handles of the large double doors.

"Oh, shit," Will said.

The door swung open, and the horde flooded inside.

Pastor Bartman never had the chance to scream.

CHAPTER TWENTY-SIX

"Go!" Will shouted to Holly, signaling toward the door to the dining room.

They went through the door and abruptly stopped. The Empties who'd tried to follow them into the church had somehow pushed the table away from the entrance and made it inside. They'd lumbered halfway across the room.

"What do we do?" Holly shouted.

Will scanned the room and saw a door on the other side of it. He grabbed onto Holly's wrist and ran toward it.

The door opened into a hallway with closed rooms on either side of the narrow space. A beam of light shined from around the corner at the end of the corridor. His hand still holding her wrist, Will sprinted down the hall. When they turned the corner, they arrived at a glass door which led outside. Without hesitation, Will opened the door.

Adrenaline pumped through him, and Will hadn't thought to check to make sure it was clear outside. The door led to the side parking lot, several yards down from the door they'd originally entered the church through. Empties now occupied this side of the lot. One lunged at Will and he dodged it. He turned to shoot it, but a bang startled him. Holly had drawn her pistol and shot it in the head. She grabbed onto Will's wrist.

"Let's go!"

They ran for the edge of the lot, dodging the few Empties that stood in their way. Will shot over the guard rail, using his hand as a catapult, and fell down, sliding down the hill on his ass. He took one look back up, to the creatures coming toward the rail, and then darted into the pipe.

Inside, he turned around and waited for Holly, catching his breath. She entered the tunnel and ran to him.

"You all right?" she asked. "You took quite the fall back there."

"I'm fine," Will said, frustration in his voice. "Why the hell did he do that?"

"I don't know," Holly said.

Will turned from her and clasped the back of his head with his hands.

"Son of a bitch!" he yelled. A bottle was on the ground, and he picked it up and threw it against the wall. Shards of glass blew back onto him but he didn't seem to notice or care. Holly stepped back, giving him his space.

"It's all right," Holly said. "Let's just get back to the car and get out of here."

Will faced her. "We drove all the way up here looking for answers. And that bastard, he knew. He knew exactly how to save people. How to end this. But he wouldn't tell us and wouldn't come with us."

Licking her lips, Holly replied in a mellowed tone. "I know you're upset. We risked a lot coming here. I'm not happy about it either. But he made his choice, and there's nothing we can do about that. He obviously was so far gone in the head that nothing we said was going to matter. Maybe we should just take his advice."

"You wanna go to Florida?" Will asked, his voice calm now.

"Where else are we gonna go? The days keep getting colder. Soon it's going to be hard for us to survive without sustainable shelter. We've still got a couple of weeks before it's going to start getting really cold here. Let's beat the weather and go somewhere where we won't have to worry about it."

After a moment's pause, Will cracked a smile and approached Holly. He hugged her, then pulled back and kissed her on the lips.

"Let's go."

***

Charlie was waiting for them outside of the SUV when they arrived back at the vehicle.

"Everything go all right here?" Will asked.

"Yeah," Charlie said. "None of those things in the street even looked back here. Did you find Bartman?"

Holly opened the back seat and hugged the children.

"What's the matter with your hand?" Mary Beth asked, pointing at Holly's bloody palm.

Charlie looked down at Will's hand. "Damn."

"Will had a small accident," Holly said.

"Did he get bit?" Dylan asked, concerned.

"No," Holly said. "Hand me that towel below your feet, Mary Beth. And you two stay in the car."

Holly pressed the towel against Will's hand.

"He had a run in with a bottle," Holly told Charlie, smiling.

"I thought I heard something down there," Charlie said. "I got worried for a second that something was wrong."

"Sorry about that," Will said. "I'm glad you stayed with the kids and didn't come check on us. I just got a little frustrated."

"Why?"

Holly grabbed the first-aid kit while Will explained to Charlie what had happened in the church.

"So he didn't tell you how that other preacher saved you?"

Will shook his head.

"Son of a bitch."

"I think I'm more frustrated that he wouldn't come with us and that he felt the solution was to open the door and let those things eat him," Will said. "From what he told us, I don't think that we'd be able to perform the ritual to draw a demon out of someone."

"Because we're sinners?" Charlie asked.

"We're all sinners," Holly said. She looked to Will. "This is gonna hurt." She stuck the needle into his hand to stitch up the cut. Will grimaced and bit down on his jacket sleeve to keep from crying out.

"Because we aren't of the cloth. We aren't priests, and we aren't pure," Will said, biting his lip. "Samuel told me only pure, or virgin, priests would be able to perform an exorcism of this kind. It's not just a possession, it's ownership of the body. He could've told us how to do it, but it wouldn't have mattered unless we could find someone else who could do it. And what are the chances of that?"

"He did tell us why Dylan lived, though," Holly said.

The children quit messing around in the back seat and listened.

"The demons have to travel to the brain to take over," Will said. "But he said that many of them move slowly. That's why it takes more time for some people to turn once they've been bit. It's also while we were able to save Dylan by thinking fast and amputating his arm."

"Well, at least we know *why* that works now," Charlie said. "So, what do we do next?"

Will grimaced again as Holly continued to close his cut.

"Almost done," she said.

Will bit down on his sleeve and mumbled, "We were thinking

of heading South."

"How far South?"

"We were thinking about Florida," Holly said.

"Can we live on the beach?" Mary Beth asked, a new excitement in her voice.

Smiling, Holly said, "Maybe, sweetie. We're not even sure if that's where we're gonna go, or what it would be like when we get there, if we go." She finished the last stitch on Will and snipped the thread. "All done."

"Thank God," Will said. He looked to Charlie. "What do you think?"

Charlie thought for a moment, and then he shrugged. "Well, then, I guess Florida will be as good a place as any. We won't have to worry about freezing."

In the SUV, the two kids cheered. Holly smiled. In turn, Will grinned. He looked down at his hand. Holly had done a good job at stitching him up for someone who hadn't been used to patching human flesh until recently. When he looked up again, everyone was staring at him. Will chuckled.

"Well, what are we waiting for? Let's go."

CHAPTER TWENTY-SEVEN

That night, Gabriel couldn't sleep. Even with the welcomed comfort of an air mattress, the adrenaline flowed too strongly through him. All he could think about was the next day, knowing that he would be sent out onto the football field for an impossible fight. Behind the scenes, Ambrose would be betting on him to win. And in all honesty, Gabriel still didn't understand why. What did Ambrose see in him?

Claire had at last managed to fall asleep, which Gabriel was thankful for. Since he'd been reunited with his friends, Claire had been crying the entire time. After what she'd seen—what all three of them had seen—Gabriel couldn't blame her. The three of them had every reason to be scared, and Gabriel knew he would have to stay strong to help keep them all together.

Gabriel had been lying on his back for at least two hours, trying to fall asleep. His back aching, he finally decided to stand. As he made it to his feet, his back yelled at him and he reached back to massage it. He walked over to the room's only door and stared out the tiny window.

He heard shuffling behind him and turned around.

"Why're you up?" Jessica asked.

"Can't sleep," Gabriel said, staring through the window again at the door across the hall.

"Yeah, I can't either."

"You sure sounded asleep."

Jessica shrugged. "In and out."

Gabriel turned to face Jessica. "I have to ask you something."

"All right."

"What did you put in that journal?"

"Everything," Jessica said. "It's the only way I've been able to cope with this madness."

"What did you say about me in there?"

"Why?"

"I just want to know," Gabriel said. "Every indication that Ambrose has given me is that he's 'chosen' me because of whatever is written in that book. I just feel like I kinda have a right to know."

Jessica sighed and looked to the ground, and then looked up to Gabriel again. "It says the truth. You and Will both held us all together. So, in case I was eventually separated from you all, I wanted to remember. And if something happened to me, I wanted the world to remember that you two were strong. If Will were here, he'd be in the same boat you're in." She bowed her head again. "I'm sorry."

"For what?"

"Well, like you said, I got you into this."

"No," Gabriel said. "We were going to be here either way. I think what that book has done has given us a chance. It's given us beds and privacy. If we had been captured and they hadn't found your journal, chances are we'd be stuck in one of those rooms with all the other prisoners. Instead, we are here, together. And Ambrose *wants* me to win. He's going to be betting on me. So, maybe I'll get an advantage that the others won't."

"What was it like?" Jessica asked.

"What was what like?"

"This 'game' you're going to be in. You said that they took you outside to see one."

Gabriel looked outside the window again, staring off into that distant place. "It was a nightmare. People in the crowd were cheering and booing like animals. And the guys on the field didn't stand a chance. There was only one weapon, and they had to race across the length of the field to get it. All before a pack of Empties was released."

"Well, I'm betting on you," Jessica said.

Gabriel looked over to Jessica, and he smiled at her. He put his arm out to hug her, and she cuddled into him, hugging him back.

When Jessica pulled away, she said, "Now, try to get some sleep. You're going to need it. We all are."

***

Gabriel had eventually been able to fall asleep, though he wasn't sure for exactly how long. All he knew was that, by the time he woke up, natural light poured through the room's single, square window. He rolled over to check on Jessica and Claire, seeing that they were both still asleep.

After allowing himself a few extra moments of lying down, Gabriel swung his legs over the side of the mattress and sat on the side of the bed. He sunk into the air mattress, as it had deflated some overnight. He couldn't imagine that anyone would come into the room and blow it up again for him, but remained thankful to even have it.

He stood up and walked to the corner of the room. After relieving himself into the bucket they used as a restroom, he dove into a routine of stretches. Given the small amount of training time he'd been given, Gabriel doubted he would get any sort of warm-up before being thrown into the arena that was the football field. He performed a variety of full-body stretches, focusing mostly on his arms, legs, hips, and neck. Feeling better already, he sat down on the ground Indian-style, facing the wall. He closed his eyes and focused to clear his mind. While he'd never been much into meditation, he had attended a few yoga classes with Katie. He'd liked those classes, more than he would've liked to admit. His favorite part had been at the end of the class when the instructor would ask everyone to either lie down on the ground, or sit Indian-style, and try to vacate their mind of any stressful thoughts. That's what he did now. Gabriel knew that if he had any chance of surviving, he'd have to walk into that arena calm and focused.

When he finished, Gabriel opened his eyes. Some light had started to peek into the room from the hallway. He allowed himself a couple of minutes to neutralize his body after having been fully relaxed, and then he stood. He turned around, and Jessica still lay on the bed, but she was awake now. Claire still appeared to be sleeping.

"Hey," Jessica whispered.

"Good morning," Gabriel said. "How long've you been awake?"

"About fifteen minutes. I almost said something, but then I realized what you were doing. Didn't want to disturb you."

"Thanks for that." Gabriel walked back over to his bed and sat on the edge.

"When do you think they'll come get you?" Jessica asked, propping herself up on her elbow.

"Not sure," Gabriel said. "I'm not even sure when the whole thing is supposed to start. Honestly, I'd rather not talk about it right now."

"Sorry."

"It's all right," Gabriel said. "Obviously, it's the only thing on our minds." He looked over to Claire. "Maybe except for hers.

You think she's going to be okay?"

Jessica shook her head. "I don't know. I think the thing I worry about most is, the longer that we're here, the more chance there is for her to do something stupid."

Gabriel shifted his attention back to Jessica. "We're going to get out of here. You know that, right?"

Staring back at him, Jessica asked, "How can you be so sure? This isn't like the hospital, or the farm. David Ellis was an intelligent man, no doubt, but he was just that: one man. We don't know how many people are here, but we do know they're well armed and that they seem pretty smart."

Gabriel shook his head. "They aren't that smart. The leader, Ambrose, he's no slouch. As for all his pawns he's got trotting around here, we shouldn't have to worry about any of them outsmarting us."

"Only that they're carrying assault rifles."

"Yeah," Gabriel said, smiling. "There is that."

They stopped talking. After a few minutes, Gabriel stood up and walked to the door.

"What is it?" Jessica asked.

Keeping his back to her, Gabriel said, "They're coming."

A face appeared in the small window, and the door handle rattled. It opened, and Lance and Derek stood in the hallway. As always, each carried heavy artillery. A pair of handcuffs clanked together in Derek's hands.

"Turn around," Derek said.

Gabriel turned to face Jessica, putting his hands behind his back. In the bed beside her, Claire had woken up. Confusion spread across her face as her eyes tried to adjust to being open.

"On your knees."

After Derek had restrained Gabriel, Lance picked him up off

the ground, pulling at the cuffs around Gabriel's wrists. He grimaced as the steel cut into his bones.

Lance laughed as they shut the door, leaving Jessica and Claire alone once again.

***

They exited through the same side door that they'd taken Gabriel through before when they'd walked to the stadium. His eyes had an easier time adjusting to the sun this time, as it had hidden itself behind clouds. Gabriel wondered if an overcast sky would lead to rain on this day when he'd have to fight for his life.

Gabriel looked across the parking lot at the stadium. No one stood at the gate taking tickets, and it didn't appear that any spectators had even shown up yet. He had time before the game would begin.

Lance and Derek led Gabriel to the field-house behind the football field. They opened the front double-doors and pushed him inside.

"Keep walking," Lance said.

They walked through a weight room. Various cardio and strength-training equipment was scattered across the room. Derek stepped in front of Gabriel just as they arrived at a door. He pulled out a set of keys, inserted one into the handle, and opened the door.

Lance pushed Gabriel through the door before it had even swung all the way open. It took every ounce of strength in Gabriel's blood not to rear back and kick Lance in the knee. He thought he'd be able to break it. Instead, he closed his eyes and drew in three deep breaths.

When he opened his eyes again, Derek stared at him.

"You done with that shit?"

Gabriel nodded.

"All right then," Derek said. "Turn around."

Turning around, Gabriel faced Lance. Aiming his assault rifle square into the middle of Gabriel's chest, Lance smiled. Gabriel glanced down to Lance's finger. His hand appeared to be shaking, his index finger resting on the edge of the trigger. Gabriel tried to remain calm, but he knew this man wanted nothing more than to kill him. Of course, he would likely be killed by Ambrose if this happened. Either way, sweat seeped from the pores on Gabriel's arms and cheeks.

Lance quickly moved the gun and made a false move toward Gabriel, startling him.

Laughing, Lance said, "You fucking pussy. You think I'd actually shoot you? I fucking wish."

"Cut that shit out," Derek said. "He'll be here any—"

Someone knocked on the door and it opened.

Ambrose.

CHAPTER TWENTY-EIGHT

It was mid-afternoon when Charlie pulled off the road. A bad storm was brewing in the air, and they'd found another exit on a desolate stretch of highway to stop at. It was a thinly populated area with only one building: a truck stop. Charlie pulled the vehicle into the parking lot and they saw a small group of five Empties hanging around the side of the lot.

"Shit," Charlie said.

"It's all right," Will said. "Take a spin around the parking lot and let's make sure there's nothing else, or no one else, here. If it looks abandoned, you can return to the front and we'll take care of them."

Charlie drove around the side of the convenience store, and then the rear. Two more Empties limped around the back side of the lot, but that was it. One of the creatures had once been a large man, wearing overalls over a shirt that had once been white and was now stained red. The other had been a thin man, younger than its counterpart, and wore a button-up shirt and jeans.

"Stop," Will said. "I'll get 'em."

Charlie stopped the vehicle a safe distance away from the two creatures, and Will grabbed the machete and jumped out. It was the first time he'd held the weapon since cutting his hand in the drain pipe, and the grip surprisingly felt as comfortable as ever in his grasp.

The two creatures stood ten yards apart. Will went to the smaller one and landed a blow in the side of its head before the

Empty could put its hands up in defense. It crumbled to the ground, and Will stepped on its chest and wedged the blade out of its skull. The nearing creature's snarl drowned out most of the wet sound that came with dislodging the machete. Will stood up straight with the thing in overalls five yards away. It lunged toward him, but he easily ducked the blow and passed behind the creature. The Empty had about five inches on him. Will lifted the weapon overhead and brought the machete down into the back of the creature's skull. It let out one last snarl before it fell forward, landing belly-first. Its face slammed against the concrete with a sickening thud. Will kicked the Empty once to confirm the kill. When it didn't move, he placed his boot on the thing's back and withdrew the blade.

When he returned to the SUV, Charlie threw him a towel.

"Not bad," Charlie said. "I think I'd give you a solid six out of ten."

Will wiped the blade down and smiled. "Catch."

He threw the towel to Charlie, who tried to wiggle away, and then Will loaded back into the passenger seat. Charlie wrangled the towel away, tossing it back to Will. Holly and the kids laughed in the back seat.

The slaying had attracted the other five Empties as the creatures made their way from the side lots. Charlie only drove about fifteen yards before he stopped.

"Guns?" Charlie asked.

Will nodded. "It's too risky with five of them. We're in the middle of nowhere. I don't think we'll attract anything or anyone. Just no shotguns or rifles. Let's stick with handguns."

"Do you need me to come with?" Holly asked.

"Stay in here with the kids," Will said. "Keep an eye on us, and if something weird happens, then come help. Keep a gun at your side."

The creatures had cut the distance to the SUV in half as Will opened his door and stepped out.

Three of the Empties stood bunched together, while the other two moved in Will's direction, leaving about a half-a-car length between their counterparts. Will stepped forward until his target stood ten feet in front of him and then he fired the first shot. It blew past the creature's ear; it had been a petite woman during its life. Setting his sights again, Will squeezed off another round and hit the creature above its left eye. At almost the same time, Charlie took down his first target with his initial shot.

The other three creatures came down without either man having to reload. Final count: Charlie 3, Will 2.

They loaded back into the SUV and Charlie parked it behind the truck stop, out of sight from any possible passersby.

As Will popped a new clip into his weapon, he said to Holly, "Charlie and I will go make sure it's clear inside; then we'll come get you guys and our stuff."

"Why don't you let me go in with Charlie?" Holly offered. "You need a break."

Before Will could protest, Charlie chimed in.

"She's right. We'll handle it, man. Just chill out for a few minutes."

Will thought of protesting until he looked down at his hands. Dirt, grime, and blood covered them. The stitches on his palm looked almost ready to bust open. His muscles ached, his head throbbed, and he felt disgusted from the repeated blood showers.

"All right," he said, looking back at Holly. "You guys just be sure to yell if anything is wrong, all right? I'll be coming right in." He took his gun by the barrel and offered it to Holly.

Popping a new clip into her own sidearm, Holly smiled and said, "I've got my own."

"Just be careful," Will said.

"We will, don't worry," Charlie replied. He looked back to Holly and signaled her outside.

After they exited the vehicle, Will let his head slam against the head rest and he closed his eyes. As hesitant as he'd been to let Holly go, he now found it relaxing that he was able to just sit and wait. Even so, he found himself becoming more anxious by the second.

He opened his eyes, then looked to the back seat. The two children sat shoulder to shoulder on one end of the bench, staring up at him.

Smiling, Will got out of the SUV and re-entered through the rear passenger side door. Dylan and Mary Beth remained silent and stared at him. He sat beside them.

"Come here," Will said, and he put his arm up, offering to let Dylan duck under it. The boy did, and Mary Beth snuggled next to him.

"Are we really going to Florida?" Dylan asked.

Running his fingers through Dylan's hair, Will said, "Yeah, buddy, we are."

"Good," he said. "I like the beach."

Will smiled. "Me, too."

"Can we go to Disney World?" Mary Beth asked. "You know, if it's open. I've never been."

"I doubt it will be open, but when it opens back up, that's the first place we'll take you guys."

After that, they sat there for several moments in silence. Will would rub Dylan's head for a minute, and then shift his hand over to Mary Beth and comfort her by stroking her hair. He took comfort in them feeling at peace with him there, like he was their father. He looked down at Dylan and wondered if the boy's parents were still alive. If they were, how must they be feeling? The thought filled him with regret for holding onto the boy instead of forcing him to travel with Gabriel to Washington. If he had, not only would the boy possibly have been reunited with his parents, but he'd still have both of his arms. Will shook off the thought, though, because if Washington was as bad as he'd been told, Dylan's fate could've been far worse than losing a limb.

Will was pulled out of his thoughts when Dylan spoke.

"Do you think things will ever go back to normal?"

Before Will had to come up with an answer, Charlie and Holly rounded the corner of the building, their weapons holstered. Holly signaled everything was clear with a thumbs up.

Will leaned down and kissed Dylan on the forehead. "Come on, bud. Let's go inside."

The inside of the truck stop looked clean. The vibrant walls and updated countertops made the place look new, even. It would be a comfortable place for them to stay the night. But the place had been completely stripped of any food or supplies worth possessing.

"I've gotta say, it's a little strange a place this nice is empty," Will said.

Charlie added, "We haven't passed another vehicle on the road in a while."

"We should really scour the place," Holly said. "Charlie and I just made sure no one else was here. Never know what we might find in the back or in the kitchen."

"Good idea," Will said. "We should look now while there's

still light outside."

"I'll take the kids and check around here in the store," Charlie said. "You guys go check out the restaurant. We only took a quick peek into the kitchen to make sure no Empties were in there."

Will nodded, then crossed the store to the restaurant, Holly behind him. Tables and chairs were still set up across the dining room. They scurried across the space to the double doors that presumably led to the kitchen.

Leaning against the doors, Will asked, "You guys looked back here and it was clear?"

Holly nodded, and Will pushed through the doors.

Much like the rest of the building, the kitchen was surprisingly clean. How had this place been left untouched? Pots and pans were in their places, the stovetop was clear, and even the floor was mostly free of debris. It wasn't until Will opened the refrigerator that he caught a whiff of anything sour. The smell of rotten meat escaped from the refrigerator like it had been just awaiting its chance to flee. Will nearly vomited before he slammed the door shut.

"Let's check the pantry," Will said, holding his hand to his mouth.

Holly moved ahead of Will and opened the walk-in dry storage.

"Damn it," Holly said.

It had already been raided. Will didn't even go inside to check. Someone *had* been here, or anyone who'd been here during The Fall had stolen the contents. Still holding his hand over his face, Will walked over to the stovetop and tried turning on one of the burners.

Whoosh.

The stovetop's eye came alive, the blue flame rising. Will removed his hand from his mouth, revealing a smile.

"Does it work?" Holly asked.

Will moved out of the way, showing her that indeed it did.

That evening, they treated themselves to a warm meal. For at least one night, they didn't have to eat cold beans or veggies out of the can. It was all the children could talk about, and that brought a sense of peace to the three adults in the group.

Will rested peacefully that night, thankful they'd survived another day.

CHAPTER TWENTY-NINE

"Hello, Mr. Alexander," Ambrose said, smiling as he entered the room.

Gabriel didn't respond. For once, Ambrose wasn't smoking a cigar. Still, Gabriel could smell the stench radiating off of him.

"Give us a moment, gentlemen," Ambrose said, speaking to Lance and Derek.

"Are you sure, sir?" Lance asked.

Ambrose's smile vanished. "Are you going to stand there and question me?" Ambrose asked.

"No, sir," Lance said. "I'm sorry."

"You're damn right, you're sorry," Ambrose said. "Now get the fuck out of here."

Lance's face went red. He exited the room.

For the first few moments, Ambrose didn't speak. He paced back and forth in front of Gabriel, who still sat on the wood bench in front of the lockers. Ambrose didn't even look at him. Even though Gabriel was unarmed, he still found it risky for Ambrose to have left him alone in the room with him. He assumed that Ambrose was armed, but that didn't mean that Gabriel couldn't attack him. Either Ambrose was too confident of his own ability to keep this from happening, or he just didn't think Gabriel would do anything. The latter was true; Gabriel had no intentions of doing anything stupid. He would eventually get out of this place, but he would have to be smart about it.

"I assume that you're prepared for today, Mr. Alexander," Ambrose said.

"Am I supposed to be?" Gabriel asked. "I only had about ten minutes of training."

Ambrose chuckled. "You don't need training."

"What about the guy you plan on sending out there with me? Did he have adequate training?"

Ambrose shrugged. "Perhaps. But who's to say that I'm even sending anyone in there with you?"

Gabriel shrugged. "I guess I figured you just wanted people to have more options to bet on."

"Makes my odds better if it's just between you and the creatures," Ambrose said. "Do you really think people are going to bet on you, Mr. Alexander?"

"Well, I guess if they're as smart and competent as you are, then they should bet on me."

A big smile crescendoed on Nathan's face. "That's my boy. You're going to make me a very rich man. I can feel it." He pulled a cigar from his pocket and lit it.

Guess I spoke too soon on that one, Gabriel thought. Ambrose took a drag off the cigar, blowing the cloud of smoke toward Gabriel.

Ambrose headed for the door. Before he exited, he turned back and said, "I'm going to give you one piece of advice." He took another deep inhale of a cigar, and blew the smoke into the air before looking back down at Gabriel. "You just worry about yourself. Be selfish. Show no mercy. Think about your family. You do that, you're gonna make both of us happy."

He left the room, leaving Gabriel alone.

***

Half an hour had passed since the guards had come in and retrieved Gabriel. In that time, Claire and Jessica had not spoken a word to each other. Claire lay on the bed, curled up and crying, though less than before. Jessica sat in the corner of the room with her eyes closed and her legs crossed. Unable to find an escape in writing, she'd begun using meditation to center herself. She was still learning this new ritual, and only able to remain still for five to ten minutes at a time. Today had been especially difficult with so many things racing through her mind.

When she'd finished, she stood up. Claire still lay on the bed in the fetal position, her back facing the room's only door. Jessica walked over to her. She sat on the edge of the bed and rubbed Claire's arm. Claire didn't look up, but she sniffled.

"I know you're hurting, sweetie," Jessica said. "But you—"

Claire flipped over onto her back, pushing Jessica's hand off of her arm. "Do you?" she snapped at Jessica. "Do you know that I'm hurting?"

"Yes, I do. I—"

"My brother was murdered!" Claire sat up. She pointed toward the door. "They let those things slaughter him. Tear him apart. Right in front of me. You have no idea what that feels like."

As Claire glared at her, Jessica thought about her own parents. The image of them lying on their bed together, holding each other's hands. The pistols between them. It had been painted in her mind forever. Claire was wrong. While Jessica hadn't seen her parents draw in their last breaths, she'd seen the aftermath of that tragedy. And it had been enough for her to imagine those final moments every day since.

And while Jessica wanted to spit back at Claire and tell her these things, she held it inside. She understood that Claire's anger wasn't directed at her. Claire hadn't gotten enough distance from her loss. And she hadn't exactly been in the best environment to grieve.

Claire's face shifted from anger to sadness as she started to cry again. She fell forward into Jessica's arms and Jessica accepted her, hugging the hurting woman. Jessica ran her hand up and down Claire's back.

"I'm sorry," Claire said.

"It's okay," Jessica said.

"I just miss him so much."

"I know you do."

Both women turned when the door clicked. It opened, and two guards stood in front of a third person. The two guards entered the room. Jessica felt something inside herself die when she recognized the man behind them.

"Hello," Bruce said, looking to Jessica. His face didn't need much lighting for Jessica to remember how disgusting he was. She didn't reply to him.

"You can't even say 'hello' to me? That's quite rude." He looked to the guards and nodded.

The two guards, one a female and one a male, pulled Jessica and Claire apart. The two women fought it until the female guard slapped Jessica across the face. Jessica pulled back and the two guards picked Claire up under her arms.

"Let me go," Claire said, fighting them.

"Where are you taking her?" Jessica asked. She stood up.

The three captors ignored her. Claire continued to scream, working to get free from the two guards' grasps.

Jessica watched as Bruce drew a pistol from his side.

"No!" Jessica yelled.

Bruce reared back and slammed the butt of the weapon into the back of Claire's head. She fell limp, and the two guards dragged her out of the room. Bruce holstered the weapon and looked up at Jessica.

"Please," Jessica said. "Please, don't hurt her. Where are you taking her?"

Bruce smiled and shook his head. "You should've just given me what I wanted."

He exited the room, locking it behind him.

Jessica fell down onto the bed and wept.

***

After he'd eaten the ground beef and potatoes they'd brought him, Gabriel put himself through a light routine of bodyweight exercises. The regimen included push-ups, squats, lunges, and sit-ups. When he'd finished, he'd spent another ten minutes stretching. Now, he sat on the bench in front of a locker. Above the locker, written in permanent marker, it said: McDaniel (34). He wondered what position McDaniel had played on the football team, and if he'd had any chance of playing college ball before The Fall. He looked around the entire locker room, reading the names of each player. On a Friday night in September, this room would've been rocking with testosterone-filled excitement. Now, it had become the final place for gladiators to reflect on their lives before heading out into the slaughter.

Only, Gabriel would survive. He told himself this, over and over again, as he waited.

The wait ended when the door opened and two guards walked into the room. Only one of them held an assault rifle. The other, while armed with a pistol mounted to his hip, walked in with empty hands.

"On your feet," the unarmed guard said. The other guard aimed the rifle at Gabriel.

Gabriel stood up and put his arms out to the side, and the unarmed guard patted Gabriel down, making sure he hadn't gathered any weapons in the time he'd been left alone. There had been nothing to arm himself with; he'd checked.

"He's clear," the guard called out.

The other guard signaled toward the door. "All right. Let's go. It's time."

CHAPTER THIRTY

A man stood in front of double doors alongside two other armed guards. He wore the same outfit as Gabriel. He was slightly taller, and slender, with auburn hair down to his shoulders. The number "77" had been drawn across his back. The two guards holding the man stepped back as Gabriel approached, and 77 looked over his shoulder. The guy couldn't have been older than 25. A stringy beard wrapped around his chin from ear to ear.

Gabriel stopped next to number 77. He could see the taller competitor out of the corner of his eye, looking him up and down. Gabriel glanced over at him for a moment, and then re-focused on the double doors in front of him.

Outside, a crowd had gathered. They cheered, likely anxious for the upcoming bout.

One of the guards stepped in front of number 77 and Gabriel.

"When the doors open, you'll step out together," the guard said. "Side-by-side."

This was different than what Gabriel remembered from before. When Ambrose had brought him here to see one of these fights, the competitors had come out separately. He remembered the crowd cheering and booing each of the competitors, depending on who they had bet on.

The guard continued. "Walk to the guard standing in the nearest end zone. He'll tell you where you'll start, and give you further instructions on how to play the game." The guard smiled. "Good luck. You're going to need it." He turned to face the doors.

Out of the corner of his eye, Gabriel could see number 77's hand shaking. He looked over and saw that he was drawing in breaths at a rapid rate. His eyes showed Gabriel how scared he was. Gabriel was fearful too, but he wasn't about to show it.

The guard standing in front of the competitors had a walkie talkie on his waist. It made a noise and he grabbed it as a voice came through on the other end.

"Ready?" the voice asked.

"Ready when you are," the guard said.

"Let them out," the person on the other end of the walkie talkie said.

The guard looked over his shoulder and smiled at both Gabriel and number 77. He put a hand on each door handle.

The door opened, and the sun blinded Gabriel as the roar of the crowd hit his ears.

Gabriel stood frozen in the doorway until someone behind him pushed him.

"Move your ass," the guard said.

Number 77 walked ten yards ahead of Gabriel and the guard demanded that he catch up. All the while, the crowd continued to rumble. Gabriel looked into the stands. The crowd appeared to be smaller than last time. Last time, there had been about 100 people in the crowd. Now, there appeared to be a little more than half that. He wondered how much this would upset Ambrose. After all, Ambrose had depended on Gabriel to bring him home a big payday. With less people there to bet, the purse would be smaller.

When he caught up to 77, Gabriel kept his focus forward. He could sense number 77 looking at him again, working to try and intimidate him. Gabriel ignored it.

Ahead, he saw the guard waiting for them. Beyond him—a hundred yards beyond him, in fact—he saw the lone ax hanging on the upright. This was the weapon that he and number 77 would be fighting for. When they reached the guard at the starting line, he put his hand up.

"Stop here," the guard said.

The guard who'd led Gabriel to the starting line stepped in front of him and unlocked the handcuffs. Gabriel massaged his wrists, with the steel no longer rubbing against his flesh.

The guard at the starting line stepped in front of both of them.

"I'm only going to say this once, so listen up," the guard said. "You both will remain behind this line until you hear a gunshot." The guard pointed to a line drawn at his feet. "If either one of you jumps across the line before you hear the gunshot, you will be shot. Once you hear the signal, you're both going to run like hell to that goal post." He pointed a hundred yards down to the ax. "That's the only weapon out here. So, I suggest that you get to it before your other competitor does if you want any chance to live." He smiled. "But before any of this, that fence you see over there is going to open. A truck is going to come out and unload hell on you guys. Your objective? To kill as many of those things as you can, and be the last one to survive. And I do mean the last one. There will only be one winner."

Gabriel knew the game. In fact, he knew the chances were slim that either he or Number 77 would survive. But he couldn't tell himself that. All he could tell himself was that he would be the one to survive, at any and all costs. And by any means necessary.

The guard continued. "There will be rifles aimed directly at you at all times. If something seems funny, you will be shot down immediately. Do you understand?"

Gabriel nodded, and could see out of his peripheral vision 77 doing the same.

"Good," the guard said. He looked into the stands at the restless crowd. "No sense in making them wait any longer." He turned back to Gabriel and 77, that same crooked smile on his face. He patted both men on the shoulders and said, "Good luck." He nodded to one of the other guards, who pulled a two-way radio from his belt.

"Let's do this," he said into the radio.

All the personnel surrounding the two competitors scattered.

Gabriel now stood alone with 77.

Still looking forward, focusing on the lone weapon, Gabriel said, "We should work together."

He sensed 77 looking over at him as the man said, "What?"

"Don't look at me," Gabriel said. "Don't let them think we're becoming friendly."

"Believe me. With the face I'm making, they won't think we're becoming friendly, because we *aren't*."

The fence opened in the corner of the field, and the same box truck, armored with scraps, drove out onto the opposite end zone. The crowd roared. Four armed guards followed the vehicle. It turned around to where its rear faced Gabriel, and the standing guards hurried to the back door.

"Do you want to stay alive or not?" Gabriel asked. "They are about to unleash hell out of the back of that truck, and they want us pitted against one another. They want us to think that our only chance to win is to be the last one standing, but that's bullshit. If we can work together and take down these things, I'd bet you that we could win the crowd over. If we do that, there's no way in hell they would kill us."

77 scoffed. "You're crazy, man. Even if that were to work, how the hell am I supposed to trust you?"

"Because I'm not one of them," Gabriel said. "I'm a prisoner —a slave—like you."

The guards slowly moved to the back of the truck, readying to open it up and unleash the Empties.

"You want me to gain your trust?" Gabriel said. "I'm going to let you get that ax. I will make it look like I'm trying, but I'm going to let you beat me to it."

"You wouldn't have to *let* me," 77 said.

Gabriel ignored the jab. "You get to that ax, and I'm going to distract the monsters so that you can take them down. I'm putting my trust in you, 77."

"My name is Chase. I ain't no fucking number."

"All right, Chase. I'm Gabriel. Now, are we gonna do this or not?"

The roar of the crowd pinched the two men's silence as the back of the box truck cracked open. A bead of sweat trickled down Gabriel's cheek as he awaited for an answer from Chase. He knew this was his best chance of walking off this football field. Otherwise, he'd likely be buried here.

Gabriel looked Chase in the eyes. Though he noticed the quake in the man's hand again, he didn't allow his focus to shift from Chase's eyes. Fear lay behind those eyes.

Chase nodded just enough for Gabriel to notice, but not so much as to tip the guards off to their joining forces.

"I'm in," Chase said.

CHAPTER THIRTY-ONE

When Will awoke, Holly wasn't by his side. He sat up to see that only Charlie was still asleep; the kids were missing, too. The sun poured in through the windows, lighting the inside of the convenience store. He heard laughing coming from outside. When he stood up and looked out front, he saw Dylan and Mary Beth running around in the parking lot, playing and laughing together. He didn't see Holly. He ran for the front door.

Will shot through the door. He was about to reprimand the children for playing outside alone before he saw Holly out of the corner of his eye. She sat against the glass with a smile spread across her face.

"Good morning," Holly said.

Mary Beth started to tell Will hello, but he cut her off.

"What the hell are you doing?" Will asked Holly.

Her smile morphed into a face of confusion.

"How could you let the kids come out here and make this much noise? There's no telling who or what they might attract."

Dylan and Mary Beth stopped jumping around, and each of their faces turned sour, as well. They each looked guilty, as if they'd done something wrong.

Holly said to the kids, "Guys, can you go inside for a minute so Will and I can talk?"

Heads bowed, the two children headed back into the gas station. Holly moved down toward the corner of the store, further out of their earshot, and Will followed.

"What was that?" Holly asked.

"What was that? What the hell were you thinking, letting the kids come play out here?"

"I didn't want to keep them cooped up inside that gas station. These kids have been through enough. They need to get outside and play, and do normal things."

"This isn't the campground," Will said. "We don't know if it's safe. We're right next to the interstate, for Christ's sake."

"The campground? Safe? Will, listen to yourself. Nowhere is safe, especially that damn campground. Look at Dylan."

Will put his hands on his hips and turned away. He thought of Dylan and his injury all the time. Blamed himself for it. He felt a hand grab his shoulder.

"I'm sorry for bringing that up," Holly said. "And I'm sorry for letting the kids play out here. I wasn't thinking."

"No, it's okay," Will said, sighing. He turned around to face her. "I shouldn't have come out here and jumped your ass like that. You've been amazing with the kids. I've barely paid any attention to them. You've basically made them your life."

Holly wrapped her arms around Will's neck. "You've been doing great. I know you're in a tough spot and *you've* done an amazing job taking care of us."

"I'm ready to stop running."

"I know," Holly said, combing her hands through his hair. "Me, too. Let's just focus on getting to Florida. We'll find somewhere to settle down, and we'll quit running."

They kissed.

In the distance, thunder sounded in the sky. It came from the North. They'd be heading South.

Will took Holly's hand and they headed back inside.

Just about an hour later, after a warm breakfast of hearty soup, they were back on the road.

***

They'd been on the road just under an hour. Holly sat in the back seat, entertaining the kids. Will drove.

Everything had been fine, until they heard gunshots.

"What's that noise?" Mary Beth asked.

"It's nothing, honey," Holly said.

At the top of a steep hill, Will slammed on the brakes. Charlie lunged forward, catching himself on the dashboard. Holly and the kids slammed against the front seats and cried out.

"What the hell, man?" Charlie asked.

Will didn't say anything. He simply looked ahead. The others joined him when the next gunshot rang out moments later. Followed by another. And another. Holly poked her head between the seats.

"What's going on?" Mary Beth asked.

A quarter of a mile down the open road, a group of six or seven humans fought against a herd of Empties. There were several vehicles around them, including an overturned SUV. The battle took up the entire width of the road. From what Will could tell from a distance, the possessed outnumbered the living by about two to one.

"We've gotta turn around," Holly said.

Will remained silent, observing the scene.

The kids became restless in the back, trying to catch a glimpse of what was going on. Dylan went to open his door and Holly shot back into her seat to scold him. She ordered him to stay in his seat and keep his seatbelt on.

Will looked over to Charlie, who held a neutral expression on his face. Charlie shrugged, and Will nodded.

As Holly appeared between the seats again, Will grabbed his sidearm to assure it was loaded.

"Check that shotgun and rifle," Will told Charlie, who had the guns by his feet.

"What are you doing?" Holly asked.

"We're going to help them," Will said.

"What?" Holly grabbed onto his shoulder. "Will, the children. We can't just run down there recklessly."

"Those loaded?" Will said to Charlie, ignoring Holly.

Holly grabbed his face and turned it toward her.

"Don't do this."

"What if that was us down there, Holly?"

"Please," Holly said. "Turn around. We'll find another way."

Will shook his head. "We'll pull to within a hundred feet or so of them. Charlie, you and I will run out and help. Holly, you jump up into the front seat. If things go south, or any of the creatures come close, you turn around and head back to the top of the hill. If things get *really* bad, then don't stop there. Keep going."

"I'm not leaving you," Holly said.

Will said, "The children."

Holly wiped her eyes and nodded.

"I wanna help," Dylan said.

"You keep Mar—"

"No, I want to help." Gunshots continued, and people screamed. "Will, pl—"

"No," Will said sharply. "You're not helping. Now, hang on."

Will hit the gas. The tires squealed, the smell of burning rubber hitting his nostrils for just a moment. The SUV sped down the hill, toward the battle.

The humans saw them coming and waved. With a better view of what was going on, Will saw that his estimates were about right. There were three men and one woman fighting against ten

Empties. Several bodies lay sprawled on the ground, indistinguishable as having been human or demon. Will stopped the SUV, not slamming on the brakes this time. He reached over and took the rifle from Charlie, who grabbed the shotgun.

"Go!" Will shouted.

Leaving the vehicle running, Will exited. He and Charlie jogged toward the fight, slowing to a walk twenty feet away from the herd. The creatures had driven the humans back around their vehicles. Most of the Empties turned their attention to Will and Charlie. When that happened, one of the men fired a rifle. The first shot missed while the second connected, garnering the attention of part of the herd again.

"We're about out of ammo!" one of the men shouted.

Will pressed the butt of the rifle against his shoulder and crept forward while aiming. He fired his first shot into the horde. It took him three shots to take down the first Empty, hitting it in the cheek. Charlie disabled one of the creatures with his second round of buckshot, blowing the thing's leg off below the knee. It howled as it fell to the ground.

The survivors smiled. The only one who appeared to still have a loaded weapon re-joined the fight. He approached one of the beasts and took it down from close range while its attention was focused on Will and Charlie. One of the other survivors drew a large knife, ran up to one of the Empties, and slammed the blade through the thing's skull. They continued the fight until only the humans remained standing. When it was all said and done, smoke lifted from each barrel. The six humans found themselves among a spread of corpses that was covering the road.

The man who hadn't run out of ammo approached Will and Charlie, stepping over the fallen bodies.

"Thank y'all," he said, mumbling with a backwoods accent. "We for sure thought we was done for."

"It's no problem," Will said.

He looked back to Holly and waved her to pull forward. Glancing back to the carnage, he observed the bodies sprawled across the road.

"We lost three people," the man said.

"I'm sorry," Charlie said.

The man looked past Will and Charlie to the SUV. "How many've you are there?"

The question made Will nervous. These people were armed, and he had yet to figure out how they'd gotten into this mess in the first place. He'd opened his mouth to respond when he heard the pump of a shotgun. He looked over to see Charlie with the shotgun aimed at the man who'd been speaking to them.

"Charlie, what are you doing?" Will asked.

"Lay down your weapon," Charlie said to the man.

"Charlie," Will said again.

"Shut up, Will."

Will was taken aback by the sudden change in Charlie's demeanor. He gripped his own weapon tight with sweaty palms, wondering if he should aim it at Charlie and threaten him into standing down.

"Where are the people who own that SUV?" Charlie asked, nodding his head toward the flipped-over vehicle.

Eyes squinted in confusion, Will looked over to the SUV. It lay on its side. The side facing the sky was wrecked, as if it had rolled. There were bullet holes in the back. Will noticed the South Carolina plates that read: CLA BEAR.

"Claire's?" Will mumbled.

"You're damn right," Charlie said. He took a step toward the man, who took two steps back and raised his hands in the air, still holding his rifle.

"Whoa, now. I don't know what you're talking about, son."

"Where are they? I'm not asking again."

"Charlie, let's just calm down and talk to them," Will said.

The man started to laugh. His yellow teeth showed from between his chapped lips and under his salt and pepper mustache.

"I'm not sure why you're laughing, but you better give me some answers now," Charlie said.

The others in their group laughed. The man, smiling, took two steps toward Charlie, gaining confidence.

"You ain't gonna shoot me," the man said. "If you shoot me, you'll never find them. Hell, you'll never know if they're alive or dead. Now, why don't we put down that gun? Huh? Come on, how about it, nigger?"

Will could see Charlie grip the shotgun tighter and his finger itched the trigger.

"Charlie, don—"

One of the men darted behind a vehicle, gathering Charlie's attention. Everything that followed happened in seconds.

Charlie shifted his aim and fired, hitting one of the other men in the stomach. As soon as he removed the gun's aim from the leader, the man lowered his hands and raised his rifle into a firing position, aiming it at Charlie.

Will, having dropped his rifle, drew his sidearm and fired. Not even a second after the bullet left the chamber of Will's gun, the man fired.

The man stumbled backward, removing one of his hands from the rifle and clutching his chest. Looking down at his hand, he found it covered in blood.

Charlie stood with the shotgun still resting against his shoulder. The man's shot had missed him.

"Fuck you, bigot," Charlie said, stepping within just a few yards of the man.

The shotgun blast startled Will, even though he knew it was coming. The man's stomach opened like a blooming flower and he fell backward.

Will looked to Charlie, who stood there stunned at what he'd done. Smoke rose from the man's stomach and the outlines of his innards showed.

The survivor who'd hidden behind one of the vehicles reappeared from behind Claire's SUV, aiming a gun at Charlie.

"Charlie!"

Charlie looked over and saw the man pointing the gun at him, and he ducked just as the survivor fired. Will's eyes went wide and the bullet whistled past his ear. He lifted his own weapon and fired until his clip was empty. He wasn't sure how many of the bullets connected, but the man fell backward, dropping the pistol out of his hand.

The one remaining survivor—a woman—remained still in the middle of the road, her arms raised. She trembled, staring toward Will and Charlie.

"I'm sorry," she mumbled. She turned and ran.

Charlie dropped the shotgun and drew his own sidearm, aiming it at her.

"Charlie, no!" Will yelled.

He lunged at his friend and tackled him, but not before Charlie could fire off two shots.

Lying on top of Charlie, Will looked down the road. Charlie yelled at Will to get off of him. The bullets had missed, and the girl continued to run.

Will jumped to his feet and raced after her.

Hearing him coming, the woman kept looking back.

"Stop!" Will commanded.

Crying, the woman continued to run. Will gained on her, having cut their distance in half. She finally stopped and turned all the way around to face him. Will slowed and stopped, standing about fifteen yards from her.

"Look, we just want to know where our friends are," Will said.

"I can't," the woman said, wiping her eyes.

"No one else needs to die."

"I can't. I can't go back. Not like this."

"Where? You can't go back where?"

"To him. He'll torture me. He'll make me play."

Will furrowed his brow. "Play? What are you talking about? Please, tell me where my friends are."

"Your friends are already dead. They have to be. I'm sorry."

"No, what do you me—"

"I'm sorry." She drew her knife from her hip and pressed it to her throat.

"No!" Will yelled. He ran toward her, but only made it in time to catch her as she fell backward.

The woman's head went limp, and Will almost threw his back out as gravity took over and she went down. Blood seeped from the wound at first, and then poured.

"Please, where are my friends?"

But the woman couldn't speak. She gurgled and coughed as blood came out her mouth.

Angry now, Will shook her.

"Tell me!"

She coughed once more and took a final breath. Then she

went still, falling completely limp in Will's arms. He eased her down onto the ground.

Charlie, Holly, and the two children approached. Will bowed his head and closed his eyes. When he opened them again, he gazed upon the knife on the ground, covered in blood. A small river ran red from her body, paving a path across the highway.

"Is Gabriel okay?" Dylan asked.

The question drew Will's attention away. He turned around to see Holly shifting her attention from Mary Beth to Dylan.

"We don't know, sweetie," Holly said, kneeling down and putting her hands on his shoulders. "But we're gonna find him."

"We need to search the vehicles," Will said. "There might be some sort of clue to where these people came from."

"How do we even know they knew where they went? What if they just found the vehicle on the road and were scouring it?"

"They knew," Charlie said.

Holly looked to Will, and he nodded at her.

Will said, "Let's check them. You guys go ahead, and I'll be right behind you." He drew his knife.

"Come on, guys," Holly said, and she turned the children away.

"Sorry, man," Charlie said.

"It's all right," Will replied. "I just want to find them."

Charlie nodded, then looked down to the woman's body. "You got that one?"

"Yeah," Will said. "Go start checking those vehicles."

"All right."

Will faced the body and kneeled down. The woman's eyes remained open, staring up at the sky. Will rolled his palm over her face, shutting her eyes. He told her he was sorry, and then he assured that she'd never stand or open her eyes again.

***

Among the vehicles left behind by the group Will and the others had just encountered was an old Winnebago. When Charlie searched it, he found a map that showed where Gabriel, Jessica, and the others had been taken.

They moved all their things into the Winnebago and left their SUV behind.

There was one stop to make before they went for their friends.

***

It took them most of the day to travel back to the neighborhood. By the time they got there, they'd almost run out of daylight. The guards looked hesitant as the Winnebago approached. Then Will poked out and told them who he needed to see.

They parked the Winnebago in the middle of the street, and a familiar face stepped out of a nearby house. Will exited the vehicle. His eyes drooped and he barely felt able to stand, a sudden sense of exhaustion traveling through him.

"Will, what are you doing back here?" Timothy asked.

"We need your help."

He explained to Timothy how they'd found the vehicle belonging to their friends.

"My God. I'm glad you guys made it out okay. How do you know that your friends did?"

"We can't be sure that they're there, but we have to go and find out."

"And where exactly is *there*?"

Will reached into his pocket and pulled out a folded piece of paper. They went into the house.

Timothy cleared off the dining room table and Will unfolded

the paper, laying it out flat. Timothy's wife, Samantha, entered the room. She frowned, puzzled by the reappearance of Will. She looked into the living room and saw Holly with the kids. Charlie pulled her aside to explain to her why they'd come back.

What Will had lain on the table was a map. Charlie had found it inside the Winnebago. It had been marked up to show the different places the raiders had scoured, but most importantly, it showed where their home base was.

"This is where you want to go?" Timothy asked.

"Yes," Will said.

"That's Shorewood. It's only about thirty minutes or so from here. Really small town. Lives and breathes high school football. So what do you need from us?"

Will told him what he needed. Timothy frowned, and Samantha immediately jumped in to protest. After a few moments, the commotion wore down. Will's gaze remained on Timothy, and when the doctor turned around, he saw the looks of the children. Dylan had started crying, mumbling that he missed Gabriel. Holly hugged him. The boy's face helped them have a change of heart.

"All right," Timothy said. "I'll gather the others."

CHAPTER THIRTY-TWO

As the Empties exited the back of the truck, Gabriel counted. He landed at the number eight.

"We can defeat eight of them," Gabriel said. "How many of these things did you have to kill out there before you ended up here?" Gabriel could only assume that Chase had spent time out in the world before showing up here. He hoped so.

"I lost count," Chase said. "A lot."

"Good. Then you know to aim for the head."

"The neck. Won't have time to be trying to draw that blade back out of their skulls."

Good point, Gabriel thought.

"I only hope the edge is sharp enough for a clean decapitation," Chase said.

The crowd erupted again. Gabriel looked above the opposite goal post to see Ambrose arriving in the bandstands. He waved to the crowd like he was their king or savior. Nathan Ambrose settled into his chair and looked down to the two competitors.

On the field, the Empties lumbered, and the truck raced off. A guard on the other side of the fence raised his hand and the crowd went silent. Next to him, another guard pointed a rifle into the air.

Gabriel scanned the stands, looking for Jessica and Claire. He checked the seats where they had been brought the last time for Thomas' game, but neither woman was there. He refocused on his own game, glancing back down to the two guards assigned with starting the game.

The guard's hand came down, and his counterpart fired the rifle.

Gabriel and Chase took off.

The crowd screamed.

Chase's longer legs gave him a slight advantage. Gabriel thought that perhaps Chase had been right and Gabriel wouldn't have had to let him win. As Chase put a few extra yards between them, Gabriel found himself thankful that he'd made the deal with his competitor. He chugged his legs as hard as he could. No way in hell would he have beaten Chase to that ax. Not unless something happened.

Then something happened.

Chase tripped at the fifty yard line and fell flat on his face.

For a moment, Gabriel thought to stop and help him.

Shit, I can't do that, he told himself. If he helped Chase up, both men would be shot; that was the rule. Instead, he kept running.

He looked back. Chase had made it back onto his feet. Another twenty yards ahead, the Empties remained gathered in a herd. Gabriel still had time to give Chase the opportunity to catch up.

Gabriel grimaced and pulled up, grabbing his leg. He didn't stop, continuing to run, but now with a limp. As he faked a cramp in his leg, Chase raced by him. Most of the crowd cheered. Perhaps they also felt as if Gabriel could not win.

Still limping, Gabriel worked his way to the right side of the field. He wanted to get as far away from the Empties as possible. Ahead, Chase reached the ax, yanking it off the upright. Again, the majority of the gallery clapped and yelled. Three of the beasts had broken off from the group and followed Chase. The other five remained focused on Gabriel.

"Son of a bitch," Gabriel mumbled.

He'd made it about ten feet from the fence, and heard the jeers from the crowd. Spectators said things such as "Fight, you pussy!" and "Quit running!" and "Stand up and fight!"

He, of course, heard the heckling, but fought to ignore it. He found himself far more concerned with the guards lining the outside of the gate.

The crowd turned their attention to Chase when he severed the head of the first Empty in his sights. The creature had stretched its arms out toward 77, but it was of no use. The single blow took the Empty's head clean off, showing that the blade was more than sharp enough to handle the creatures. He immediately drew the ax back up over his shoulder and swung at the next creature. This one put its arms up, and Chase chopped the thing's hand off at the wrist. He pulled up again and buried the ax into the side of the Empty's face. It fell to the ground, and he pulled at the ax as it slipped out of the creature's face. If it had gotten stuck, the next Empty in line would have gotten to Chase.

With the group of five creatures only ten yards from Gabriel now, he figured that he'd sold his fake leg injury long enough. It was time for him to proceed with the plan. Licking his lips, Gabriel pushed off and ran around the side of the group of Empties.

Chase was about to swing at the last Empty in front of him when Gabriel shouted, "Hey!"

The creature turned, and Chase decapitated the beast.

As the crowd cheered, Gabriel looked around the perimeter of the fence. The guards raised their weapons and fixed their aim onto Gabriel.

Above the nearby end zone, Ambrose spoke into a walkie

talkie. He looked down to Gabriel and smiled. When Gabriel looked around the fence again, the guards had all backed away and lowered their weapons.

Turning his attention to the other five creatures, Gabriel waved his arms. The small horde turned to him, and he worked to position them where all their backs would face Chase. All five creatures followed his lead.

Holy shit, it's working, Gabriel thought.

When the entire group had faced Gabriel, he called out, "Now!"

Chase lifted the ax over his shoulder and beheaded another creature. Everyone in the crowd stood now, and all cheered and clapped for both men. The demise of the fourth Empty drew the attention of two others in the group. Chase quickly executed the next one, burying the ax into its head. Only, this time, the weapon didn't come back out.

"Oh, shit."

While two of the remaining creatures remained focused on Gabriel, the third monster extended its arms toward Chase. It dragged him down to the ground. From what Gabriel could tell, it hadn't bitten him, yet.

The two remaining Empties stood between Gabriel and the ax—the key to saving Chase. The key to saving himself.

Gabriel squatted. He called out like a warrior and ran forward.

Lowering his shoulder, Gabriel bowled into the two creatures in front of him.

The creatures snarled as they stumbled backwards, falling onto the ground. Gabriel almost fell with them, but managed somehow to stay on his feet. Chase, still struggling with the empty on top of him, looked up at Gabriel.

"Help me!" Chase cried.

Gabriel looked down to the last Empty that Chase had attacked. It lay on its stomach, the ax buried into the back of its skull. As he reached for the handle of the ax, a hand grabbed onto Gabriel's ankle. He looked back and saw one of the snarling beasts holding on to his leg. Again, he nearly fell, but managed to stay on his feet. He shook the creature loose and hurried to grab the ax.

Placing his foot on the creature's head for leverage, Gabriel pushed down while simultaneously pulling at the ax. The blade made a grotesque wet sound as it drew from the beast's skull. When the blade of the ax finally dislodged, Gabriel stumbled backward a few steps.

"I can't hold him much longer!" Chase yelled. Nearby, the two other Empties had started to make it back to their feet.

Gabriel ran to Chase and kicked the beast off of him. It snarled as it rolled off of Chase. Gabriel raised the ax over his head and brought it down into the creature's face before it could raise its hands up in protest. Gabriel stomped his foot down in the middle of the Empty's chest and dislodged the ax from its skull.

On the ground, Chase sat up on his hands and pushed himself backwards, pedaling his feet. He panted, working to catch his breath.

Gabriel had no time to worry about Chase. The two remaining Empties had made it to their feet and were headed toward Gabriel. One of the creatures lunged at him, and Gabriel ducked out of the way, causing the creature to dive past him. He turned around and decapitated the creature from behind

He turned around to face the final creature, and it was already coming at him. The beast extended its hands toward

Gabriel, who brought the ax up across his chest and blocked it. The Empty grabbed onto the handle and Gabriel kicked the creature in the gut. The force of the blow was just enough to push the creature back, and it let go of the ax. With every ounce of energy he had left, Gabriel brought the ax up over his head and then slammed it into the top of the creature's cranium.

The beast fell down on its back.

The crowd erupted.

Gabriel turned back to Chase, who still lay on his back. His hands gripped the turf. He looked up to Gabriel, the same fear still present in his eyes. Gabriel approached him and extended his hand.

Chase reached out and grabbed Gabriel's hand, and Gabriel pulled him up to his feet. The crowd cheered the loudest that Gabriel had heard yet.

On the perimeter of the fence, the guards raised their weapons and pointed them toward the two competitors. Gabriel looked up to the bandstand at Ambrose, who now stood, holding his walkie talkie to his mouth.

Gabriel and Chase put a little bit of distance between themselves, and Gabriel dropped the ax, raising his hands into the air and surrendering.

The crowd continued to cheer.

"Let them live!" one person shouted.

"Mercy!" called another.

This wasn't the game, but Gabriel's plan had worked. He and Chase had won over the crowd, and they'd put Ambrose in a tough spot. Ambrose wouldn't want to ruin his game, but he also couldn't make the spectators angry by not giving them what they wanted.

A different kind of commotion came from the crowd as they

pointed behind Gabriel. He looked back just in time to see Chase about to swing the ax at him, and he ducked.

Chase stood in a fighter's stance, slightly crouched and holding the ax with both hands. His teeth gritted, he stared down Gabriel.

"I can't believe you actually trusted me," Chase said, laughing.

"I saved your life," Gabriel said.

"Yeah, well, that's your fucking problem."

Chase faked another swing, moving just enough to throw Gabriel off balance. He then swung again, aiming for Gabriel's midsection. Gabriel caught his balance quickly enough to jump back, but tripped over his own feet. He ended up on his back, where he looked up and watched as Chase brought the ax up overhead. Chase slammed it down into the ground, just as Gabriel rolled out of the way.

Gabriel got back to his feet and the two men circled each other.

"There's no way you're going to win this," Chase said. "If you give up now, I'll make this quick and painless."

Not responding, Gabriel remained focused on his opponent.

Chase reared back to swing the ax again, but this time Gabriel was the quicker of the two. As Chase swung the ax back over his shoulder, Gabriel kicked him in the stomach. Chase doubled over, but managed to keep the ax in his hands. Gabriel almost had his hands on the handle of the weapon when Chase raised it straight up, hitting Gabriel in the chin. Gabriel fell backwards, landing on the body of one of the fallen Empties.

The crowd exhaled a collective gasp.

Dazed, Gabriel came to in time to see Chase bringing the ax down once again. Gabriel rolled away, dodging another blow.

Instead of the ax going into the ground like it had before, the head of it buried into one of the Empty's skulls. Chase couldn't pull the ax out of the thing's head.

Gabriel saw an opportunity.

He jumped to his feet and tackled Chase. Both men tumbled to the ground and the gallery erupted again.

Gabriel fell on top of Chase and landed one good punch right off the bat, clocking Chase in the chin. Before Gabriel could land another, Chase managed to block his face with his hands. He then found Gabriel's collar, pulled toward him, and head-butted him. Even through the wall of the crowd and Chase's grunt, Gabriel could hear his nose crunch. Blood shot off from each side of his face. He rolled off of Chase's body, landing on the turf next to him. Gabriel held his face as the broken cartilage screamed at him.

Chase fought to his feet, staggering as he stood. The crowd booed. With Gabriel writhing in pain on the ground, Chase shouted at the crowd. He told them to "Fuck off" and shot them the bird. He turned around and kicked a still ailing Gabriel in the ribs. Gabriel coughed and rolled onto his side.

"Look at yourself," Chase said. "You don't stand a fucking chance against me, and they're booing me. I guess everyone *does* love to root for the underdog. But the underdog never wins."

Gabriel looked up at Chase, who'd diverted his attention away from him. Chase eyed the ax, still buried in the skull of the nearby Empty. He stepped on the chest of the creature, and pulled out the ax. Gabriel heard the blade withdraw from every tissue and layer of flesh. The skull crackled. Gabriel rolled onto his back, splaying his arms out like he was about to make a snow angel. He tried to blank out the sound of the raging crowd as he closed his eyes.

He thought of Katie and of Sarah. He wondered if he would see them soon. He thought of Jessica and Claire, hoping they would make it out of this hell. And he thought of Dylan, trusting that the boy was all right in the hands of Will and Holly.

The audience had gone quiet, and Gabriel could hear the grunt Chase bellowed. He slit his eyes open to see 77 lift the ax over his head. The sun shined down, blocking Gabriel's view of Chase's face, but he could imagine what it looked like. The prisoner likely either gritted his teeth, or held a malevolent smile from ear to ear.

Chase swung the ax straight down.

Eyes wide, Gabriel rolled to his right, stopping when he was on his back again.

The blade of the ax planted into the grass again. Gabriel pulled his leg back and drove his boot into Chase's knee. He didn't have to hear the leg snap; he could feel it.

Chase crashed to the ground, hands gripping his injured knee. The stadium exploded, and everyone appeared to be standing on their feet. Gabriel slid his forearm across his face, leaving a crimson streak from his elbow to the top of his wrist. He rolled onto his stomach and pushed himself to his feet.

On the ground, Chase writhed in pain. Gabriel spun around, looking to the crowd. People had begun to chant.

"Fin-ish him! Fin-ish him! Fin-ish him!"

They stomped on the bleachers in conjunction with each syllable. Many people clapped. Others pumped their fists.

Turning to the opposite end zone, Gabriel stared up into the bandstands. Ambrose stood, clapping his hands to the same rhythm of the crowd. A smile stretched across his face. He nodded at Gabriel, and raised his hand to his throat, sliding it across his skin like it was the tip of a knife.

Gabriel pulled the ax out of the ground and stood over Chase.

He could now see the damage he'd done to 77's leg. The limb contorted below the knee. Gabriel had broken either the tibia or the fibula—perhaps both. Chase rolled on his back like it was a turtle shell, trying desperately to relieve the pain in his leg with his hands. It would be of no use. He would need serious medical attention to fix it. That, or he could suffer the same fate as a horse would with a similar injury. The crowd preferred the latter. Ambrose had demanded it.

Chase stared up and caught Gabriel's gaze. He stopped writhing and just stared up. His lip quivered and his eyes were bloodshot. As Gabriel lifted the ax overhead, he didn't speak. Chase closed his eyes, and mumbled through tears.

With his arms up, the blade of the ax behind him, Gabriel looked around to the crowd. People continued to pump their fists. Some cupped their hands over their mouths, shouting at Gabriel to kill Chase. Around the fence, the guards held their guns down, and they watched.

Diverting his attention to the bandstand, Gabriel watched Ambrose nod down at him again.

Gabriel nodded back.

He screamed.

He swung the ax straight down.

CHAPTER THIRTY-THREE

Near complete silence had fallen over the stadium. Gabriel still held the handle of the ax, his body bent over, the blade buried into its target. He closed his eyes as he drew in long, deep breaths.

When Gabriel opened his eyes again, he saw Chase with his hands covering his face. Blood covered Chase, and the piss stain on his pants was unmistakable. He made the only other noises Gabriel could hear aside from his own breathing. Panting, Chase uncovered his face and looked up at Gabriel. He looked over and saw the blade of the ax buried into the turf, inches away from his head.

Gabriel had missed.

Still standing, Nathan Ambrose looked upon Gabriel, dumbfounded.

Keeping his gaze focused on Ambrose, Gabriel grunted as he turned and threw the ax as far behind him as he could.

Gabriel then walked with a swift gait past Chase and came to a stop on the ten yard line. Around the perimeter of the fence, the guards had all raised their rifles and aimed them at Gabriel. He breathed so heavy that his shoulders rocked up and down. Faces in the crowd ranged from shock to disappointment. A few people even smiled. They'd remained silent.

"Is this what you want?" Gabriel yelled as he circled around to look into the faces of the spectators. "You want me to bury that ax into him?" He pointed to Chase, who remained on the ground gripping his injured leg. "And for what, your few moments of entertainment? I am not a killer of human beings. I would guess that I have killed dozens more of those creatures than any of you have. Because while you've all sat here, watching these bloodbaths, I've been out in the world. I've seen hell, and still, I've held on to the one thing that makes us human. Compassion! I've failed to let empathy escape me."

Many spectators' faces turned blank, as if they were realizing how shameful they'd become.

Gabriel turned to face the bandstand and look at Ambrose.

"I refuse to become some sort of animal for the benefit of a monster."

Ambrose's face soured. His eyes narrowed, and his lips looked thin.

Gabriel walked back over to Chase.

"I will not kill this man. If you want him dead, you will have to come down and do so yourself. And you can take me with him."

Drawing in a deep breath, Gabriel closed his eyes and waited for the sound of guns blasting around him. Waited for the lead to enter his body. The sound and the pain never came.

Then someone spoke.

"Let him go." It was the voice of a woman, somewhere off in the crowd.

Someone else, a man, shouted, "Forgive us!"

As one, everyone started a simple chant, started by someone among the vast array of people.

"Let-Them-Live! Let-Them-Live! Let-Them-Live!"

With this, Gabriel opened his eyes. He looked around the crowd, examining the faces. Most in the crowd were looking toward Ambrose. They knew that he was in charge, and that only he could decide whether Gabriel and Chase would live or die.

Gabriel awaited Ambrose's signal.

Ambrose looked down at Gabriel, holding his thousand yard stare as he lifted the two-way radio to his lips.

The guards along the fence lowered their weapons. The gate at the corner of the field swung open, and the armored truck returned to the field. Gabriel backed up, stopping next to Chase.

"What's happening?" Chase asked.

Gabriel didn't respond.

The truck stopped five yards away from Gabriel and Chase. The back door opened, and four guards came running around the front of the vehicle. Two of them stopped at Chase.

"What are you doing?" Chase asked.

The two men knelt down, and Chase yelled out. They picked him up, showing little concern for his broken leg. One of the guards even grabbed him by his legs. He screamed.

The other two guards grabbed Gabriel and led him away from the truck. They headed back toward the field-house. And the entire way, Gabriel listened as the crowd clapped and cheered.

The crowd continued to cheer as the guards led Gabriel back to the field-house. He looked back and watched as people in the stands began throwing things onto the field. Guards around the perimeter of the fence shouted into the grandstands, urging the people to calm down. One of Ambrose's men fired a shot into the air, and the crowd screamed.

Another guard shoved Gabriel through the doors of the field-house and he managed to stay on his feet.

He turned around to face the field, and watched as a guard pointed his rifle into the stands. The doors to the field-house shut just before the gun went off.

Though it was muffled, Gabriel could hear the panic in the

crowd outside. More gunshots followed.

A guard shoved Gabriel into the middle of the room.

"You hear what you've done, asshole?" the guard said to Gabriel.

Gabriel spit in his face.

The guard reared back his fist and punched Gabriel in the cheek.

Gabriel lunged at him, but the other guard grabbed Gabriel and threw him against a locker. With Gabriel pinned, the guard who Gabriel had spit on walked over and punched Gabriel in the gut. He then spit in Gabriel's face.

"How's that taste, bitch?"

He punched Gabriel in the cheek again, landing the punch in the same spot. Gabriel felt the skin split on his cheek and the blood trickling down to his chin. He looked down and watched the first drop hit the ground.

The guard was about to hit him again when the interior door on the other side of the room opened.

Leaning against the locker, just trying to stay on his feet, Gabriel looked to the door.

Ambrose entered the room, bringing with him Lance and Derek.

The two guards moved away from Gabriel and faced Ambrose. When the man let Gabriel go, he nearly fell to the ground. He managed to stay on his feet, though, using the wall of lockers behind him to stay upright.

The guards stood at attention to Ambrose, and he sneered at them, a fire in his eyes.

"What the fuck is this?" Ambrose asked the guards.

"He tried to escape," the guard who'd been spit on said.

Gabriel laughed. "So now you're gonna lie to him?"

"Shut the fuck up!" the other guard shouted. He turned around and punched Gabriel in the stomach, again.

Gabriel doubled over, clutching his stomach. He coughed and watched as more blood trickled from his face to the ground. The two shots to the stomach made it difficult for him to breathe. He'd closed his eyes, searching for the strength to stand, when a noise deafened him, and he felt something warm splash onto him. He opened his eyes and watched as the guard who'd just struck him fell onto the ground near him. The top of the man's head was gone, and blood pooled around it.

When Gabriel stood up, he saw Ambrose aiming a revolver at the other guards. Smoke rose from the barrel.

"You gonna be next?" Ambrose asked the guard.

The man trembled. "N-no, sir."

Ambrose lowered his weapon, and signaled toward the door.

"Get the fuck out of here," Ambrose said. "Go outside and help get that crowd in line."

"Y-yes, sir."

The guard wiped his face and hurried out of the room. He didn't look back at Gabriel.

Shaking his head, Ambrose re-holstered his gun and shifted his attention to Gabriel. He leaned in and examined the cut on his cheek. It continued to bleed. Gabriel could feel it streaming down his cheek.

"He opened you up pretty good," Ambrose said.

"Yeah, your guys don't mess around."

Ambrose smiled. "No, they don't."

He turned around and nodded at Lance and Derek.

Gabriel's eyes went wide as the two men approached him. Derek punched him in the ribs, and he fell down this time.

"Get him the fuck up," Lance said.

Gabriel found himself being lifted to his feet, his arms pinned behind his back. He coughed, opening his eyes to see Lance standing in front of him. A crooked smile stretched across his face.

He turned his Eagles hat backwards.

"I've been looking forward to this."

Lance reared back and came forward. He didn't have much time to appreciate how hard Lance had hit him because another fist struck him across the cheek just seconds later. Gabriel felt his body go limp, and he wanted to fall down, but Derek wouldn't allow it. He held him up, leaving Gabriel there like a punching bag. Lance continued his assault.

Eventually, Derek's arms tired out and he let go of Gabriel, letting his dead weight just fall to the ground.

Half conscious, Gabriel lay on his stomach watching the blood pool around him. Time stood still and his vision was blurry. He could hear the boots moving towards him, but the sound was fuzzy. When his body was lifted up again, he felt as if he was floating.

When he stood this time, he could barely open his eyes. He could hardly see, but he could make out Ambrose standing in front of him.

"I thought we had a deal," Ambrose said. "I don't like when people break my deals."

Gabriel spit blood onto the floor below him. He managed the words, "It's not like you're going to live up to your end of the bargain."

Ambrose smiled and laughed. "Yeah, well, that's your mistake for not trusting me. Now, you've gotta pay for that mistake."

Gabriel wrapped his tongue around the inside of his mouth,

checking for all of his teeth. His tongue was numb, but he could still taste the blood. None of his teeth seemed to be missing.

He wondered if these were his last moments. In a lot of ways, he hoped they would be. He was tired of dragging through this world filled with nothing but death and hatred. If being alive meant spending another minute at this school with these maniacs, then he would welcome death.

"Do what you've gotta do," he said.

Ambrose reached to his waist and Gabriel closed his eyes. Waited for the cold steel to press against his forehead. Waited for an ending.

Instead, he heard static, and Ambrose spoke. "You there?"

Gabriel opened his eyes. Ambrose held a walkie to his mouth.

"I'm here, sir."

"Bring me the girl. The dark-haired one."

Jessica.

CHAPTER THIRTY-FOUR

Lying on her side with her back facing the door, Jessica couldn't sleep. She'd tried, but her mind kept racing about where they had taken Claire. She also wondered if anyone would ever come and take her out to watch Gabriel's fight. She hadn't been told she was going, but had just figured the people would want her there to see her friend die. Jessica wanted to believe that Gabriel would come back. Had made herself believe it. But deep down, she wasn't sure. She had seen what had happened to Thomas: how he'd been torn apart by the Empties. Even though Gabriel still had his legs, Jessica knew that Ambrose wouldn't make it easy for him.

She shot up and looked toward the door when she heard what she thought to be gunshots.

Jessica ran to the door and looked through the small window. A small group of guards ran down the hallway, passing by her room.

"Hey!" she shouted, banging on the door.

The guards ignored her.

"What's happening?" she mumbled.

When no one passed by again, she sat back down on her bed.

Over the next few minutes, she only heard the gunshots once more. She trembled. All she could do was think of Gabriel and hope that he was all right.

Jessica wasn't paying attention when the door handle clicked. The door opened and one of Ambrose's guards entered the room, stopping only a few steps in. A second guard stood behind him, remaining in the hallway and holding the door open.

"Get up," he said.

"Where are you taking me? To see Gabriel?"

The guard took three more steps toward Jessica. "Ask another question without doing what I say," he said, threatening her. "Go on."

Jessica glared at him, but she stood.

The second guard came forward and handed his counterpart a set of handcuffs.

"Up against the wall, back to me," the guard said. "You know the drill."

Jessica stood against the wall and waited for the guard to restrain her. He approached, but he stopped when more gunshots rang out. These were continuous. They were louder, and sounded closer.

"What the hell?" the guard in the hall said.

The radio on the nearby guard's waist came alive.

"Attention, we need all forces to the front of the building, now! We're being attacked!"

Jessica looked back over her shoulder and saw the guards looking at each other.

"Do we still bring Ambrose the girl?" the guard in the hall asked.

The other guard shook his head. "I'm not sure." He brought the radio to his lips. "What of the girl? Over."

More gunshots fired off outside, and no one replied over the radio.

"Fuck this," the guard said. "We can come back for her."

He hurried out of the room and the other guard let go of the door. They ran down the hall.

Jessica's eyes went wide as the door closed slowly.

She ran for it, diving across the floor.

Jessica caught the door just before it closed all the way.

She stood up, looking back and forth down the hallway. It was clear; she was free.

With gunshots continuing outside, she went to look for Claire.

***

When Gabriel's eyes fluttered open, he was on the floor with his back against a wall. He couldn't recall passing out, and his vision was still fuzzy when he looked up.

All three men in the room had their backs turned to Gabriel. Ambrose shouted commands into his walkie talkie while Lance and Derek stood nearby, awaiting their boss's word. The gunshots continued outside.

Lance looked back, and Gabriel had enough sense to close his eyes again.

"We've gotta get you to safety, sir," Lance said.

"You come with me," Ambrose replied. "Derek, stay here with this piece of shit until I signal you."

"Why don't we just kill him now?" Lance asked.

"Just shut up and come on."

Gabriel listened as the two men scurried out of the room.

He wanted to open his eyes, but was worried that Derek would be looking down at him. So he kept them shut tight, waiting.

Boot steps moved across the floor, heard only between the gunshots. Derek whistled.

Gabriel opened his eyes.

Derek stood on the opposite side of the room, examining a poster on the wall. It showed a weight lifter handling an impressive amount of weight and had a cheesy inspirational quote plastered across the middle.

Gabriel shifted, wanting to work himself to his feet, when suddenly Derek turned away from the poster. Gabriel fell limp, closing his eyes again.

Boots moved across the room once more. They moved closer to Gabriel, stopping next to him. One of the lockers near him opened, and then another.

"You'd think there'd be something left in one of these," Derek said to himself.

He continued to open lockers, and Gabriel awaited the perfect moment.

"Jackpot," Derek said, a tinge of excitement in his voice.

The pages of a magazine turned above Gabriel.

"Damn, girl. I'm not sure your daddy would like seein' this."

Derek moved again. When Gabriel opened his eyes, Derek stood only a few feet in front of him, his back turned.

Gabriel bit his lip, tasting the blood residing there. He saw his chance.

Gunshots continued to blast outside, drowning out the inside of the locker room. Gabriel eased himself to his feet, all while Derek kept his nose buried into the magazine he'd found. Gabriel's entire body ached. His face felt as big as a watermelon. Blood had started to dry on his cheeks. He feared looking into a mirror to see his nose. But his legs felt fine, and those were what he needed right now.

As gunfire rained outside, Gabriel ran forward. Derek hadn't a clue what was happening until it was too late.

Gabriel grabbed onto Derek's coat with one hand and the back of his head with the other, gripping a wad of his long hair. He used his momentum to carry Derek toward the nearby wall.

The gunfire outside ceased, and Gabriel heard Derek's face break as he slammed it into the wall.

Derek's body dropped from his grasp and landed tangled on the floor. The impact of his face on concrete had left a blood splat on the wall. Gabriel kneeled next to the guard and rolled him over.

His nose was completely mangled. Teeth were missing from his mouth. Blood poured from both places.

Gabriel checked his pulse.

Nothing.

Gabriel sighed, shaking his head as he closed his eyes. Even with all he'd been through at the school, it didn't make killing easy. He collected himself and gathered Derek's weapons. The rifle he'd held had fallen onto the ground nearby, and he wore a handgun on his waist, along with a knife. He took the weapons and went to stand.

"Don't fucking move."

The voice was familiar, and Gabriel swallowed hard. He turned back and saw Lance with a Glock pointed at his head.

"Throw that shit over here," Lance said. "And I'll know if you're bullshittin' 'cause I know everything that asshole carried."

Gabriel closed his eyes and sighed. He threw the rifle onto the floor and slid it toward Lance. He gripped the handgun on his waist.

"Try anything and you're dead."

"I'm dead anyway," Gabriel said.

"That might be so, but not quite yet."

Gabriel pulled out the handgun and slid it across the ground, followed by the knife.

"Stand up."

Gabriel stood.

"Face me."

He turned.

Lance's eyes shifted down to Derek, and he smirked. "Dumb motherfucker."

"At least you've got the balls to look me in the eyes when you shoot me," Gabriel said. "I'll give you that."

Lance scoffed. "Shoot you?" He lowered the Glock, tossing it onto the ground.

Gabriel tilted his head to the side, confused.

"I'm gonna kill you with my bare fucking hands."

Lance charged.

***

Jessica moved down the hallway with a stealth-like ability. She looked around each corner, making sure it was clear before moving further. Each room she passed, she looked through the window, checking to see if Claire was inside. Every room so far had been empty.

Outside, the gunfire continued. The further she moved away from her room, the quieter the firefight became.

She was walking down a long hall when a door opened ahead. Jessica ducked into a nearby doorway, concealing herself behind the end of the row of lockers. Footsteps clicked across the floor and Jessica turned to check the door. It was open and she went inside, careful to shut the door behind her.

Jessica froze against the wall, listening as the person walked by. She waited until she heard the footsteps no more, and then exited back out into the hallway.

Two doors down was the room the person had come out of, and Jessica hurried to it.

She looked through the window and gasped.

Claire lay in the middle of the room on a stretcher.

The door opened when Jessica pushed down on the handle and she entered the room, rushing to Claire's side.

"Claire?" Jessica put her hands on Claire's shoulders and shook her, but she didn't move.

Jessica laid her head against Claire's chest to check for a heartbeat.

It was faint, but there was one.

"I've gotta get you out of here," Jessica mumbled.

Jessica had unlocked the wheels and started for the door when it opened.

A man entered, reading a piece of paper on a clipboard. Jessica froze as she saw him.

He looked up, and a smile extended across his disgusting face.

"Well, fancy seeing you here, dear. You remember me, right?"

She, of course, did.

Bruce.

***

If Gabriel's head had hit the ground when Lance tackled him, then he likely wouldn't have ever woken up. But his back slamming against the concrete floor was enough to send a bolt of pain down his spine. It disoriented him long enough for Lance to land the first two punches.

The wounds on Gabriel's face came alive again, and he raised his hands to block further blows. He remained in the defensive position, trying to keep Lance's fist away from his face.

"Fight, you fucking pussy," Lance spat.

Lance grabbed ahold of Gabriel's arms, pinning them down. When he let go of one of them to try and connect with another blow, Gabriel struck, hitting Lance's in his injured nose and knocking him off of Gabriel.

Gabriel rolled onto his side and both men staggered to their feet.

Blood streamed from Lance's nose. He covered it with his hand, then looked at the blood on his palm.

Gabriel clutched his ribs, which still ached from the earlier abuse. It was hard to breathe, but he drew in fast breaths.

"You ready to die, Alexander?" Lance asked, still wiping blood away from his face.

Without speaking, Gabriel raised his hand and waved Lance toward him.

Again, Lance charged.

Waiting until the last possible moment, Gabriel sidestepped him. Using Lance's momentum, Gabriel pushed Lance from behind. He threw Lance into a door, which busted open. Lance fell into the room beyond it. Sporting gear filled the small supply closet. Much if it came spilling down onto Lance as he went head and shoulder first into a shelf, falling face first to the ground. When the balls, helmets, and bats had stopped falling, Lance lay still.

The fight continued outside, and Gabriel grimaced and held onto his aching ribs again. He turned around and limped to where Lance had dropped his gun. He picked up the Glock, the outside gunfire sounding much closer now. He checked to make sure the gun was loaded. It was.

He'd made it halfway to Derek's rifle when he heard movement behind him.

When he turned around again, Lance reared back a baseball bat and screamed.

Gabriel's eyes went wide and he ducked just in time. Lance's swing missed, the bat crashing into a locker behind Gabriel's head.

Gabriel raised the Glock, but Lance turned around and hit him in the forearm with the aluminum bat. He cried out and dropped the gun onto the ground. With Gabriel gripping his arm, Lance drove the butt of the bat into Gabriel's gut. Gabriel doubled over and held his stomach. He fell to his knees, shutting his eyes as the pain passed through him.

When he opened them again, he watched Lance's shadow move behind him.

Lance stood at Gabriel's back. Unable to move, Gabriel remained on his knees with his shoulders slumped. The Glock had slid to the other side of the room.

Gabriel felt the cold aluminum touch his neck as Lance rested the bat on his shoulder.

"Any last words?" Lance asked.

Silence.

"Well, all right then."

Standing executioner style behind Gabriel, Lance raised the bat.

Gabriel closed his eyes.

Lance swung.

Gabriel went face first to the ground, and Lance swung all the way around, having missed the shot. He'd swung so hard that the bat left his hands, crashing into the lockers behind them. His momentum carried him all the way to the ground.

The bat bounced off the locker and landed next to Gabriel. His eyes went wide as he grabbed onto it and stood.

Disoriented, Lance landed on the other side of the room. Gabriel saw the Glock lying within reach, and Lance went for it.

Grabbed it.

Lance went to his knees and lifted the gun as he turned

around toward Gabriel.

He faced Gabriel just in time to see the bat coming, but not soon enough to evade the blow.

The aluminum bat crushed the top of Lance's skull, and he fell limp, dropping the Glock. Gabriel watched as his body sank to the concrete, and his Philadelphia Eagles hat fell beside him.

The sound of aluminum hitting concrete echoed throughout the tiny space as Gabriel dropped the bat and fell to one knee. He wasn't sure how he'd managed to stay on his feet at all, but knew he now had to garner the strength to leave. He grabbed the bat again, using it as a cane to stand.

He got to his feet, but before he could grab any guns, the door opened.

Gabriel readied the bat on his shoulder as a man appeared in the doorway, a rifle aimed at him. He'd been about to swing when he suddenly loosened his grip.

The man standing in front of him lowered the rifle and squinted his eyes.

"Gabriel?"

Gabriel spit blood and mumbled, "Will."

***

Rolling the stretcher, Jessica stepped backward as Bruce came toward her. He smiled, showing his yellow teeth.

"There's nowhere you can go this time," Bruce said. "No one is gonna save you."

When her back hit the wall, Jessica pushed Claire to the other side of the room, away from both herself and Bruce. Nothing stood between them now.

"I've been waiting for this," Bruce said. He licked his lips. "I haven't been able to get you out of my mind."

Jessica moved down the wall, but knew she had few to no

options on where she could go.

Bruce faked a lunge toward her, and Jessica almost lost her balance. He laughed.

"Now, come on. Let's just make this easy, all right?"

"Stay away from me."

Jessica came to the stretcher and had no place else to go. She was sure to keep herself between Bruce and Claire.

"Stay back," Jessica said.

Bruce came forward and tried to grab her, and Jessica slapped him. She dragged her hand so that her nails scraped across his cheek, breaking flesh. He stepped back and held his face. When he pulled it away and looked at his fingertips, he saw the blood.

His taunting smile turned to a glare of hateful lust.

"You stupid bitch."

Jessica screamed as Bruce came at her again. She swung her arm again, but he caught her by the wrist this time. Using his other hand, he backhanded her across her face. Jessica fell to the ground.

"Get the fuck up."

He grabbed onto the back of her coveralls, yanking Jessica to her feet. Tears streamed down her face as he turned her toward him, binding both of her arms with his strong grip.

"Please, just leave us alone," Jessica pleaded.

"We're far past that, darlin'."

He struck her again. Hard enough to turn her around. She caught herself on the edge of the stretcher, bending over. Behind her, she could hear Bruce groan.

"You like it this way, huh? Fine by me."

The sound of him unzipping his pants was like glass shattering. Soon, his hands were on her waist, moving up her body. He squeezed her breasts and pinched her nipple. Jessica cried out. Further violating her, he slapped her on the ass. It burned, but not as much as her pride.

"It's a shame your friend can't watch," he said, laughing.

His hands slid to the front of her coveralls and reached for the zipper.

"Please," Jessica cried. "Don't do this."

Bruce grabbed the back of her head by the hair and pulled it back.

"If you don't shut the fuck up, I swear to God that I'm gonna twist your goddam head off your chicken neck." He pushed her head back down toward the stretcher.

Jessica continued to cry, looking down to Claire. Her friend didn't move. Jessica turned her eyes away from Claire's face. That's when she noticed something pinned under her friend's arm.

The plunger of a syringe poked out from under Claire's wrist. Jessica couldn't tell if a needle was attached to it, but it would be her only hope.

Bruce opened the front of her coveralls, squeezing her breast again, over her sports bra. She felt him as he rubbed up against her and he moaned.

"Goddam, I feel like I could cum now."

This was Jessica's last chance to hold onto any dignity she had left.

She grabbed the syringe and twisted, burying it into Bruce's neck, pushing down the plunger. The tube was just under half-full, and whatever was in there went under his skin. He stumbled back, eyes wide. She'd swung as hard as she could, sending the entire length of the needle into him. Bruce fell to his knees, his hand gripping the plunger.

Out of the corner of her eye, Jessica saw something that caught her attention. A small bottle sat on a nearby table. She squinted her eyes to read the package.

DANGEROUS: CONTENTS ARE POISONOUS.

Bruce pulled the plunger out and looked at it. Then his eyes went to Jessica, and he fell forward, landing face first on the tile floor.

Jessica zipped up her coveralls and looked back to Claire on the stretcher. Her eyes were still open, but it was clear that she wasn't there. Jessica turned over her friend's wrist and saw the place where they had inserted the needle. Jessica pressed her index and middle fingers against Claire's forearm, searching for a pulse.

She waited, and felt only a faint pulse.

She was pulled away from her friend when the door opened.

The guard Derek entered the room first, aiming a rifle at Jessica and shifting his gaze down to Bruce.

Ambrose entered the room behind him.

"Stay right there," Derek commanded Jessica.

She remained still, with no intention of moving.

With Derek's gun pointed square at Jessica's chest, Ambrose moved past him and kneeled down next to Bruce. He placed his fingers on his neck and waited. After a moment, he scoffed and looked up at Jessica.

"You did this?"

She made no signal and gave no response.

Ambrose laughed. "Damn, girl. You didn't write in that diary of yours just how much of a badass you were." His eyes shifted to Claire on the table behind Jessica. "What about her?"

Derek went to Claire and placed his fingers on her neck. "She's barely alive."

Ambrose shrugged. "Well, your girl for my guy, I guess, right?" He stood and patted Derek on the back. "They come with us."

Jessica looked up, and Derek reached out and took her by the wrist. He forced her to walk between himself and Ambrose while he pushed Claire along.

They headed down the hallway, and the firefight continued outside.

CHAPTER THIRTY-FIVE

Gabriel held Will's embrace, mostly just so he could stay on his feet. His face pulsated, his ribs ached, and his legs wanted to give out on him. Will eventually pulled away, but allowed Gabriel to hold onto him. Holly and Charlie stood behind Will, smiling. Holly came to him and hugged him.

"What happened?" Will asked.

Gabriel shook his head. "I'll explain later. We've gotta find Jessica and Claire."

"Where's Thomas?" Holly asked.

Gabriel shook his head.

"Damn it," Holly mumbled.

"We can still save the girls," Will said. "Do you know where they are?"

"Hopefully they're still back in my room. Are we able to cross the parking lot and get into the school?"

"Most of the fighting is happening at the front entrance of the school," Charlie said. "We cleared out this end of the parking lot."

"Ambrose's headquarters is in the school's main office," Gabriel said. "They're probably protecting him."

Will furrowed his brow. "Who is Ambrose?"

"He runs this place. He's evil. We've got to find Jessica and Claire before he hurts them."

"Can you walk?" Will asked. "You look like shit."

Gabriel signaled his head toward Lance on the floor. "You should see his face."

Will eyed the baseball bat. "You ready to trade that for a gun?"

Gabriel nodded. He gestured toward Lance and Derek's weapons, and Charlie picked them up.

"You said you cleared out this side of the lot?"

Will nodded.

"All right," Gabriel said. "Directly across the lot, there's a side entrance to the school. We've gotta go down a couple of hallways, and we'll be at our room."

"You and I will lead the way," Will said. He looked to Holly and Charlie. "You two watch our six, okay?"

"Got it," Charlie said.

Gabriel went to the door and drew in a deep breath as he gripped the handle. His ribcage screamed at him with each breath, and he fought to ignore it.

He opened the door.

People screamed and bullets soared, but it all came from the front side of the building. As Will had said, this side was clear. The proof was in the bodies that lay sprawled across the parking lot. Fresh blood pooled on the ground next to them. Gabriel scanned the area to make sure it was clear. Then he pointed to the school's side entrance and hurried across the lot.

The side door was unlocked, and the group spilled into the stairwell.

"Were any of those people out there with you?"

"Two of them," Charlie replied.

"Who are they?"

"Just a group we met. Good people," Will replied. "Where's your room?"

"We stay downstairs. Come on, this way."

They put their backs to the adjacent wall as Gabriel opened

the door to the hallway. He nodded at Will, who spun into the doorway, rifle ready.

"It's clear," Will said. "Let's go."

Again, Gabriel and Will led the way while Charlie and Holly guarded their back side.

They turned one corner and arrived at another vacant hallway.

"How many people are here?" Holly asked.

"I don't know," Gabriel said. "I've seen several guards, but I'm not sure how many people are here total."

"We only brought about twenty-five people with us," Will said.

"Sounds like they're holding their own pretty well out there."

They arrived at another corner, and Gabriel peeked around to check the hallway, clutching his ribs. Like everywhere else, it was vacant. He led the others around the corner, slowing to a walk.

"We're this room right here," Gabriel said, pointing to a nearby door.

He went to the room, expecting the door to be locked. Instead, it was just barely open, the mechanism sitting against the plate. Gabriel readied his handgun and turned with his fingers to his lips, signaling for the others to be quiet.

He drew in a deep, painful breath and drove his shoulder through the door.

The beds remained in place, their blankets tossed where they'd left them. Neither girl was there.

"Shit," Gabriel said.

"You said they were both here when you left?" Charlie asked.

"They must've taken them hostage."

Gabriel walked over to one of the cots and sat down on the

edge. Adrenaline was wearing off and he could feel the aches all over his body, each one defining itself.

"Do you know how to get to the lobby from here?" Charlie asked.

"Yes, but they're sure to have numbers on us. Ambrose probably has all his people guarding those doors so that no one can get inside."

"Are you gonna make it?" Will asked. "You look like you're in a lot of pain."

Grimacing, Gabriel said, "I'll be fine."

Standing at the door, keeping it propped open, Holly said, "All right, so we should—"

She was cut off by shouting coming from down the hallway. Will grabbed her and yanked her inside the room, being sure to ease the door shut so that whoever was coming wouldn't hear it.

They remained silent and still in the dark room, standing against the wall. Shadows filled the room as several people passed the window. It was impossible to tell how many. Their boots kept moving down the hall, eventually fading out to nothing. Gabriel came off of the wall and peeked through the window. He saw no one in the hallway. He turned to face the group.

"They must've found out that you killed their side entrance guards," Gabriel said.

"Good thing we made it in here before they got to that door," Charlie said.

"We can't stay here," Will said. "We've gotta try to find Jessica and Claire."

Suddenly, Gabriel had an idea. He smiled, almost mad at himself that he hadn't thought of it before. Will noticed his face light up.

"What?"

"Come on," Gabriel said. "I've got an idea."

***

When they came to the door, Gabriel looked through the window. He fumbled for the keys in his pocket before finding them. He tried three keys before getting the door to swing open.

There were six men inside the room. Two lay on the floor, not acknowledging Gabriel and the others. The other four men looked up. One of them was standing, and he raised his hands at the sight of Gabriel's rifle, looking confused as he eyed Gabriel up and down.

"Are you here to kill us?" the man asked, a tremble in his voice. "We hear all that commotion outside. If that's why you're here, just get it over with."

"No," Gabriel said. "We're here to ask you to come fight those sons of bitches with us."

He entered the room with Will, Holly, and Charlie filing in behind him. The man stepped back until he was against the wall, still appearing hesitant.

"It's all right," Gabriel said. "I've been a prisoner here, just like you all."

"We brought a group here and they're out there fighting to bring this place down," Holly said. "That's the commotion you hear."

"We've gotta hurry," Will reiterated.

Gabriel eyed the conscious men in the room. "Are you able to move? Can you fight?"

One of the men on the ground, a black 30-something guy, said, "They've hardly brought us any food. That's why those two aren't awake. They don't have any strength." He licked his chapped lips. "But I think I can muster up enough energy if it means that I might live."

"It does," Gabriel said.

"Do you know how to use a gun?" Charlie asked. Only one of the four men said they didn't.

Being sure to keep their heavy artillery to themselves, each person in the group handed over a handgun so that each of the prisoners had ones. Charlie gave the one guy a quick crash course on using a pistol.

"I'm sorry that we don't have something heavier to offer you," Gabriel said. "But if you wanna make it out of here, this is gonna have to do."

"Doesn't matter to me," the black man said. "If I'm going to hell today, it can't be any worse than this place. I'm just gonna make sure I take as many of those motherfuckers with me as I can."

Gabriel couldn't help but chuckle. He slapped the guy on the shoulder.

"Then let's go give you your wish."

CHAPTER THIRTY-SIX

When they arrived near the lobby, Gabriel slid into an empty nearby room that had once served as a lounge.

"Stay here," he told the others. "I'm going to peek my head around the corner and try to see how many soldiers are out there."

"Do you want me to go?" Will asked.

Gabriel took his hand off his aching side and stood up straight. "I'll be fine."

"Just be careful," Will said.

Gabriel exited the room, being sure to check both ways before entering the hallway, and hugging the wall as he moved. Most of the fighting had settled down, as he only heard the occasional gunshot. He came to the tall, open archway of the lobby, and ducked his head around the corner.

The glass doors and windows stretching across the front entrance of the school were practically nonexistent now. Three guards sat on the ground behind the desk near the entrance. Others stood with their backs against the wall on the far side of the lobby, out of sight from the people outside. The guards against the wall were facing his way, though not looking at him. Gabriel had to shift out of view again before he was noticed. He headed back to the lounge and rejoined the others.

"Are they still fighting? I don't hear anything," Holly said.

"They're at a standstill right now."

"Were you able to see how many of them there were?" Will asked.

Gabriel shook his head. "I had to duck out of view before they noticed me. I counted at least seven, but I'm sure there are more." Gabriel used the white board on the wall to draw a map, pinpointing the positioning of the guards he'd been able to see.

"I'm assuming there's going to be more guards on this wall." He pointed to the wall that was next to where he'd peeked into the lobby and been unable to see. "The door to the office is on that wall and it curves in, so I couldn't see. It's likely that Ambrose is in there, so they'll probably have it well-guarded."

"What if he's not in there?" Charlie asked. "What if he's hiding somewhere else in the school?"

"He'll be there," Gabriel said. "He's not a coward."

"He's right," said the black man, who had revealed his name to be Joe.

"We've gotta take out the guards behind the desk and on the far wall first," Will said. "Then we'll worry about whoever is in front of the office."

"We'll go in first," Joe said.

Gabriel shook his head. "You don't have to do that."

"Man, if you guys didn't come and get us, we'd be sitting in that room right now, just waiting to be slaughtered. It's cool, right?" He looked to the other survivors, and though they looked scared, they each nodded. "You just be ready to back us up with some heavier artillery."

"You're all okay with it?" Gabriel asked the other men.

They nodded.

Gabriel sighed. "All right." He looked to Will. "Do we have any extra clips we can give them?"

Charlie reached into a satchel he carried and pulled out two extra clips for each of the four men. Gabriel looked to Joe again.

"And you're sure you wanna do this?"

He nodded. One of the other men said, "We're gonna be getting our hands dirty either way. Not sure it's really that different if we lead you in."

"You just be ready to raise hell," Joe said.

Gabriel was.

They shook hands, and Joe led the others out the door. Gabriel, Will, Holly, and Charlie followed, stopping in the hallway just outside the door.

Joe and the others crept to the archway, and he looked back and said something to them. Then he smiled, and he went around the corner.

He fired the first shot.

The other three prisoners stepped out into the hallway and opened fire. It only took moments for Ambrose's men to fight back, and one of the four survivors hit the tile floor almost immediately.

Gabriel, Charlie, and Will positioned themselves just outside the archway, and shot at the guards.

When one of the other prisoners hit the ground, Joe yelled out. Then he ran across the lobby toward the door to the cafeteria. He screamed like a warrior, firing his gun as he ran.

A bullet caught the left side of his body and he fell down.

"Shit," Will said.

"That came from the office," Gabriel said. "There's definitely people over there."

The final standing prisoner fell, but not without getting off another shot that took down the last guard that Gabriel and the others could see.

The lobby went silent, and the group stood still.

"I'm gonna look and see how many are left," Gabriel whispered.

"What about Joe and the others?" Holly asked.

"It's too risky," Gabriel said. "We're gonna have to wait to help them."

"Be careful," Charlie said.

Gabriel crouched down and went to the archway. He put his back against the wall, his rifle ready in his hands. He looked to the four prisoners. Only Joe appeared to still be moving, as Gabriel watched him slide his leg across the tile floor.

Drawing in a deep breath, Gabriel looked around the corner.

To his surprise, the ambush had worked. The three guards who'd been sitting behind the desk now lay motionless on the ground. Against the wall, one guard lay sprawled on the floor and another was slumped against the wall. Shots rang outside, but no sound came from inside the lobby as smoke rose into the air, following the short battle.

Gabriel looked to the others and signaled them to follow. Before they could protest, he moved around the corner. He remained crouched and close to the wall. When he arrived near the corner to where the wall caved into itself, he stood up straight and stopped.

"Gabriel, wait for us," Holly hissed.

He looked back and put his finger to his lips.

Will yelled, "Gabriel!"

Gabriel turned back to see Derek raising a handgun, at point blank range from him. Just as the barrel reached the height of Gabriel's head, he grabbed onto Derek's wrist and pushed the gun away from his face. Derek pulled the trigger. The shot went off in Gabriel's ear, and he immediately heard the ring. But the bullet missed, soaring past him.

Still holding onto Derek's wrist, Gabriel drew the pistol from his side. He shoved it under Derek's chin and turned his eyes as he pulled the trigger.

He let go of Derek's wrist as his body fell limp.

"No!"

The scream came from Will. Gabriel turned back and saw Will kneeled next to Holly, his hand pressed against her shoulder. She was slumped against the wall, and Will's hand was red with blood. The bullet from Derek's gun had missed Gabriel, but it had hit Holly in her right shoulder. Gabriel ran to her.

"Oh, shit."

Tears rolled down Holly's face. "It hurts."

"It's gonna be all right," Gabriel said.

Glass fell to the ground at the entrance of the school as the front doors opened. Gabriel turned and pointed his gun, but Will put his hand on his friend's shoulder.

"It's okay," Will said. "They're with us." Will stood up. "Timothy, come quick!"

An older man ran over and kneeled down next to Holly.

"When did this happen?" Timothy asked Will.

"Just now."

Timothy looked over his shoulder to one of the men with him. "Go get Doug and tell him to bring his medical kit, now!"

"Is she going to be okay?" Will asked.

"She should be fine," Timothy said. "She's obviously just in a lot of pain."

"You've gotta go help Joe and the other prisoners," Holly said. "I can wait."

"Holly, no."

"I'll be fine."

"Someone just needs to keep pressure on her wound," Timothy said. "I can go check on the others."

"We've gotta go in there and get Jessica and Claire," Gabriel said.

"I'll go with him," Charlie said. "You stay here with Holly."

"No," Will said. "I'm going with him. You stay with her and do what the doctor asks. Here, come down here and take my spot. Keep pressure on it until Timothy can stop the bleeding."

Charlie took over and Will stood up.

"You sure?" Gabriel asked.

"Yeah," Will said. "Let's go get them."

"Just the two of you?" Timothy asked.

"It's better this way," Gabriel said. "If we go storming in there like an army and he is indeed in there with our friends, then there's no doubt; he'll kill them immediately."

"Be careful," Holly said.

Gabriel and Will looked at each other and nodded, and then they headed toward the office.

Gabriel opened the door.

CHAPTER THIRTY-SEVEN

For the second time, Gabriel walked through the school's office. It looked untouched and exactly the same as it had the last time he'd been there. Though no one was in the main office, he knew that Ambrose stood behind the door in front of him.

"Ambrose," Gabriel called out. "We know you're in there. Your men are all dead; it's over."

No response.

Will said, "Just come out."

"Nothing is over," Ambrose said.

"You think he's in there alone?" Will whispered. Gabriel shrugged.

"I've got two things in here you want. Or should I say, two lovely ladies I know you want."

Gabriel's heart skipped a beat.

"Don't hurt them," Gabriel said. "Let's talk."

"Talk? Your friends come in here, guns blazin', and now you wanna talk?" He laughed. "Yeah, we'll talk."

Gabriel looked over to Will. "He'll kill them."

"Then we gotta get in there, now."

Will started to brace to charge the door, but Gabriel grabbed onto him. "Wait."

"Put down your guns, and open the door slowly," Ambrose said.

Will looked at Gabriel and shook his head.

"The blonde one is hurt," Ambrose said. "She needs medical attention, so I suggest that you hurry up and do as I say."

Keeping his eyes locked on Will's, Gabriel pulled the rifle over his head and set it down onto the ground. Will still looked hesitant to do as Ambrose demanded.

"Tell your boy there that he better put that shit down now, or I'll blow Jessica's brains out."

Gabriel looked above the door and noticed the camera. He tapped on Will's arm and pointed to it.

"That's right, I can see you. Now, put down the fucking gun."

Will sighed and cursed. He took off the rifle and lay it down.

"Good," Ambrose said. "Is that all you have? Show me the holsters."

"That's all we've got, Nathan," Gabriel said. "You've got our friends in there. Think we're gonna risk them?"

"Show me."

Shaking his head in frustration, Gabriel flashed his empty holster to the camera. He told Will to do the same, and he did.

"You tell the truth," Ambrose said. "Good. Now, step toward the door."

Gabriel went to the door and Will followed.

"Slowly come in."

Pushing down on the handle, Gabriel opened the door.

Ambrose stood on the other side of the desk, using Jessica as a shield as he held a revolver against her rib cage. Gabriel scanned the room, looking for Claire. He was about to ask Ambrose if he'd lied about her being there when he noticed the feet on the ground. He went to peak around the desk, but Ambrose stopped him.

"Don't move unless I tell you to," Ambrose said. "I can assure you: that's your friend."

"What is it that you want?" Will asked.

"Well, I don't believe that I've gotten your name."

"His name is Will," Gabriel said.

Ambrose smirked. "Well, well, you're Will. I have to tell you that I've been so anxious to meet you. Jessica here had some fun things to say about you in her diary. She really likes you, you know that? Is it true that you were bit and survived? Because I'd sure like to know how that's possible."

Will didn't respond. He left his firm glare on Ambrose.

"Just tell us what you want," Gabriel said.

"I already told you what I wanted before. But you had to go and fuck that up, didn't you?"

"I'm just trying to survive," Gabriel said.

"Aren't we all?" Ambrose laughed. "I gotta give you some credit, though. That shit you pulled, getting the crowd on your side; it was smart. You knew I couldn't kill you without having a riot on my hands."

"As I said: I just want to live. So, how do we all get out of here alive?"

Ambrose smiled. "You've got to be out of your fucking mind if you think you're making it out of here alive. The only question I'm asking myself is which one of you assholes I'm gonna kill first."

Jessica closed her eyes and bit her lip. When she opened them again, Gabriel told her that everything was going to be okay.

Ambrose scoffed. "You just keep telling her that. Maybe I'll just kill them first and make you watch. How about that?" He jammed the gun into Jessica's ribs, and she squirmed and squealed.

Will stepped forward, stopping only when he reached the edge of the desk. "If you're gonna shoot somebody, asshole, shoot me. Leave them out of this."

"Will, stop," Gabriel said.

A bigger smile grew across Ambrose's face. "As you wish."

He pulled the gun's barrel away from Jessica, lifting it and pointing it at Will's chest.

"Don't do this," Gabriel said.

Ambrose shook his head. "It's too late."

Aiming the gun higher, Ambrose now pointed it at Will's head.

"You got any last words?" Ambrose asked Will.

"Fuck you."

Gabriel kept waiting for the gun to go off and kill his friend, but then he heard the first snarl.

There was a low rumbling growl, and Ambrose turned his attention away from the prisoners and looked onto the floor.

"What the—"

A snarl was followed by a crunch which sounded like someone biting into an apple. Ambrose grimaced and his legs buckled. The aim of the gun shifted above Will's head and went off, sending a bullet into the wall.

"Jessica, move!" Gabriel shouted. She did, running to the door and exiting the room.

Even through all the pain, Gabriel leaped over the desk and tackled Ambrose, sending the gun flying out of his hand. They fell to the ground, and Ambrose continued to scream. Gabriel heard ripping and tearing, and the smell hit his nose immediately. He rocked back when Ambrose punched him in the face.

"Get off me!" Ambrose shouted.

Gabriel looked down to his feet and saw Claire tearing into Ambrose's leg. Blood spit out from the wound. Gabriel fought to get up, but Ambrose had thirty, perhaps even fifty pounds on him.

Claire pulled away from Ambrose's leg and looked up. Her eyes had gone pale and vacant. Blood covered her mouth and cheeks. It dyed her blonde hair. She snarled as Gabriel looked into her cold, dead, Empty eyes.

She dipped her head again, and Gabriel felt his heart jump. He waited for the pain of her teeth diving into his leg, but instead Ambrose screamed again. He grabbed hold of Gabriel's shoulder. The hand moved down to Gabriel's throat.

Gabriel's eyes bulged as Ambrose choked the life out of him.

"You're coming with me," Ambrose said. He gripped Gabriel's throat harder. "You're coming—"

There was the bang of a gunshot, and Ambrose's grip loosened. His head went limp, slamming into Gabriel's nose.

Another gunshot married with a scream, and the snarling at Gabriel's legs ceased.

Ambrose's weight came off of him, and he saw Will.

"I couldn't get a good shot," Will said. "He was all over you."

With Ambrose off of Gabriel, Will reached down and offered his hand. He took it, gripping Will's wrist as he was lifted off the ground.

The door opened and Jessica rushed back into the room.

"Oh, God," Jessica said.

Gabriel looked to her and saw that she had noticed Claire's body on the ground.

"They poisoned her," Jessica said. "She might have been dead long before you guys got here."

"How's Holly?" Will asked.

"She's gonna be all right," Jessica said. "Timothy and Charlie are with her."

"And the others?" Gabriel asked.

Jessica shook her head.

"Shit."

As they exited the office, Gabriel listened. The gunfire outside had ceased.

"Is it over?" Gabriel asked.

Timothy nodded. "Whoever was left surrendered. My people have a small group of prisoners outside."

Gabriel looked to Will. He patted Will on the shoulder and said, "Thank you for coming to get me."

He pulled Will in for an embrace, and then Will went to be with Holly.

"What are we going to do with the prisoners?" Timothy asked.

Gabriel pondered this for a moment. He thought about his time at the school, and everything these people had done to him. Then he thought of Timothy. Some of his people had been killed, coming to rescue him and Jessica.

"How many people did you lose in the fight?" Gabriel asked.

Timothy bowed his head and shrugged. "We're not quite sure yet. But I think it was at least a dozen. One of my guys is out there trying to find all the bodies right now and gather names."

"Well, you're as much a part of this decision as I am," Gabriel said. "Your people came here and sacrificed for us. So we have to make this decision together."

For several minutes, they thought about it before collectively arriving at a decision. Together, they left the office, heading outside the school.

When they walked outside, Gabriel felt like he should pinch himself just to see if he was dreaming. Bodies lay sprawled everywhere. They spread out from the parking lot, up the stairs, and all the way up to the front door. Blood surrounded his feet.

Sitting around the flagpole were the prisoners, each with their hands behind their head. Timothy's men stood with assault rifles and shotguns fixed on them. A few of Ambrose's men were awaiting medical attention, but Timothy had somebody tending to his own injured people first.

Gabriel turned his attention back to the prisoners sitting around the flagpole. Their eyes shifted toward him as he approached.

"Are you gonna kill us?" Gabriel hadn't seen this man during his time at the school.

"What do you think we should do with you?" Gabriel asked.

"With all the shit that Ambrose put you through? Well, I suppose that if I was in your shoes, I'd probably kill me."

"Then I suppose you're lucky that I'm not you." He looked over to Timothy's men. "Let them go."

One of Timothy's men scratched his face. "Let them go? They killed a dozen of our people. And you expect us just to let them go?" He looked over to Timothy. "Timothy, we can't do this."

"Brian, let them go," Timothy said.

One by one, Ambrose's men stood up. Gabriel approached the man he'd been talking to.

"Don't think about coming back here and trying to build this place back into a prison. My people here will be watching this place closely, and there's a lot more of them than what showed up here today. Got it?"

Ambrose's man smiled, and not a friendly smile. "Yeah, we got it."

Timothy said to a small group of his men, "Lead them a few miles down the road. Then come back here and guard this place until we can get back. If they try to return, shoot 'em."

Timothy's men nodded.

Ambrose's men who'd been injured were loaded into the back of the pickup truck. It followed the rest of the guards out of the school. When they were far enough away, Timothy's group would let the men take the truck, but not give them any weapons.

Gabriel turned to Timothy and extended his hand. The doctor accepted the handshake.

"I can't thank you enough."

"Well, your friends here are good people. They helped us out, and we like to help look after good people." He glanced at the bodies on the ground. "It doesn't look like there's many of those around anymore. We need to stick together."

They spent some time scouring the school for things they could use. They found food, medical supplies, generators, and more weapons than they could even take with them. Later, they could come back for what they couldn't take on the first trip. They also went back to the room where the male prisoners were. The ones who hadn't been able to help in the fight. One of the men was beyond saving. Timothy gave him enough morphine to make him comfortable. He died before they left. The other man was carried up front with the other injured people. He would be taken back to Timothy's community.

Jessica also showed them to another room where there were women prisoners. One of them had died, and the others looked terrified when they saw the group. Jessica assured the women that they meant them no harm, and it was proven so when they let them loose. It took some time for the women to warm up to the group. When they did, they agreed to head back to Timothy's community.

Within two hours, they were all heading out of the school's parking lot.

Gabriel rode with Will and the others. He took one last look at the school as they pulled out of the lot. He shook his head, thankful that he could look forward now. Forward to getting to Washington and finding his family. And, more immediately, forward to seeing Dylan once again.

CHAPTER THIRTY-EIGHT

Will thought Gabriel might jump out of the moving vehicle when he saw Dylan waiting for him on the front porch. When the vehicle did finally come to a stop, the boy was already halfway across the yard. Gabriel was the first one to exit the vehicle, and Dylan ran to him. They had explained to Gabriel what had happened to Dylan's arm, but Gabriel still cried when he saw it was missing as he held the boy close.

Mary Beth appeared in the doorway. She ran across the yard to join them, sprinting into Jessica's arms.

As Will watched the reunion, he began to cry. Especially when he witnessed Gabriel examining Dylan's missing limb for the first time. Though Charlie and Holly had told him different, Will still blamed himself for the accident.

He wiped his cheek with his arm as Timothy arrived from another vehicle.

"We're going to move Holly inside to remove the bullet and stitch her up," Timothy said. "She should be feeling better by this evening, or the morning at the latest."

"Do you need my help?" Will asked.

Timothy shook his head. "We can handle it."

Together, they looked on as Gabriel and Dylan continued their embrace.

"Gabriel really cares for that boy, doesn't he?" Timothy asked.

"He does," Will replied. He turned and shook Timothy's hand again. "Thank you for everything."

As they shook hands, the doctor said, "I want you to stay. All of you." He looked around. "We've got plenty of room. I could let you have three separate houses."

Will looked over to Dylan and Gabriel again. Dylan was now hugging Jessica, but Gabriel had left his hand on the boy's shoulder. Dylan looked back to Will and smiled. Will returned the gesture and waved.

"I appreciate your offer, but I can't pull them apart again. We'll stay here for at least the night, maybe a couple of days, but Gabriel is going to want to get to Washington. It's all he's wanted since all this happened."

"Are you sure?" Timothy asked.

Will sighed and wiped the sweat from his brow. "We've separated from Gabriel twice, and this is the second time we've been reunited. I think the universe wants us to stay together."

Timothy put his hand on Will's shoulder and he smiled. "Not the universe, but God."

TO BE CONTINUED...

Want to be the first to know when the final Empty Bodies book is coming out?

Join my new release mailing list for news, exclusive content, members only giveaways and contests, and more!

Click or visit:
http://bit.ly/zbblist

ACKNOWLEDGEMENTS

Thank you to all the readers who've come along this journey with me!

Thank you to Jimmy Chew for all the awesome information on field amputation.

Thank you to The Empties!

Thanks, as always, to Johnny Digges for another great cover, and to Jennifer Collins for another fantastic edit.

ABOUT THE AUTHOR

Something about the dark side of life has always appealed to me. Whether I experience it through reading and watching horror or listening to my favorite heavy metal bands, I have been forever fascinated with the shadow of human emotion.

While in my 20's, I discovered my passion to create through playing drums in two heavy metal bands: Kerygma and Twelve Winters. While playing in Twelve Winters (a power metal band with a thrash edge fronted by my now wife Kathryn), I was able to indulge myself in my love of writing by penning the lyrics for all our music. My love of telling a story started here, as many of the songs became connected to the same concept and characters in one way or another.

Now in my 30's, my creative passion is being passed to willing readers through the art of stories. While I have a particular fascination for real life scenarios, I also love dark fantasy. So, you'll find a little bit of everything in my stories, from zombies to serial killers, angels and demons to mindless psychopaths, and even ghosts and parallel dimensions.

My influences as a writer come primarily from the works of Clive Barker, Stephen King, and Blake Crouch in the written form; the beautifully dark, rich lyrics of Mikael Akerfeldt from the band Opeth; and an array of movies, going back to the root of my fascination at a young age with 70's and 80's slasher films such as *Halloween, Friday the 13th,* and *The Texas Chainsaw Massacre.*

I live in Nashville, Tennessee with my wife Kathryn, our daughter Haley, and our German Shepherd Guinness. When I'm not writing, I enjoy playing hockey, watching hockey and football, cycling, watching some of my favorite television shows and movies, and, of course, reading.

Connect with me online:

Website: www.zachbohannon.com
Subscribe: http://bit.ly/zbblist
Facebook: http://www.facebook.com/zbbwrites
Pinterest: http://www.pinterest.com/zbbwrites
Twitter: @zachbohannon32
Instagram: @zachbohannon

Made in the USA
Monee, IL
29 March 2021